LAST ONE OUT

STEPH NELSON

Published 2025 by Ticking Clock Press

ISBN: 979-8989615414

PRAISE FOR STEPH NELSON

The success of dark narratives often hinges on their ability to generate empathy in readers, and Steph Nelson nails it...

— *NEW YORK TIMES* REVIEW OF *THE THRESHING FLOOR*

Last One Out is a stunner that will have everyone talking. You'll love it.

— GREGG OLSEN, #1 *NEW YORK TIMES* BESTSELLING AUTHOR OF *IF YOU TELL*

This thriller is as clever, pulse-pounding, and heart-breaking as they come.

— NOELLE W. IHLI, BESTSELLING AUTHOR OF *ASK FOR ANDREA*

This novel contains violence, coarse language, off-page child trafficking, and non-explicit references to pedophilia. Please read with care.

PART I

AUGUST 1999

CHAPTER 1
CHLOE

I HOPE *we don't die tonight*—that's what I'm thinking as I crack open the window of Amy's car. I need fresh air, and even though the wind relieves my nausea, it does nothing for the pulsing anxiety about what we're doing and how dangerous it is.

I stare at the short guardrail along the side of the road while Amy drives. It's the only thing standing between us and a steep drop into fast-rushing whitecaps of the Payette River. The edge is close. Way too close, and the Payette is wild enough to white-water raft.

Amy, Kristi, and I aren't here to raft, though.

My friends and I drove over an hour from Boise to take a midnight soak at the isolated Skinny Dipper Hot Springs. A last blast before we start our senior year—Amy's idea. None of our parents know. They'd flip their lids because not only is Skinny Dipper far away, but it's tucked into the Boise National Forest, only accessible by a steep half-mile hike.

Nobody tries it in the dark. In fact, people don't even come out here this time of night. It's secluded enough that you don't need the cover of dark.

Amy parks her Corolla and turns to her twin sister, Kristi, in the front seat. "Let's do this!" she says in that chipper tone that's equal parts cute and demanding. It's her don't-argue-with-me voice.

Kristi claps her hands and they both get out.

I watch from the back seat as Kristi busts out this squirmy little happy dance on the empty road, but I don't buy that she's this excited. Like me, she was nervous when Amy first floated the idea. She's either changed her mind or is pretending. Either way, I'm sure the goal is to avoid upsetting Amy.

Amy and Kristi may be fraternal twins, but they're inseparable and it's like they made some agreement in the womb where Kristi obeys without question, and in return, Amy makes sure Kristi, who is painfully shy, has friends.

As I slide out of the car to join them, the white noise of the plunging river below is deafening, and the way it sits against a backdrop of night makes my stomach turn again.

Being up here feels worlds away from the safety of snuggling on the couch and talking about it.

The girls move to the other side of the deserted two-lane highway, using a flashlight to search for the trail up to Skinny Dipper. My eyes track up the steep mountainside and I let out a little gasp.

I expected a hike and a late-night soak in the woods, but I didn't sign up for this.

This is isolation and wilderness and everything bad that could happen. I'm grateful for the full moon, so at least we can see a little, but that doesn't remove the fact that we're choosing danger. And while the risk is kind of the point, I'm having second thoughts. Where are the hot springs, even?

"I found the trail!" Amy shouts and plants a Nike runner on a patch of dirt while shining the light in my face.

"Hey, stop that." I shield my eyes.

"Well, hurry up," Amy groans.

It's not like I'm lagging. I'm just a few steps behind them, but Amy gets annoyed with everything I do lately. Even when I'm following her ideas and trying hard to be what she wants, she complains. Her voice has a manic edge right now, like she's afraid I'll pull the cord on this whole idea.

I want to, but I also don't want to piss her off, so I tread carefully.

"That hike looks super hard. Worse than I pictured," I say. "Plus, it's creepy enough right here that we can just say we did it. We don't have to go all the way up."

"No," Amy says. "You're not weaseling out of this. We're here, so we're gonna do the whole thing. This little walk isn't going to kill us."

It might though, I'm afraid. It may very well kill us.

After all, it's so ... vertical. Switchbacks are supposed to make an uphill hike easier, but they don't do much for this trail. I alternate my gaze between the dirt ribbon leading up and the twins, who are both in one-piece swimsuits covered by jean shorts. Amy's brown hair is in a sloppy bun, and Kristi's is in a French braid. They're a whole head taller than me and I find myself once again envying their long legs. I hate being so short.

I follow as the girls start up the trail, because what else am I going to do? Stand out here alone in the dark, next to the road? That's just as scary.

The wind is cooler than I expected for summer, which makes me wonder why I didn't wear a tee shirt over my bikini top. These Umbro shorts aren't cutting it, either; the fabric is so thin. I drape my beach towel over my shoulders so my hands are free in case I need to catch myself, but it adds a little warmth, too.

We go single file, and I stay behind Kristi, trying to watch where she steps to avoid slipping on the dirt and scree, but she's moving so fast it's nearly impossible to keep up. I have to leech off her flashlight or I'll fall off the trail, so staying close isn't optional. I should have brought my own flashlight.

After a while, even Amy in the lead has to stop to catch her breath.

Thank god.

"This is so much harder than you said it would be," I mutter.

"Well maybe you should have come to the soccer workouts this summer."

I don't reply because whatever comes out won't be nice. I couldn't go because my mom is single and works all day. Unlike Amy, I don't have my driver's license, and even if I did, Mom can't afford to buy me a car. Plus, Amy and Kristi live too far away to pick me up. Not like I'd ask them for a ride anyway because it'd be one more thing they'd hold over me. So, yeah, no soccer workouts. Instead, I spent the summer with my cousin, Frankie. Which was fine by me. Sure, she's two years younger, but she's my best friend in the whole world, even though the twins never want her around. I'm pretty sure they're jealous of how close we are, but the official reason is Frankie's too young to hang out with us. So dumb since she's going to be joining us in high school this year.

Amy and Kristi are hiking again, and Amy acts as if she didn't just say something super rude to me. I follow along in silence, willing this spark of irritation to ease up.

Soon, we're far enough up the mountain that the trees muffle the sound of the river, and the telltale sulfur scent of natural hot springs hits my nose.

My stomach jolts and I pause on the trail for a moment, feeling sick.

"You okay?" Kristi calls from a few feet ahead, shining her light back on the trail so I can see where to step. "We're almost there. Looks like this path dips down to a tiny pool. It's not big enough for all of us, but Amy thinks there's another one above it."

Awesome. More climbing.

"Yeah, I'm fine," I say.

Fine.

I sigh at my word choice because, yeah, I'm fine as in *not ill.* But that doesn't mean I won't throw up.

I've been throwing up for weeks because I'm pregnant.

CHAPTER 2
CHLOE

I DON'T KNOW how far along I am. I've been tired for what feels like forever, but I'm still not showing. Mostly I try not to think about it because I don't know what to do.

The baby is *his*.

I refuse to even think his name in my mind because I hate him so much for doing this to me. I have to figure it out, but I keep putting it off because it's so overwhelming.

If I have the baby, my life will be over. I can't even think about his response to it because a deep hole digs into my gut when I do. He can't find out. But if I don't have the baby ... no way to think about that either because while I'm not ready to be a mom, I also don't want to end the baby's life.

Every option feels bad, and so these thoughts keep dancing circles in my mind, all the while the baby grows, which only stresses me out more. I feel paralyzed, which is why I haven't told anyone I'm pregnant. Not even my mom. Definitely not Frankie. She would be so disappointed in me, and I can't handle that because I'm already so disappointed in myself.

Steam threads up toward the starlit sky and the pools come into view.

I take in the entire scene as best as I can in the dark. It looks like a trickling waterfall landing in shelves, or pools, in the crevice of a mountain. It reminds me of an oversized backyard water feature, but much less perfect. My stomach flips when I see that the pool we're aiming for has an edge that ends in a cliff. You could be in the pool and overlook everything below, which would be an incredible view if it were daylight. There's the mountain we hiked—you can even see the tiny highway below. If it weren't so dark, I bet I could find Amy's car.

I focus on the path over to the pools again. To get there, we'd have to lily-pad-hop across a few big rocks.

Kristi shines her flashlight on a makeshift carved wooden sign that says "Skinny Dipper Hot Springs," and this weird summer-camp feeling crawls over me. It's not the s'mores and day-hikes kind. More like the horror-movie kind.

A whisper of fear skims against my neck, and I shiver. "We shouldn't be here," I say quietly.

Amy groans and moves the light along the rocks and brush to highlight the empty liquor bottles and beer cans littering the area. I even see a used condom, and that makes me wince thinking about what people do up here. Then she trips while rock-hopping across to the larger pool and teeters over the cliff for a beat, but catches herself and lands on her ass.

I gasp—that was such a close call.

Kristi yells her sister's name, and then she goes across, being more careful than Amy was and hunches over, shining the light on Amy's knee. There's a smear of dirt and red liquid beads pushing through a small cut.

"You okay?" I call out.

"Yeah, it's only a scrape."

"You could have fallen over that cliff and died. Maybe we should go back," I say.

"No, I'm fine," Amy says, pushing Kristi's helping hands away.

"Truth?" Kristi puts her hands on her hips.

"Yes, Truth. It's a baby scrape. And I *didn't* fall over the cliff." Amy stands and brushes away dirt and blood.

Truth with a capital "T" is how we operate. High school is full of so much bullshit, so much preening and pretending, that the three of us made a pact last year, swearing that we would always be honest with each other.

Even if it hurts.

Even if it causes a fight.

Because lying would cause fights too—probably more. We pricked our fingertips with a safety pin and solemnly swore.

So, my friends and I don't lie to each other.

Mostly.

I think of my pregnancy, but immediately dismiss it because that's different. It feels much bigger than lies about who we have a crush on or who we're mad at. My lie is necessary. And anyway, is it even lying? It's more like not confessing.

"Come on, Chloe!" Amy calls out, shutting off her flashlight and dropping it on the ground. She removes her shorts.

Kristi points her flashlight on the rocks I need to move across, and I go slowly, even more carefully than she did, until I'm standing next to the pool.

Amy steps into the water and Kristi shucks down to her swimsuit, entering the water without hesitation. "God, it feels so good!" she says with a sigh.

The sulfur scent triggers my nausea a bit, but I have to get in or the girls will wonder why. It does sound nice to soak, and I should enjoy this moment. Let my worries fizzle away for now. When I finally do slip in, my body practically sighs with relief after that intense hike, and I can feel tight muscles relaxing.

Nobody speaks, and I look at the twins, both of them with eyes closed, like they're in heaven. I take a deep breath and, for the first time tonight, stare at the sky and enjoy the quiet.

After a few minutes, something rustles above us on the mountain. I catch it in my peripheral vision and startle.

"Did you see that?" I whisper, pointing to a small locust tree bursting through two boulders. A few of its branches are still moving against the moonlight. The girls strain to see what I'm talking about, but it doesn't happen again.

"It's just the wind. You need to chill out, Chloe," Amy groans.

There's no wind up here. We're sheltered in this crevice.

Minutes pass in silence where nothing happens, and I guess I should take Amy's advice and calm down. The air feels even colder now thanks to my wet skin, so I crouch lower into the water and sit still until my face throbs. It's actually really hot in here.

The baby.

What if this high temperature is harmful to it? I pull myself out and sit on a rock's edge, dangling my feet in. I reach to the side for my towel and nearly knock my shoes into the water.

"Why did you get out?" Amy asks. "What are you doing?"

I sense a challenge in her tone, so I remind myself again to be careful with my reply.

"Oh, I'm good. Just got a little too hot. And I don't feel great."

Amy looks at Kristi, and I swear a little smirk passes between them. Right in front of my face.

"Why are you always sick, Chloe?" Kristi asks in a voice that sounds more like Amy. It catches me off guard. This isn't her. She's usually more non-confrontational.

"Yeah. It's not normal to get the flu for weeks and weeks on end," Amy adds.

What the hell?

Before I can come up with something to say, Amy speaks again, moving closer to me in the pool. "Are you pregnant or something?" But her tone—there's a certainty that makes my gut flop. It feels like she already knows the answer.

"Chloe had sex," Kristi adds.

"Are you having *sex*, Chloe?" Amy whispers in a mocking voice.

"What? No."

"Whatever, *mama*. So much for Truth. We found the used pregnancy test in our bathroom trash can. You didn't even try to be discreet. But don't worry, we haven't told—"

A small avalanche of rocks falls behind us, coming from the spot I saw movement before.

I slip back into the water and duck down as if to hide.

We all stare at each other in silence, and I swear I can feel their panic rise to the same level as mine.

The twins know about my pregnancy and that's a huge, scary deal, but it's overshadowed by this fear thrumming below my skin. Who or what made that noise?

"Guys," I whisper. "That is *something!*"

The air grows charged while we sit as still as possible, trying to make ourselves invisible. I'm fighting the urge to go inspect, if anything, to discover that I'm wrong and it's nothing.

"Get the flashlight," I whisper to Kristi, pointing at it.

"You get it! You're closer," she protests quietly.

"Jesus Christ, you two, it's nothing. I'll show you," Amy says, moving through the water toward the light.

She pulls herself up onto the large rocks that form the rim of the pool, when there's a whirring noise—something flying through the air. It hits her in the back.

An arrow. I can see it sticking out.

Everything slows down and Amy turns as if she's simply changed her mind about the flashlight and now she's getting back into the pool. But her movements are stilted, her face contorts in fear, and then she lets out a shriek of terror that makes it feel like the blood stops pumping in my veins.

I should go over there and help her, but I'm stuck in place. My body won't move.

Amy falters, flailing her arms as if to grab hold of something, but there's nothing. Just the edge of the pool before the massive drop to the bottom. She loses balance and disappears over the cliff.

CHAPTER 3
CHLOE

ALL NOISE DAMPENS, funneling into a quiet hum that zings in my ears. Kristi's mouth is open as if she's screaming, but I don't hear anything.

I reach for her hand and grab her by the wrist instead. I want to tell her to stay here. Stay at the back of the pool where we're hidden from above, where the arrow came from. But I can't get anything out.

She shakes off my grip, and I watch her lips form her sister's name, but it's muffled. She repeats it over and over while sloshing across to the place where Amy fell.

No. Stay down. Don't go over there.

The warning is there, but the words stay stuck in my throat.

We need to run. Get out of here. But still, I'm locked in place.

Another arrow flies through the air and lodges into Kristi's chest. She stumbles, crying out as her body goes limp and slides back into the pool.

Everything spins, dreamlike, as if I'm outside of myself watching this happen. As if there are two Chloes, and the first Chloe moves through the water, ducking low to both hide from whoever is hunting us and to grab Kristi to turn her face up so she doesn't drown. The other Chloe sits, unmoving and observing like an idiot. Someone sobs.

But I'm the only Chloe. I'm the one pulling at Kristi, turning her over, and I'm the one crying. A dark blotch of blood where the arrow sticks out soaks Kristi's pink swimsuit and seeps into the water. Her eyes are open, blinking, and blood trails from the corner of her mouth down her cheek. I wash it off gently, as if that's important. Her mouth gapes open. Is she dead? No— can't be. She's blinking.

Then she's not.

I whimper, looking around and trying to figure out what to do.

Kristi is dead.

What about Amy?

What about me?

If I stay put, *I'm* dead. But if I get out, he may shoot me like the others. Plus, the steep trail back down the mountain would be impossible to run in the dark. How would I do it without falling? Either way, I die.

These thoughts ping in my mind rapid-fire. I have to do something. I can't stay here.

Branches snap from above in the same place the arrows came from. Then I hear nothing. He knows I'm here and he's waiting me out.

Something about that terrifies me even more. I gasp and cover my mouth.

Think.

An idea sprouts and I remove my locket from my neck. I throw it to the other side of the pool, opposite of the trail and into the bushes. If he thinks the movement is me, he'll shoot off another arrow and I may have a split second while he reloads. That's when I'll run.

But nothing happens. The locket is too small to make any noise when it lands.

I pick up a rock and throw it in the same direction, and it crashes against a pine tree.

He doesn't stir. Doesn't take the bait at all.

He can see us.

Whoever this is, he's not going by sound, he's going by sight. And I have to take my chances and run down the hill or he could close in on me. Possibly cut off my access to the trail if I don't move now.

I take a deep breath and rocket out of the pool. The cold air is an instant assault, but I ignore it, crouching to make myself smaller. It's a short incline up and then all downhill switchbacks to the car. If I could get over the hump, the mountainside would shield me. Unless he follows.

I make it past the short incline, and on the way down the trail, I slip on hardpack dirt over and over. Every time, I get a new scrape or open cut on my legs, feet, hands. I move down the mountain, barefoot, drenched with sweat and blood, the whole time trying to focus on what to do next. Need to keep my mind from squirreling off to thoughts about my friends. I lose my balance and skid, but stick my legs out to gain footing again. My whole body throbs with pain.

He's not shooting at me. Why?

Almost to the car. But—shit! The keys are in Amy's pocket!

Can't think about that. I have to keep going, avoid tumbling to my death, figure out what to do next, and also somehow stay out of firing range.

Where is he?

Don't look back.

It'll slow me down, but I want to figure out why this person isn't trying to shoot me. In fact, I can't tell that anyone is chasing behind, and that's way too good to be true.

The road below comes into close view. There's Amy's car,

and behind it, a truck with its headlights on, purring while it idles.

No. I stop dead in my tracks. Is that the shooter's truck?

Doesn't matter because I have no choice. I have to go that way, and so I push harder down the last leg of loose scree until I trip and fall, torquing my ankle so hard I can't help but scream out in pain.

Instinctively, I touch the injury, but even that hurts. Standing up is impossible because I can't put any weight on the leg.

But I'm almost there; Amy's car is just ahead, dark and quiet. I know I left my door unlocked. If anything, I can get into the car.

That's not a plan! My instincts scream, but I crawl toward it, dragging my wounded leg. My vision is blurry, blinking in and out, as if I might faint.

Focus. Get to the car. Push a little more.

Then someone is behind me, panting, and there's a slight growl on the exhale. It's deep, like a man's voice even though he doesn't speak. A rag comes over my face and I try not to breathe the sickly sweet smell, but his arms are a vice grip, and eventually I have to.

Everything goes black.

CHAPTER 4
FRANKIE

As I take the stairs down to the kitchen this morning, a jealous thread twists inside me at the thought of Chloe going up to Skinny Dipper with Amy and Kristi, and without me.

I cried in my bedroom after hanging up the phone with her yesterday, all because of this. I don't know why, but I thought Chloe would invite me. It's not like I'm in junior high anymore, but I guess that doesn't matter. Chloe said the twins wanted to spend time with only her, but I know she just said that to spare my feelings. The twins hate me, and I don't know why.

Then I was so grumpy about it that Dad grounded me, making it so I wouldn't have been able to go even if the twins said I could.

What is up with Dad? He's so easily irritated ever since Mom died a couple of years ago. I guess I haven't been the same since she passed away, either. Maybe I should cut him some slack.

Dad is sitting at the little round kitchen table reading the paper when I get into the kitchen. I find the microwave for the time. Nine a.m. This is late for him. He's usually had his coffee and read the paper by now.

"Morning, Dad," I say in passing as I head to the pantry. Honey Bunches of Oats are a first order of business.

"Hey, I'm glad you're up. I got a call from Aunt Bertie. Do you know where Chloe is?"

Aunt Bertie is my mom's sister. Or she was my mom's sister. She and Dad have stayed close since Mom died, but mostly because Chloe and I are together all the time.

"Probably at Amy and Kristi's," I say, trying to keep the sass out of my voice, but also feeling that prickle of envy again.

"Bertie says she's not over there."

That gets my attention and I whirl around to figure out what he means. "What?" My voice goes high and gives away my surprise.

Dad squints at me. "You know where she is."

"No I don't."

Defensive. Way too defensive.

I really don't want to rat Chloe out because Amy and Kristi's parents would find out they lied too, and then the twins would hate me even more.

But then a bigger thought steamrolls that one.

What if Chloe is in danger?

Why isn't she back? Did something happen to her?

"Okay, your reaction is scaring me," Dad says. "You look like a ghost. Tell me what you know."

"What did Amy and Kristi say?"

"All three girls are missing. Apparently, the twins told their parents they were staying at Chloe's, and Chloe said she was staying at their place. This morning, when Aunt Bertie called over there to tell Chloe to come home, she found out Chloe had lied. She's not there. The twins aren't at Chloe's either."

It's the way he says it. Sort of annoyed that I didn't get it the first time, but also slowly realizing for himself the same thing I just thought of: Chloe could be in danger.

"All three girls are missing."

My knees feel like jelly. I move to the table and pull out a chair to sit next to Dad. I have to tell him the truth.

"They went up to Skinny Dipper."

Dad's eyes narrow like I spoke a different language and he's trying to match words up with a mental dictionary.

"You know, the hot springs on the way to Garden Valley," I add.

"Why on earth ..." He doesn't finish his thought and instead stands up, his chair screeching against the linoleum. "I have to call Bertie."

A flash of hot panic surges through my body. What if she got hurt? Or worse? I've never been to Skinny Dipper, but Chloe told me all about it the other day when she was over here. About the steep hike, how secluded it is.

"Dad? We'll find them, right?" I turn in my seat to face him.

He picks up the beige phone and starts dialing. "God, I hope so," he says. But his voice is a little shaky.

Dad is talking on the phone almost immediately, and I start crying. I'm not handling being without Mom very well. How will I live if something happens to Chloe, too? She's the only one who's been there for me since my mom died. The accident that took Mom came out of nowhere, tearing her from my life. I still can't talk about it.

Just the other day we were up in my bedroom, sitting on the floor with "These Are Days" by 10,000 Maniacs playing loud. It's Chloe's favorite song and she was singing. I always love listening to her sing because she has the most amazing voice. I was following along with the words in the CD jacket when I started crying so hard.

It was embarrassing. I hate crying in front of people.

"It's okay to express your feelings," Chloe had said. "Just let it all out."

But I don't want to let it out. It feels like if I give that sadness any space, it'll take over and I'll never be able to tame it again.

"Losing your mom is about the shittiest thing anyone can experience," Chloe went on when I didn't answer. "You should scream into a pillow. That's what I do when things aren't fair. Here, try it out." Chloe tossed a pillow and it clocked me in the face.

"Ouch," I said, even though it didn't hurt.

She chuckled.

I held the pillow, considering Chloe's suggestion, but ultimately, I shook my head. It was better to swallow it down. That always worked.

Chloe tilted her head in curiosity and grabbed another pillow off the bed, shoved her own face into it, and screamed. The intensity of the smothered shrieking shocked me, and all I could do was watch as she alternatively gasped for air, then returned to the pillow for more screaming. When she finally put the sunshine-yellow pillow down, her face was glistening with sweat. Her eyes were red, as if she'd been crying.

"Your turn," she said.

"You're crazy." I started laughing, and it felt good.

Chloe shoved her face into the pillow and did it again. When she came up for air, she said, "I think I'll do this every day, actually. I feel amazing."

I threw my pillow at Chloe and she scooted over and wrapped her arms around me. "You can't hold it in forever. It's not healthy. You don't have to face it today, but you have to process it eventually. Your mom would want that."

Tears run down my face and I don't feel like eating cereal anymore. Dad is still on the phone and pacing the kitchen as far as the coiled cord allows. He sounds worried and it makes me feel untethered. Like someone unhooked me from a dock and I'm floating out to sea.

They'll find Chloe. They have to.

I can't live without her.

TWENTY-FIVE YEARS LATER

CHAPTER 5
FRANKIE

I WAKE UP SWEATY. It's still dark out but I'm too tired to check the time. When I move slightly, it's obvious my sheets are drenched, so I touch my hairline, where perspiration beads up. My tank top sticks to my bare chest, and there's not a single inch of dry fabric.

It's the perimenopause song and dance, and my signal to wake up and change. No rolling over to the dry side of the bed and ignoring it. My big "welcome to 40" this year was night sweats and crazy Chloe dreams. Both make sleep a battleground.

Stumbling across the hallway to my bathroom, I avoid turning on the light. I've got a night light to see by and as long as I keep it relatively dark while I pee and change, I can still hope to nestle into oblivion when I get back to bed. It's wishful thinking, bordering on delusion, because sleep never comes that easy, but it's what I tell myself every time.

The vivid dream I just woke from presses against my brain, demanding to be inspected, and it feels impossible to keep my mind blank and sleep-focused.

So much for oblivion.

I give in and rewind the details of the dream, closing my eyes to focus and bracing myself against the bathroom sink.

Chloe and I are speeding along in a truck, but the brakes and accelerator don't work. Chloe's in the driver's seat, but it doesn't look like her. She's older, and drinking straight from a tequila bottle. I tell her to pull over so we can switch places. Not because Chloe is drinking and driving, which would make sense, but because I'm worried that she doesn't know how to drive. She never learned.

"I got this," Chloe says, smiling at me.

She looks so beautiful and young, but she's our age now, and she's happy.

I squeeze my hands against the cold tile countertop, and when I open my eyes, there I am, back in reality. Long, brown hair hanging in semi-greasy strands thanks to skipping a shower yesterday. My freckles stand out like pinpricks through skin. I move to the toilet, and when I'm done, I go back into the bedroom where I pull off my tank top and underwear and feel around in my drawer for something fresh to wear.

Every time I have a dream about Chloe, it feels so real. Like I'm building a new relationship with her, as adults, but in the dream world.

It's not real, I keep telling myself.

I feel around in a drawer for my good underwear, but all I come up with are grannies. Period panties. Mental note: Do laundry.

When I slip back into my queen-sized bed, I scoot to the dry side.

Sleep. Sleep. Sleep, I command my body.

But it's not happening. I'm wide awake, and my mind is working hard against my will to recall the rest of the dream. They feel like intrusive thoughts, as if I have no control over what enters my mind.

You're obsessed with what happened to Chloe.

This is what Jensen thinks, but it's not true. It's just that time of year, and I'm always a shitshow when this week rolls around.

I flop over to my other side and hug my pillow tight, then groan. I'm not going to be able to turn my brain off.

The anniversary of what happened that night at Skinny Dipper Hot Springs is the day after tomorrow, and every year, I put on a benefit for the girls. Even though I've done this for over a decade, memories of Chloe always feel amped during this particular week, and I face minor depression, irritability, and fresh sadness. Sometimes I cry even if I haven't shed a tear over Chloe since the last anniversary. Without fail, my body remembers the deep grief of those early days. It's been twenty-five years, and you'd think I would be able to move on. At least that I wouldn't be so shattered. But this time of year, all bets are off.

I'm not sleeping anymore tonight and at this point it's time for me to call it. I'll definitely need a nap later. Do I have time today? I lie in bed a minute longer to mentally review what I have going on, which consists of checking in on Dad's cat and going over final details for the memorial event. With this two-a.m. head start, a couple hours of shut-eye are probably in the cards. Maybe I'll actually cash them in this time, even though I never do. But the possibility itself is enough of a thought to propel me out of bed, and I wrap a hunter green robe around myself, tying it tight. It's bunny-soft, and on days I have nowhere to be, I stay in it until evening.

Next stop: coffee.

My kitchen is wallpapered in 1980s powder blue geese, every fifth one wearing a huge rose-pink bow around its neck.

"Morning, guys," I say when I walk in, greeting them like usual. I've known them for a long time. Much longer than I've lived here.

This house is my aunt's old place, where Chloe grew up, so the wallpaper reminds me of childhood. As I spoon coffee grounds into the filter, I wonder whether I'll have the heart to update the wallpaper. I should, considering I flip houses for a living and that's why I bought it. I'm not usually attached to the houses I remodel, but of course, this one is different. I waited years for the owner to put it up for sale so I could buy it. Aunt Bertie hadn't lived here in decades, but the owners after her took good care of it. They changed hardly anything, and when they finally put it on the market last winter, I acted fast to buy it, telling myself it was simply another trendy mid-century home that I could flip for a good price.

Yeah right. As if I'd flip this 1,800-square-foot nostalgia bomb. It's like something in me knows this because I moved all my stuff in. Typically I bring the minimal amount of things I need in order to live for a few months. This house took me by surprise. Right when I walked in, I couldn't believe the vibe of the place. It feels exactly like how it was when Chloe lived here, and it's the first time I've felt so connected to her in years.

Maybe that's why I'm dreaming about her so much lately.

This kitchen alone holds so many memories. Chloe and I baking cookies during Christmas break. Scarfing toast and eggs that Aunt Bertie pushed on us before we got on bikes to disappear for the day during summer. Trying to do homework at the table but failing miserably thanks to endless laugh attacks. Crying over cocoa because Chloe's latest crush had been an asshole to her.

Maybe I'm right there's a connection between moving into this house, and the anniversary of the Hot Springs Murders causing such a fresh case of Chloe-on-the-brain. I was doing so good living my life too. Well, good enough for me. My business is successful, and I've got money in the bank. I still feel like some part of me is stuck in the past where Chloe lives because I can't find any closure.

Amy and Kristi's parents got closure. Their bodies were found at the site the next day.

But not Chloe. Twenty-five years later and there's still no trace of her.

CHAPTER 6
FRANKIE

IT's ONLY two p.m. and I've already been up for twelve hours. I'm wiped out from working through my event to-do list, but I manage to drag myself over to Dad's to check on his orange marmalade cat, Sundown.

If I'm being honest, I think Sundown's kind of a dick. But Dad asked me to pop in and check on the cat's food and water while he's gone for the summer. I may not be in love with the cat, and I may be annoyed with my dad's self-centeredness— leaving an animal to fend for itself for three months is case in point—but it's not the cat's fault. At least he has a cool name. Dad has had a lot of animals over the years and he always names them after old folk songs. There was Bojangles, a little brown terrier. Woodstock, a fat pit bull. Leroy Brown, a black cat who Dad always called Lee. Scarborough, or Scar. Then there was Moonshadow, Smackwater Jack, and ... well, a few more that I can't remember.

When I walk into Dad's house, Sundown is nowhere to be seen. There's the half-full water dish on slate tile flooring in the hallway, along with the huge bowl of kibble. I keep it overfull in case I'm ever delayed in getting over here.

I tried to get Dad to buy one of those automatic dispensers, but he refused. "Then how would I get you to come and check on him while I'm gone? Sunny will get so lonely."

As if he cares about that.

Sundown comes trotting into the kitchen and gives a little *purrup* as he sharks between my ankles in a lazy figure eight. He's using all of his cute cat power to convince me he's the sweetest floof in the world so I'll bend down and pet him. Then he can have the everlasting joy of scratching me. I still have a mark from the last time I gave into the temptation. The cat is pretty damn cute.

"Hey, jerk, I'm not falling for it again," I say, dodging him to grab the dish and fill it with water at the sink. I feel bad for being rude to him, but it's also kind of second nature to keep pets—and people—at a distance. It's weird how once you wall yourself off, it gets easier and easier to do it. I'm at the point now that I'm not sure I'd know how to take the wall down even if I wanted to. Getting close to people feels uncomfortable like a too-tight waistband.

I set the water down in front of Sundown and reach for the scoop in the food bin to top off his dish for good measure when my phone buzzes in my back pocket.

What should we do for dinner tonight?

It's a text from Jensen, my neighbor.

I smirk to myself thinking of that word to describe him. Jensen is more than a neighbor. I've known him forever—we were at the same high school although he was Chloe's age. When I moved into Chloe's old house a few months ago, I learned he lives around the corner, so we struck a friendship right up. Now, he's like my best friend—plus sex. He wants to be more than that, and would probably even put a ring on it despite that it's only been eight months of us hanging out, but

I'm not ready. Plus, I like the dynamic we have. As long as I think of him as my neighbor, it puts a safe distance between us.

At this point, being vulnerable with someone is like a foreign language I'd have to learn from scratch. Is there Duolingo for becoming fluent in intimacy? I text him back.

> Pizza and beer at mine?

> That sounds perfect. Tell me you found the sink of your dreams.

I've been on the hunt for a Mamie pink sink that's true to Chloe's—I mean *my*—mid-century home. The whole bathroom is like a Pepto explosion, and it's such a rarity in an old home that I plan to keep it that way for the most part. Unfortunately, the sink has a crack and is chipped beyond repair, so it needs to be swapped out.

I stretch my neck and reply to Jensen's text.

> Not yet, but I know it's out there.

> It could also be right in front of your face, and you refuse to see it.

His text arrives immediately like he had that one queued up, and how wonderful. Now we're not talking about the sink. We're talking about *us*. Our situationship that Jensen wants more from.

> Pretty sure I'd notice a pink sink in front of my face. ☺

I feel a tinge of worry that Jensen will confront me more directly on this topic and force me to make a decision. I shove the phone into my jeans pocket.

Sundown sits next to his dish, staring like he's judging me for my inability to allow anyone in. He's not wrong. Most women would die to have a guy like Jensen wanting to take things to the next level. He's got a steady job as a high school math teacher, he's funny in a sarcastic way, and he's good looking. But I'm not most women. I'm broken.

Even with Jensen, I never truly open up. I know it's because I still haven't processed my trauma. I've read enough self-help books to pinpoint that as the issue. I hadn't even wrapped my brain around my mom dying when Chloe went missing.

Yet, for better or worse, Jensen is undaunted when it comes to me. He won't believe me when I say I'm not ready for a relationship. I haven't had the guts to tell him I don't think I ever will be. At least not with him. I've tried being rude to him, and ghosting him. Turns out it's insanely hard to ghost someone who lives around the corner. And I hate to admit it, but I'm always relieved that he shows up again. I don't have anyone else, and I'm afraid of being alone.

"Am I the Asshole?" I ask the cat, who starts licking a paw in response. I should ask the subreddit, but I'm afraid of what they'd say.

As I'm getting into my truck to head home, my phone pings again. Probably Jensen with another smart comment.

But it's not a text. It's a Reddit message, and it says:

I KNOW WHAT HAPPENED TO CHLOE WEBSTER.

THEN

CHAPTER 7
CHLOE

THE DARKNESS IS thick when I first open my eyes. My mouth tastes like a penny, and one cheek presses against a mattress that smells like dust and mold. I cough, and the resulting echo startles me. A shock of pain from my leg brings me into the moment.

My ankle.

The baby.

I touched my bare stomach and shivers wrack my body thanks to damp hair and wearing only a bikini in this cold room. But I'm not tied up, not restrained at all, and my eyes are adjusting so they can make out a cheap twin mattress covered in 101 Dalmatians sheets. Tiny spotted puppies all around. Blankets folded in a stack nearby. There's a paper plate with two slices of pizza and a plastic water bottle.

Panic drives my breathing more shallow and much faster. Where am I?

Where are Amy and Kristi?

A rustling movement across the small room startles me.

"Is someone here?" I whisper.

A figure emerges, shadowed but wearing a mask, and it's—

oh god. A chill bolts up my back, making my small hairs stand on end. The mask—it's a huge, over-smiley Bill Clinton face. The exaggerated gaping mouth is probably supposed to be funny, but somehow it's way scarier than a horror mask would be.

"Eat," the man demands.

I look at the pizza and my stomach growls, but I don't feel like eating. My hesitation is too long, and the man says, "Chloe, eat the pizza. Drink the water. Now."

He knows my name.

This makes me freeze, and I strain to see him better, trying to tell who he is, but that stupid mask makes it impossible to identify him.

"How do you know my name?" I whisper, sitting up.

"Eat. I'm not asking you again."

I reach for a slice, but stop. Why does he want me to eat so badly? Is there something in the food? Drugs, or maybe poison? I inspect it but can't tell.

"I'm not hungry," I say, setting the slice on the plate.

He comes toward me, muttering, "Fucking hell."

Terror rips through my body as he closes inches between us, but again, I don't move. I couldn't anyway; my back presses against the concrete wall and the only door is located on the other side of this man. It's metal with no window.

He grabs my right hand and wrenches it behind my back. The sharp movement makes my body jerk, twisting my hurt leg, and I cry out. But my voice is weak, and my throat is hoarse like I've been screaming for days.

I move to my knees and he pushes my face onto the mattress so my cheek smashes against it. He takes my other arm and yanks it back too. Then he secures my wrists with zip ties.

I cry out again, both in pain and desperate fear, taking big breaths and coughing.

He doesn't say anything, and I can't see him since he's behind me, but I hear the *slurrp* of duct tape pulled loose from a roll.

I scream again, this time trying to call for help.

"Shut up," he says.

The man flips me on my back, and the pressure of my zip-tied hands against my arched spine sends new riots of pain shooting through me. He straddles me at the hips, and the truth of my situation bears down. He's going to kill me.

I stare at him, my eyes blurry with tears. The piece of duct tape hangs near the mouth of his mask like a silver tongue out of Bill Clinton's menacing smile. He shoves something into my mouth. A pill?

Two, actually.

I try to spit them out, but only successfully dislodge one. My tongue finds the other, but before I can spit it out too, he puts his hand over my mouth, forcing a swallow.

He groans in annoyance and feels around my chest for where the other pill landed, grazing my breasts until he comes up with it in his fingers. I gasp at the touch, a new level of fear striking.

This time, he shoves the pill into my mouth, but follows up with duct tape to seal my lips closed. He holds a warm palm over it, and I can smell glue from the tape mixed with his nasty hand.

I try hard not to swallow the second pill. Whatever he's giving me, I don't want it, and besides, who knows what he might do to me while I'm high? What would that do to the baby? But the saliva backs up so much that I have to swallow or I'll choke.

"Atta girl," he says, watching my neck bob.

It grosses me out, the way he says it, and I try to fight, thrashing on my back. Then I watch him as he moves to sit next to me.

I dart my eyes around the room. Hot tears run down my cheeks and into my ears. What's he doing? Seems like he's just watching.

"Takes a few minutes to kick in," he says. "Relax. I increased the dose so it'd take faster, but you're better off not fighting it."

My body slowly goes heavy until I don't know how much time has passed. Then it's all I can do to keep my eyes open. The urge to sleep is insanely strong and I can't fight it. Panic tries to spur my body toward movement, but then it dulls. Everything dulls.

The man grabs me, and I register a feeling of weightlessness as he carries me toward the door. I try to struggle, but it does nothing and I pass out.

———

WHEN I WAKE UP, I'm in water. It's warm. My hands are free and they're draped over something cold. There's pressure against my biceps and I realize I'm in a dingy, standing bathtub. I'm completely naked, suspended in the water, except for my wounded ankle. That leg is hanging over the edge and bandaged. My skin is littered with cuts and bruises. I blink a few times to clear my vision so I can figure out where I am.

Paint is flaking off the walls. It looks like it was once white, but now it's nicotine-yellow and curling away from concrete. In the far corner is a large mattress on the floor. Double the size of the one in the room where I woke up before.

I try to move but can't. Behind me, in one of the corners, I hear low grunting and a skin-on-skin sound—gentle slapping and quick breathing.

What is that noise? It takes effort because I'm groggy, but I finally see black clothing from the waist up, and pink skin exposed beneath. It's the man in a Bill Clinton mask. He has his hand on himself–*ohmygodohmygod*–stroking up and down until he lets out a moan.

"Shit," he mutters when he sees me looking, rushing to put himself back into his pants like he's ashamed of being caught.

I can only whimper because I still can't really move. The man shoves another pill into my mouth, holding his hand over it again. I'm much too weak to fight, and my mind spins.

I'm stuck. I can't run. I can't scream. And worst of all, I'm completely at this man's mercy. If he has any.

CHAPTER 8
FRANKIE

I CAN'T STOP THINKING about today's date: December 17, 2000.

Sixteen months of Chloe missing, and also her nineteenth birthday.

The second birthday she hasn't been here for.

But she's somewhere, I remind myself.

There's no way Chloe is dead. I don't believe that, and to celebrate her birthday today, I convinced Dad to help me hang Chloe posters all over town. I made them myself, even riding my bike to Kinko's to make 200 copies using the last of my babysitting money for the month. I put Chloe's senior picture on them. The one that was featured as a memorial in our yearbook instead of a sendoff into adulthood.

When Chloe first disappeared, people hung up posters in local cafes and restaurants and all over town. But those are gone now, and I need to keep her memory fresh in everyone's minds so the world doesn't give up on her.

Dad and I haven't talked much today while we've been doing this. We've worked our way downtown, block by block. I wanted to split up and cover more ground, but Dad insisted on sticking together even if it takes longer.

I didn't argue because this is the first time he's seemed to want to hang out with me in months. He's a guidance counselor at my high school, and when he's not working, he's busy volunteering as a coach—basketball and baseball—and in the summer he helps at Paradise Point, a youth camp in McCall.

"Honey, you know we may never find out what happened to her," Dad says as we enter a little bistro that has a bulletin board. When he staples the poster, it makes a *ka-thunk* sound and every time, I picture Chloe that much closer to home.

I don't answer him, and instead turn to walk back outside and into the cold, acting busy with the stack of fliers, as if I'm sorting them with mittened hands. I want him to think I didn't hear him. I hate this conversation.

He touches my arm so I have to look up. Tears warm my icy cheeks, but only for a second before they turn cold.

I already know all of this. He's been telling me for months. The odds of finding a missing person after the first forty-eight hours and all that. Adults repeat this like it's some magic pill I can swallow in order to bounce back into life as a happy high schooler. As if Chloe is disposable and all I have to do is *try* to make other friends to replace her.

"You need to start thinking about your future. We have to talk about college, about what you want to do with your life. You have to move forward."

Move forward.

He means forgetting about Chloe.

"I can't give up on her. She wouldn't give up on me," I say, handing him another flier and pointing to the traffic signal. I pull the Scotch tape out of my backpack.

"It's not giving up. It's facing reality." He takes the poster. At least his voice is soft instead of filled with annoyance like it usually is when we talk about what he calls my fixation on Chloe's disappearance.

I clench my jaw to force myself to think before speaking.

Because what I want to say is, it's only been a little over a year! How can I simply move on like that? It feels completely impossible, as if someone were demanding that I build a computer on the spot when I don't even know how they work. And besides, I'm absolutely right that Chloe would never give up on me.

She always has my back. And not only that, but it seems like Dad is always telling me to let stuff go. Not only Chloe, but bad things that happen too. Does he even care about me?

Like the time in elementary school when I was in third grade, and Chloe was in fifth, and I was going to her house for a sleepover. I had a note to ride her bus home and I beat her there and sat in the back—Chloe's usual spot.

But Matt Fisher followed and stood in the aisle, blocking me in my own seat as if he were going to sit next to me.

"What are you doing back here, Shorty?" he said.

My stomach churned with anxiety. He was huge. And so mean.

"Going home with Chloe."

He scoffed and took the seat in front of me, turning to say, "Tweedle-Dee and Tweedle-Dum are gonna go play dollies?"

I ignored him and stared out the window, searching for Chloe, and trying to hide that my eyes burned with the threat of tears. I could not cry. Not right now.

"Or maybe you play with stuffed animals instead?" Matt asked.

He wasn't going to leave me alone, so I stood up to move toward the front. Find a seat away from him. Chloe would be fine with not sitting in her usual seat. But Matt put his hand on my shoulder and shoved me down into the vinyl again.

"I didn't say you could move."

"Matt, leave her alone," a voice came from behind his huge body.

It was Chloe, standing there, so short that Matt had to look down to make eye contact even though they were almost the same age.

I started crying at this point because of the sheer relief of the moment. Chloe was here. Surely he'd back off. Chloe was popular—everyone liked her, even if she was short.

But Matt didn't back off. He moved into the aisle and turned to face Chloe, who was standing in the aisle behind him.

"What did you say to me, Tiny?" he asked.

She repeated the words.

Then it happened so fast, like the pop of a balloon.

Matt punched Chloe in the ear. She doubled over, holding her ear and crying. She wouldn't let anyone pick on me, but she couldn't hold her own against him either, so there was no way she'd fight back.

The surrounding kids started yelling and it caught the bus driver's attention, which put a stop to it all. I'll never forget how brave she was.

When I got to Chloe's house that day, I called my dad to tell him about it and he didn't do anything. He should have taken my side and maybe even called Matt's parents to tell them he'd been harassing me. All he said was, "Let it go." I never forgot that, either.

"Even if I accept that she's gone, I have to know what happened," I say finally as an answer to Dad's request that I let Chloe go. "Someone must know something. It feels like I won't be able to get past it until I find out either way."

"I understand," Dad starts, now facing me, using his hands to talk so that the poster flails around. "But it's not good for you to hang on to it like this. It's not healthy. You have to accept that we may *never* know."

"I can't handle that," I say. "I can't live without answers."

"What does that mean?" His question comes with urgency, as if he thinks I may do something drastic.

"I feel stuck. Like I can't move forward."

"You'll make new friends."

I shake my head and try to calm the anger that always rises when anyone says something like that. Chloe was closer to a sister I never had, and besides, I suck at making friends, so how would I be able to now, in the midst of the creeping gray fog that is the loss of Chloe Webster? I can't see through it. Can't even begin to wonder how to clear it. Instead, I have to muddle my way each day, feeling out the steps and taking the hits as they come.

Chloe's birthday.

Expecting to see her coming around every corner at school.

Another girl in Chloe's position on the soccer team.

Aunt Bertie slowly losing her mind from grief.

A pair of Chloe's jeans surfacing from under my bed when I clean my room.

Every moment brings fresh and unexpected pain. When my mom died, it was final. But we can still find Chloe. That means it's not over. There's still hope.

NOW

CHAPTER 9
FRANKIE

All I can do is stand in Dad's front yard, staring at the words on my phone screen:

I KNOW WHAT HAPPENED TO CHLOE WEBSTER.

My first instinct is, of course, to take the bait. To reply and beg for more information. But I hesitate because of all the bogus tips I've gotten in the past. Years after Chloe went missing, and the police had given up, and Aunt Bertie's mind was going so she no longer had the capacity to search for her, I set up a page on Reddit for anyone to reach out with information about Chloe's case.

The Hot Springs Murders got some national attention because of the brutality. The fact that the twins were shot with crossbow arrows instead of a gun, mostly. And because Chloe had seemingly gotten away. Or somebody took her. We still don't know.

Because of that, there have been so many people claiming to know her whereabouts over the years. So many "sightings" that seemed legit so I ended up wasting precious days of my life hoping, just in time for the big reveal: They didn't know jack shit the whole time.

Granted, the leads have tapered off significantly over the past ten years, but here I am again, face to face with this.

Maybe because it's the first lead in what feels like forever, or because of the timing being so close to the memorial event, my stomach feels like a hurricane, and my mind is going *this might be it this might be it this might be it*. I clench my jaw and exhale a long breath before shooting off a reply:

I'M ALL EARS.

Then the weirdest thing happens. I'm staring at my phone when I feel like someone is watching me. This has been happening lately. It's this sense of being inside a house with all the lights on while someone observes you from outside in the dark. I feel like I'm in a fish bowl.

I glance around, but can't tell if anything is out of the ordinary. Across the street, Dad's neighbor, Ellen, is on her knees in her garden, facing away from me. Mr. Garcia is in the house next to hers, and I can see him in profile while he watches TV. But he's pushing ninety and I doubt he could see this far anyway.

There's a woman about a block away, walking toward me with her black lab. That must be it. She's the only one facing my direction, although it doesn't seem right. It's not the same feeling: someone noticing you in their line of view versus someone spying on you. And I definitely feel the second one.

No matter. I shake it off and check my phone again.

There's no response from the Reddit person, so I jog a couple steps to my truck. I need to get home to my laptop so I can do some digging. Who is this person messaging me?

The second my car starts, Natalie Merchant's voice croons loud on the radio singing "These Are Days." Chloe's favorite song.

The truck idles, waiting for me to put it into drive, but I linger for a minute and listen to the words of the song.

It's a weird coincidence, hearing it immediately after receiving that Reddit message. I shouldn't assign more importance to it than what's there—it's just chance. Randomness.

I tell myself this, but who am I kidding? It feels like something. I just don't know what. Or why, for that matter.

The five-minute drive from Dad's house back to mine goes quickly, and I keep hoping for a Reddit notification.

It's a whole lot of nothing all the way home, and when I burst through the front door, I go immediately to the bedroom to get my laptop.

The big bedroom is the one place I actually didn't spend a lot of time in as a kid because it was my aunt's space. I rummage around the floor for the computer. My long hair is in the way, as usual, so I stand to loop it into a topknot and see my computer peeking half-out from under the bed.

I grab it and head back toward the kitchen, which is my makeshift office. With it open, I pull up Reddit, where I stare once again at my own message with no reply from this person, Punkass99.

What is up with that name, anyway? Does he really expect me to take him seriously?

My stomach growls, so I look at the time. It's three p.m., and I haven't had more than a few cups of coffee and a bowl of cereal today. A meal would be good, but I hate cooking and can't be away from this for the time it would take anyway, so I go to the pantry, scoop up a handful of trail mix, and plop down in the chair to make eye contact with my laptop again.

My own words sit there, staring right back at me.

I click over to study Punkass99. He has the generic Reddit alien for a profile pic, and the page is generic too. Hardly any achievements, even though it does have some post karma, which means this person is posting somewhere on Reddit. Yet, there are no posts in the feed. It's like he's chosen to hide them all from view. But that handle, Punkass99, is tugging at me. The year Chloe went missing was 1999.

It feels like it means something and my heart beats frantically.

Come on, come on. Answer, Punkass.

When there's still no indication of movement on the other end, I read over my message again. I should have come out of the gate a little more friendly. I scrunch up my nose and groan. Chances are it's another false lead anyway and I shouldn't get my hopes up. I'll get all excited about the possibility of learning more information about Chloe only to be thrown against a wall and shattered when nothing comes of it.

It's been so many years since Chloe disappeared. I can't imagine this person having anything to say that's helpful.

This inner battle rages for a while, the whole time my stomach growls, so I remember the thing about a watched pot not boiling and I force myself to walk away for another handful of trail mix.

When I return to the laptop, there's still nothing. Irritation flares inside me, so I try again.

CLEARLY YOU KNOW NOTHING.

I pop a couple peanuts and raisins into my mouth. I already combed all the chocolate out of the bag days ago.

Maybe I'm scaring him off by sending messages before he has a chance to reply. Maybe this is absolutely nothing. *Chill, Frank. Just chill.*

I open another tab and do a search for original mid-century light fixtures to get my mind off of this, but it doesn't do the trick. Still, minutes pass. A lot of them until it's already after four p.m.

I realize I've been nervously jostling my leg so hard it's making the table shake, so I stop and peer outside at the neighbor, one of the last of the elderly on this street. The whole neighborhood is growing old and passing away. This man is slowly pushing a lawn mower out of his garage and onto the yard. He doesn't get very far before a younger woman runs out the front door and pries him away from it. She guides him inside and immediately comes back to turn on the mower and proceeds to cut the grass. Must be his daughter. Or a paid caregiver, maybe?

I'm staring, watching this whole thing happen, and it makes me realize how goddamn tired I am.

I check the message thread again and there's still nothing. Whatever. This is another false lead, and I shouldn't have expected anything more.

That's when a message appears.

I KNOW PLENTY. I WAS THERE.

CHAPTER 10

FRANKIE

My stream of unanswered messages stand there, all in a neat row. More minutes pass with no response. I need to be patient and stop barraging this person. But I can't help it; hope is about to pin self-protection for the win, because this feels different from other leads. Normally, people reaching out like this are so hungry for a response from me, for my attention, that they engage immediately. They always think they have some tidbit nobody has thought of, and then quickly reveal they only know the same shit that's public information. Or what they have isn't actually a lead according to the police, so they come to me.

This feels more like the person might be having second thoughts about reaching out. It's strange to be the one bombarding with messages.

That doesn't mean this is legit. It just means I haven't had to pull messages out of anyone before. I need to keep it together, but it's hard because Punkass claims to have been there. What does that mean?

Time for a new approach. Maybe being more direct will work, so I start typing again.

TONS OF PEOPLE CLAIM TO KNOW WHAT
HAPPENED TO CHLOE.

WHY SHOULD I BELIEVE YOU?

No response.

"Come on, come on," I whisper, as if that can coax this person out of his shell.

The sound of my newly installed Ring doorbell startles me into a yelp.

I pull up the app on my phone and Jensen stands sideways, looking up like he's gazing at the stars in the middle of the day. Apparently he got his hair cut. It's still longer on top, but neatly trimmed around the ears. He's wearing a tee shirt that says "208 Born and Bred," and it has a picture of orange, red, and yellow mountains along with an outline of the Idaho panhandle. Like an off-brand version of the Patagonia logo.

Jensen was born in Idaho, yes. But that's not why he's wearing it. It's his own private joke. His way of making a passive aggressive statement against Idahoans being so up in arms about people moving here from big cities. It's easy to understand why locals are mad about what they see as an invasion into Idaho's comfy little campfire of great housing prices and family values. It's hard to watch your small town grow into something unrecognizable. But that's life. I agree with Jensen that people can move wherever they want, but it's a hot-button issue I wish he would stay away from.

Wait, why is he so early? We're doing pizza for dinner, but it's not dinner time yet.

I rush to the door and fling it open without even greeting Jensen before I race back to my computer.

"Hello to you, too!" Jensen announces to the empty entryway.

"Sorry, I got a message about Chloe. Come here."

Jensen comes to stand behind while I stare at my laptop screen.

"Another fake lead, right?" he says, reaching into the bag of trail mix at the counter and popping a peanut into his mouth. He surveys the kitchen. "Where's the pizza?"

I furrow my brows at him, ignoring his last question. "It doesn't seem like a fake. This one's different. Here, take a look."

He leans over my shoulder and I get a strong whiff of sandalwood and deodorant. His clean, earthy scent.

He scans the message thread. "They didn't actually say anything."

"They said they were there! You think that's nothing?"

"Hm." Jensen reaches for another handful of trail mix, and I can feel him thinking the words *Chloe obsession*. Being a math teacher, he's logical about the odds of Chloe ever returning. Even I understand that they're zero at this point, but I've never been one for math.

"Well, it's also not very much to go from," he says.

I know that but it's annoying that he doesn't seem to see the significance either. Or maybe he doesn't care. Sometimes it feels like the things that are important to me aren't that important to him. I never make a big deal about it because we aren't in a real relationship, so I don't expect him to be invested in that way. It still grates on me though.

"But for real. Why are you here so early?" I ask, changing the subject.

"Got my workout done and errands finished." He goes over to the fridge and opens it. "No beer either? You're really letting me down on that pizza and beer promise." He flashes a smile, but it doesn't make me any less annoyed. Why isn't he at least a little intrigued by these messages?

"Two words: Uber Eats," I reply. "Did you think the pizza and beer would materialize on their own?"

"That's one word."

"Huh?"

"UberEats is one word."

"Nope. It's two words. Look it up."

"Nah. You're always right about grammar. But you know what I'm right about?" Jensen leans on the table, snuggling up next to my computer, trying to get his face in line with the screen in a bid for my attention.

I pause, hoping he doesn't bring up our relationship and how he wants more from it. That seems like the obvious thing he'd claim to be right about.

"Food," he says. "I'm always right about food, and this chocolate-neutered trail mix isn't cutting it. Let's go out for pizza."

My shoulders drop, relaxing. I dodged the bullet I know is coming at any point: A come-to-Jesus about our "friendship." I can feel the tension building as the days go by and as he drops hints about wanting more from me.

"You're just trying to get me away from my computer and stop obsessing over Chloe, but what you don't realize is I have this little thing called the Reddit app on my phone." I hold it up and smile.

"Actually, I'm trying to get some pizza. You can look at whatever you want in the process. I know better than to think I can get you to do anything."

I sigh and close the computer. "Fine, let's go."

CHAPTER 11

FRANKIE

I'm two pieces of extra-large pineapple and pepperoni deep—Chloe's favorite—and considering a second glass of beer. Flying Pie makes the best pizza in Boise, but that doesn't distract me from the fact that Punkass still hasn't replied to my last message.

Jensen is coming back from the bathroom when an older man with a beard and ball cap stops him.

"I like your shirt." The man points to Jensen's ironic tee. "I grew up in Parma. Lived around here all my life. Sure wish they'd close the Idaho borders and send those Californians back. Where were you born?"

Boise. Jensen was born in Boise, but still, I brace myself for it—the most awkward interaction of the week. It will make Jensen's day.

"Napa Valley area," he responds. There's a little dare in his voice.

The man shifts his weight, sniffs, and stuffs his hands into his worn jean pockets. It feels like five minutes have passed. "You mean *Nampa*? Idaho?"

Jensen grins and I can't take it anymore. I reach for another slice of pizza, acting like I don't know him.

"No, sir. Napa Valley, *California*," he lies.

I don't even have to be watching this to sense the shift in the air. I can imagine the poor man's surprise, like he just got a punch in the face.

"Well, then ... Why are you wearing that shirt?" the man fumbles. "Says you were born here. In Idaho."

"Oh, I just liked these colors when I saw it at the store."

The man groans and walks past him, aiming for the bathroom. Jensen slides into the seat across from me wearing his thousand-watt smile, but I look at my phone, hoping that my mystery person will come through soon.

Jensen takes a huge swig of his beer and eyes me like he's waiting for applause for his performance, which could be titled something like *Man Pokes the Bear Yet Again*.

"I still don't get what the point of that is," I say. "They have no clue you're playing a joke on them. They just think you're an asshole."

"Well, that's the fun part." He reaches for another piece of pizza, and I notice his cheeks are very rosy. It's not hot in here. In fact, the AC is making it a bit chilly. Our pitcher of beer has about one swig left, and I've only had one glass.

"Are you drunk?" I ask, leaning across the table.

"What? On Coors Light?" He scoffs and waves a hand.

"That was definitely not Coors Light, and you know it. Why are you getting IPA-drunk on a Thursday night?"

He shrugs and breaks eye contact.

It doesn't matter. I don't care when or how much he drinks, but it's not like him to go this hard on a weekday. Jensen slides out of his seat again.

"Where you going?" I ask.

"Beer's gone. Need more."

"Let's grab a six-pack on the way home," I say just to get him out of here. But I immediately realize that won't work either. I can't stay up all night drinking because of the event tomorrow, and even if I don't get drunk, at my age, sleep deprivation is as bad as a hangover. I'm already running on so little sleep today.

A family in the booth next to us is staring. What if Jensen makes a scene? It's not like him, but still.

"I want a roady," he says.

"I've got a beer in the truck," I lie, reaching for his arm. As if I'll be able to budge him at all. He's over six feet tall and I barely break five-two.

He screws his face up. "You have a beer. In the truck."

"Yep. Just for you. Let's go."

"I'm not *that* drunk, Frank. I know you're just trying to get me out of here."

"Is it working?"

He runs a hand through his hair and eyes the single slice of pizza on the pan. "Fine, but I'm bringing this."

I sneak another glance at my phone, and it's still crickets. I probably need to let it go considering this person may never, ever reply.

Jensen is already walking out the door ahead of me, so I hit the key fob to unlock the truck before he gets there. My stomach is a burst of anxious butterflies but I also feel an undercurrent of anger. Why is Jensen acting like this? And why doesn't he seem even slightly curious about the messages from Punkass? Jesus, if Jensen brings up the topic of our relationship right now, I may lose it. It's the day before the event and he knows how important it is to me. That, coupled with his obvious disinterest in the possible lead about Chloe has my frustration growing faster than I like. Any mention of *us* and I'm afraid I'll snap.

When I step out into the heat, this crawling sensation moves down my neck. It's that feeling again—like someone is watching me. What the hell?

I glance around, but all I see are cars zooming by on busy Fairview Avenue. Nobody is even out walking. It's August, late in the day, so of course, most people are hanging out in air conditioning somewhere.

A young woman comes out of the shop next to the pizzeria, but she doesn't even notice me before she gets into her Subaru.

What is wrong with me? Am I being paranoid?

When I get into the truck, Jensen sits in the passenger seat without a seatbelt. His head leans against the window, and his eyes are closed. He doesn't say anything the whole way home, which is surprising, but I'm grateful. It gives me a chance to cool down too.

I pull into his driveway instead of mine, fully planning to drop him off because he's acting so weird and I think he might be mad at me. I don't have much to do for the event, and I was hoping to spend the evening with him. Just not staying up all night. But whatever, I guess I'll go home.

He nods in defeat even though I didn't say anything, and reaches for the door handle, but then turns toward me and says, "At some point, you have to stop living in the past. She's gone, Frank. Chloe is never coming back and you've already wasted half your life on her. Time to move on."

He grips the truck handle as if moving to get out, and it's my signal that he doesn't expect a reply. I'm surprised to find tears pricking at my face instead of frustration. Especially since he sounds exactly like my dad. But I'm so exhausted that I don't have the energy for an argument.

"You coming in?" he says, turning to face me. "We have another episode of *Chimp Crazy* to watch."

I nod and shame floods me. I should go home because it feels like staying over is taking advantage of him. But I don't want to be alone either.

THEN

CHAPTER 12
CHLOE

I'm back in the 101 Dalmatians room. It's not bright in here by any means, but I can see more clearly, and I quickly take inventory of the space.

There's a window to the left, but it's boarded up. Light peeks in around the edges of the warped plywood. It must be daytime, and that's why it's brighter.

The room is small, with concrete walls.

A bucket and a roll of toilet paper are nearby. That must be for—I swallow down a sob. It's so degrading.

I don't remember getting back to this room. I remember being naked in the bathtub, but now I'm wearing sweats that are too large but clean, and my hair is wetter than it was before. It smells like soap.

He washed and dressed me.

I groan at the thought of it, but I can't linger there in my mind. I have to sit up and get moving, but when I try, my body feels heavy. It's not until my stomach heaves that I summon enough strength to push myself up in time to vomit beside the mattress. The sudden motion makes my leg cry out in searing pain, and then I'm dizzy, out of sorts, but memories surface.

The hot springs.

Arrows flying through the night.

Amy and Kristi.

The thought of them knocks the wind out of me this time. How could they have survived the arrows? Amy fell off the cliff and Kristi stopped blinking. I don't think they made it, and a wave of emotion swells, threatening to choke me so I shake my head to clear those thoughts.

I have to get out of here, so I force myself to focus on the man. The scary Bill Clinton mask, and his hands on himself, jerking off while I was naked in the water. I whimper; a pit grows deep inside and the memory fills me with shame and horror.

I start hyperventilating, my short breaths growing louder as if I'm sprinting, and my heart comes up into my throat until I sob and moan, feeling like I can't get ahold of myself at all, but I have to.

I move carefully—so slowly—in order to lean my back against the concrete wall and create as little agony to my leg as possible. I've twisted an ankle before, and this is worse. Much worse. I gently feel around, barely grazing the skin but the pain is unbearable and it's too swollen to tell. It could be broken.

Then I think of the baby and touch my still-flat stomach awkwardly, like it belongs to someone else. "I'm so sorry I got us into this."

Sorry's not good enough.

It isn't. I have to do more than be sorry. I have to get out of here.

I take a slow, deep breath, then exhale. No time to cry; I must grow up. And now.

I shift to one knee, extending the hurt leg behind so I can favor it as I crawl to explore.

My body shakes, trembling so much that I can barely push myself forward.

A bright light suddenly illuminates around the only door.

Low murmuring on the other side. Someone is talking.

My first instinct is to call for help, but I don't because how stupid would that be? It's probably the man with the Bill Clinton mask—I'll just call him Bill. And he must be the one who shot my friends too.

The door cracks open a bit, sending a blast of light at my face, and I cover it, trying to stifle cries I can't help because of the shooting pain in my leg.

My eyes adjust, and Bill steps in, standing there holding a camping lantern which shines on half of him. The other half seems to blend into the rest of the dark room. He's tall with broad shoulders and my eyes fixate on that mask again. He approaches, and I push back against the wall until there's no space. Bill crouches on the ground across from me, sets down the lantern and then a paper plate with pizza. It might be the same two slices from before. He reaches into the front pocket of his black sweatshirt and pulls out a small water bottle, setting it next to the plate. Then he stands up again.

I stare at the pizza, remembering the last time this happened, and fear grows inside me. Then I feel a warm sensation soaking my sweatpants. I've never peed myself before, and I shake uncontrollably.

"Ready to eat now?" His voice is low and gruff.

"Are you going to hurt me?" I whisper.

"Eat." He ignores my question.

"Is it drugged?"

He doesn't answer, just stays there, much too close, covered in head-to-toe black.

I glance at the food. I should eat it, but what if it's drugged? I need to keep my mind alert.

"Do I have to force you like last time?" Bill asks.

"No! No. I'll eat it. Please don't do that again."

He stands there watching as I take a small bite of the cold pizza.

I keep my breathing steady while I eat, letting my eyes wander beyond him and to the door he came through, which still stands open. It's light out there—another lantern maybe—and across the way, I see prison bars.

I wonder if this is a jail, and if so, could I run past him and escape? I pull my feet underneath to test my leg, but no way it can hold my weight. I moan in pain. Plus, Bill is huge and standing squarely between me and the door. I'm not going anywhere. At least not right now.

"Pepperoni and pineapple, your favorite," he says.

He knows my favorite pizza.

The realization makes me shake so hard I can't hold the slice without him seeing me tremble.

"You're cold," he says, mistaking my fear.

"A little." It's not totally untrue and I'd rather he think this than know how scared I am, although surely he must know.

"Use those blankets," he points to the untouched stack. "I'll bring you clean pants since you pissed those."

A wave of shame covers me and I want to cry again, but I swallow down the urge.

He grunts and moves toward the door to leave. As he does, I notice something I didn't see before. There's a girl behind the prison bars across the hallway. My view isn't clear, but the red curly hair framing a pale face makes me certain I'm not seeing things. The girl lies on her side, facing me, but her eyes are closed. There's duct tape over her mouth.

I want to call to her, wake her up and get her attention somehow, but there's no time. The lantern light slivers as Bill closes the door.

NOW

CHAPTER 13
FRANKIE

It's already the night of Chloe's event, and I've heard nothing else from the mysterious Reddit lead.

I absolutely hate that I'm letting it get to me when it's probably nothing, but I've been compulsively checking my phone for notifications since Punkass showed up in my life days ago.

The band I hired for the event is killing it. Treefort Music Hall is a venue with a raised stage for concerts and fundraisers. It can hold about a thousand people, and the turnout is as good as I expected. We won't raise an earth-shattering amount of money, but it'll be enough to spread across a few different organizations for missing children.

Most people gather in the open area in front of the stage. There's bistro-style seating along the edges of the room, and a full bar across in the back, next to doors that open directly to downtown Boise.

Jensen has passed the evening wandering around, offering to buy drinks for people and thanking them for coming out. He's wearing the black slacks and button-up gray shirt I told him to wear. It's rare to see him dressed up, especially in the summer. He looks good.

I'm in a knee-length sundress, but it's black and that gives a more formal feel. My hair hangs in loose curls and I'm trying not to give in to the urge to put it back and out of my way.

Before I know it, the band is on the second to last song of the night, which is my cue to get on stage. My nerves are going haywire. I speak briefly every year at the end to say a few words about the girls—mostly Chloe. But I hate being in front of people and have never gotten used to it. I snake through the crowd and toward the stage so I'll be standing by when the song is over.

My phone vibrates in my hand, sending my heart surging into my throat.

A new Reddit message, and it says:

IF YOU WANT INFORMATION, I HAVE IT.

Of course Punkass decides to message me right at this moment. I type a response quickly.

GREAT, SPILL IT.

Is this person just fucking with me? It feels like he's being purposefully coy.

After a few seconds of waiting for a reply that doesn't come, I roll my eyes. I swear the mixture of nerves about going on stage, and the adrenaline from this, will give me a heart attack.

I feel like screaming and throwing my phone on the floor in some grown-up tantrum. But instead, I grip the phone tighter and fix my eyes on the stage. I need to pull it together so I'm not a mess when I get up there in a few seconds. Jensen is already at the bottom of the stairs, like he's waiting to give me some last-minute encouragement as I go up, and when I slip through the crowd to get next to him, he says, "You ready?"

I nod and glance at the phone again.

Still nothing.

My hand shakes, and the pump of blood slams against my insides. It's all too much. I may come unraveled.

Jensen wraps his arm around my shoulders and leans in close. "Breathe. It's okay, you got this."

"Punkass sent another message, but it's confusing," I say.

I show him the phone and he takes it, shaking his head. "Ignore him. Whoever he is, *he's* gonna wait on *you* this time."

"Thanks. Can you babysit my phone while I'm up there? Watch for a message?"

He nods.

I feel grateful to have him by my side right now and I climb the stairs and look out into the dark room. I know it's full of faces even if I can only see the ones in the first few rows.

Words leave my mouth—a thank you to everyone for coming out—and then I can't remember the speech I practiced. It's totally gone. Something about giving back to the community and supporting others who have lost loved ones tragically. But the rehearsed words aren't in my mind. Other words are.

"I know what happened to Chloe Webster."

"I was there."

I look at Jensen, who is alternating his face between me and my phone. He shakes his head.

No message.

I clear my throat. It's been an awkward moment, and I have to say something even if it's not what I planned. "Grief is weird," I start, then wait to see if the crowd has any reaction. Of course they don't. They have no clue this isn't what I planned to say. "Grief without closure is even weirder." I give a nervous chuckle. "Maybe *weird* isn't the right word, but when you lose someone and you don't know if they're alive or not, it feels like being suspended in time. Funny because time is supposed to heal all wounds, but how can a wound heal when it's not actually treatable? I can't bandage or nurse the gaping hole Chloe's absence left, because that would be what they call 'moving on,' and to me, it feels like giving up. It always has."

I glance over faces and read confusion. Then I think of a way to tie it together and get myself out of such vulnerable territory. "Sorry, maybe that metaphor doesn't work, but what I mean is it's hard to let go without closure. And yet, we often have to say goodbye to people before they're actually gone. There are a lot of reasons for that, and a loved one disappearing like Chloe did is much more rare than other situations. More often our loved ones 'disappear' into themselves in other ways. Sometimes because substances—like drugs or alcohol—alter them beyond recognition. We don't know if they'll ever overcome addiction and be the person we once knew and loved. We're stuck in limbo."

Dots connect like lightning when I see Joan and Mark Overland, who have two children living on the streets with severe mental illness. "Some of us have loved ones who refuse the mental help they need in order to function in society. In a way, it's like they're not with us anymore, even if their warm bodies are right there, within reach. We try to do everything in our power to support them, and in a sense, to bring them back to themselves, to us, but ultimately it's out of our control. We are excruciatingly helpless."

Tears well up and fall down my cheeks. "I'm sorry," I sniffle and look up at the ceiling like that will help. "I didn't expect to cry, but Chloe was my person, and twenty-five years doesn't make it any easier. Whoever said time heals all was full of shit."

Nervous laughter trills through the crowd.

My eyes find Jensen again, who seems to have forgotten his duty to my phone and is instead watching me, his eyes wide with compassion. Or concern. He might be worried that I'm about to come unhinged. I can't tell.

"But at least we can do this." I motion my hand around the venue. "We can come together to find community and show strength in solidarity, while raising money to support other families experiencing this limbo type of loss. Thank you for coming tonight, everyone. Please get home safely."

The band starts playing the same final song they always play. "These Are Days" by 10,000 Maniacs.

In a flash, I'm down the stairs and my phone is in hand again. Of course, no new message.

"You did great," Jensen says, intertwining his fingers with my free hand and gently squeezing. It's an intimate gesture that makes me uncomfortable, but I'm too amped up to fight it.

"I need a drink," I say, mostly to get away and find my composure.

I weave through the crowd and toward the bar.

The door opens and sunlight drafts in from the outside. It blinds me a little, but when the person doesn't enter and instead stands there in the open doorway, I get curious and step closer. Who comes to a benefit at the very end?

Then I see her.

Long, straight hair, perky nose, and just as short as ever.

It's Chloe Webster.

THEN

CHAPTER 14

CHLOE

ONCE I'M ALONE AGAIN, I call out to the redheaded girl. "Hey! Can you hear me? Are you okay?"

Nothing in response.

She doesn't reply, but maybe it's because her mouth is still taped shut. Her eyes were closed when I saw her. I don't even know if she's alive.

My stomach churns with dread at this thought and I tell myself, no, she was only sleeping.

But even so, the situation is bad.

Dread turns to nausea, which floods my system, and I lean my face away from the mattress, waiting to see if I'll throw up. Thankfully, I don't.

I can't tell if I feel sick because I'm scared to death or because I'm pregnant. It seems like I should be feeling better by now. But of course, I don't know. I'm clueless about being pregnant. And I've been so focused on keeping it a secret, so scared about anyone finding out, that I've done no research.

Amy and Kristi knew.

Who else knows?

I'm so stupid to have left the used test at their house. But bringing it home in my bag was a bad idea too. I should have taken the test at school. But then, what if someone saw it in my backpack before I got to the bathroom? Tears turn into sobbing quickly, but this isn't helping.

No sense in wasting tears on self pity, so I lift my chin and swallow hard. I'm still alive, and so there's still time.

I crawl across the room toward that boarded-up window, dragging my bad leg. Every movement hurts, but I clench my teeth and keep going. I must learn everything I can about this room. Find a way out.

When I reach the window ledge, I pull myself up, supporting my weight on the good leg.

Nausea again. This time I vomit what little was in my stomach, then cough and wipe my mouth. I run my hand along the plywood until I find a corner that seems loose. My fingers work that spot, picking at it until I manage to tear off a piece. It's not thick wood. If I tried hard, I could probably break it all off eventually.

Excitement bubbles inside me. I could break the glass next, and then maybe escape out the window.

I try to pull more wood off, but other than that one corner, it's much harder to dislodge. The part I removed is the size of a peephole, so I slowly bend down to line my eye up to see out.

Immediately, any hope I had dampens because bars cover the window. Vertical, metal bars, like the ones I saw the girl behind.

Tears form in my eyes all over again, and I blink to free my vision.

My hunch was right. I'm in a prison. And the plywood isn't there to keep me trapped. It's for secrecy. To keep me hidden from outside view.

I don't know why it matters because there are only pine trees out there. I stare at the sky and notice it's fading to a light blue. It feels like dusk.

I sigh and stagger along the rest of the walls, hand dragging flat. I want to inspect and to find some way out, even if I don't have a lot of hope for that either.

Turns out there's nothing else in here. Besides the main entrance, there's no other door, no other windows or anything.

I make my way back to the twin mattress against the back wall, almost tripping on the sloping floor. My feet touch something metal, about six inches in diameter.

It's a drain of sorts, but it's getting too dark in here to tell.

A drain. For some reason, the thought of it makes a shiver crawl up my spine.

———

THE BRIGHT LIGHT around the edges of the plywood in the window tell me it's morning. I scan the room again, this time with more visibility, and my eyes fix on the floor drain.

Is this some sort of cleaning supply room?

I glance up and there's a huge square on the ceiling. This is the most light I've had in the room and I can't tell what's up there, but it looks like a door. It's big. Maybe takes up a fourth of the ceiling.

Wait. There's a crack of space running all around it, so yes, definitely a door. But why? It's almost like a trapdoor.

My eyes trace from the ceiling door to directly below. The drain. Then I notice a mechanism on the wall across from me that's attached to the ceiling door. Like a big hinge.

I bet that's how the door opens. It could be a chute of sorts. Like a laundry chute.

But why would they have such a big laundry room in an old prison like this?

Then it hits me. It's not laundry that drops through that door.

I remember from school that Idaho used hangings to execute prisoners well into the fifties.

I'm not in a prison cell, I'm in an execution room.

A scream so visceral it surprises me comes out, followed by wailing that I can't control. It feels like an exorcism of terror and pain, and when it finally dies down into soft crying, I pull my good leg up and hug it to my chest. Then I lay my head down.

I'm in a killing room, where who knows how many people have died over the years. And not just any people—murderers and rapists. The ones worthy of a death sentence. And this brings another thing to mind. This prison clearly isn't in use. It's abandoned enough to hold girls hostage without anyone knowing. Am I even in Idaho anymore?

The devastation these thoughts bring into my body make me want to give up. There's no hope.

But I can't give up. Someone may still find me. For example, if the police find Amy and Kristi's bodies at Skinny Dipper, but not mine, that could lead them to look for me.

Poor Amy and Kristi.

I can't think about them either. My brain fuzzes out of focus, like it's trying to either protect me from more hopelessness or save mental energy for the nightmare I'm currently living.

A blade of light moves across the slit at the bottom of the door to the room, and then out of nowhere, a girl cries out.

I crawl across the room as fast as possible and cup my ear to the cold metal door.

The redhead comes to mind, but she had duct tape over her mouth, so maybe the girl crying isn't her. How many girls are here?

The girl yelps again and then cries out in desperation. "Please. Please don't."

"What the fuck?"

Bill's voice. I recognize it and my heart races.

Duct tape screeches, and then all I hear are moans.

"You said I could do what I wanted with her." A different man's voice.

Someone else is here! Someone who probably isn't locked in a cell.

Should I call out for help? I hesitate, considering the situation. This other guy doesn't strike me as friendly.

"You can't punch them!" Bill yells. "Now she's gonna have a big-ass shiner and I'll have to take her out of the rotation until it heals. Nobody wants to fuck a girl who looks like a punching bag."

"Fine. When can I have her again?"

"So you can fuck her in addition to fucking her up? No way. You're out."

The other man laughs. "You can't do that. I know too much."

There's a pause and then he speaks again and his voice sounds different. Scared. "Sorry, I didn't mean that, man. Put that thing down."

"What's the magic word?" Bill taunts.

"Please. Please!"

I picture Bill pointing his crossbow, how he shot Amy and Kristi, and I inhale sharply.

"I've got so much dirt on you I could backfill a sinkhole. Give me my money and fuck off," Bill says.

"I already paid you up front."

"You're paying double for the way her eye looks."

I pull away from the door, icy terror ripping down my back.

"Nobody wants to fuck a girl who looks like a punching bag."

Bill is selling the girls for sex.

That's why he hasn't killed me. I'm going to be in the rotation too.

A cold numbness comes over me, as if all my adrenaline has

run out, and I sit there, with my back against the door, staring into the dreary room.

I'm going to be abused over and over, maybe until I die. I want to lie down and never wake up.

I close my eyes.

Then something happens—movement in my lower abdomen. Like a tapping sensation. Or tiny bubbles. It's different from hunger pangs or cramping.

I place a hand there and watch, waiting.

It happens again, and for a second I forget about this dark cell. My confinement. The looming torture before me.

"Oh my god," I whisper, tears streaming now. "Is that you?"

Is this what it's like to feel the baby move? I must be farther along than I thought, but this tunnels everything about my situation into sharp focus.

I have a real life growing inside of me. I always knew that, but this is proof, and it's enough to steel my resolve.

Fuck the odds. Fuck Bill.

This is my reason to fight.

NOW

CHAPTER 15
FRANKIE

FOR A SECOND, all I can do is stare at her. Chloe Webster, who steps inside Treefort Music Hall, and then shrinks toward the back wall as if she's trying to make herself invisible. Nobody else seems to notice that she walked in.

Chloe wears a prairie dress that hits her mid-calf, and I can't tell what the pattern is from here, but it's light colored—maybe a shade of yellow. She wears what look like Birkenstock clogs, and a baggy dark cardigan sweater even though it's summer out, along with black-frame glasses.

Chloe didn't wear glasses or contacts before. Am I sure that's her? But then she turns, as if surveying the crowd and the way she does it—the way she tilts her head in curiosity—it's Chloe. *My* Chloe.

My stomach leaps in urgency, loosening my feet so I can close the distance between us. *Go, go, go. Before she disappears again.*

I walk fast toward her, carefully weaving around people while trying not to draw too much attention to myself. I don't want anyone else to notice Chloe Webster is here. There'd be a commotion for sure, and that's fine, but I want her all to myself for a while first.

When I'm about ten feet away, Jensen intersects my path and tries to take me into a hug, saying, "I'm so proud of you."

I feel a burst of frustration at him for interrupting my mission. I pull away and brush past him with as much gentleness as I can conjure in the moment, tossing a "Thanks" over my shoulder. I'll explain later. Surely he'll understand.

I'm getting closer to her and when I'm finally there, Chloe's back is to me as she strains to see the crowd. I bet she's searching for me. I touch her arm gently, and she whips around, half startled.

"Oh my god. Frankie!" she exclaims, then makes praying hands and uses them to cover her closed mouth as if she's trying to contain herself.

"Chloe? Is that really you?" I say.

She nods, wiping her eyes. She has streaks of gray in her hair.

I dive at her for a hug, almost pushing her over, but we find our footing in tandem and I nestle my face into her exposed neck before a stab of embarrassment hits me for such an intimate gesture. I turn my face away and lay my head on her shoulder instead.

Calm down, I tell myself.

But calming down is impossible to do while my body trembles, breaking at the sheer overload of this information to my senses.

Chloe is home. She's back.

I knew it. I always knew she was alive, and it's both glorious and supremely unbelievable at the same time. I squeeze harder, trying to ground myself in this moment.

"Are you okay? Where have you been?"

"Better now that I found you."

There are so many more questions to ask, but all I can do is stare at this person—my cousin—while my mind tries to absorb this new reality.

Everything feels like it's happening so slowly, like I've been standing here with Chloe for hours, but the last song is just now ending. People start socializing and milling around, and the urge to take Chloe out of here, to be alone with her is so strong; I can't resist it anymore. I don't want to share her yet, and I need to make sure she's truly okay. God, where has she been all this time?

"Let's get out of here and go somewhere we can talk," I say.

Something flashes across Chloe's face. It almost looks like disappointment, but she recovers quickly and smiles, saying, "Yeah, that sounds great."

I move an arm toward the back door, a few steps away to indicate I'll follow her out, and when she turns to go, I hate the thoughts that are pushing against my mind because they're dumb and petty.

Chloe looks frumpy. As if she completely forgot how to style herself. Her clothes are way too big and the dress looks like something you'd find on a religious cult compound. Was she in a cult? And those glasses! They have such thick lenses. Nobody really wears Coke bottle lenses anymore, even if the prescription is heavy. Her hair is the same length it was before, but she has thick bangs that almost hang over the glasses.

When we're outside in the warm night air, and Chloe turns to wait for me, the words come streaming out of my mouth. "Chloe, where have you been all these years?"

"Frankie!" Jensen calls my name from behind. I'm sure he's wondering why I'm leaving so abruptly when I'm usually the last to leave. I don't want to hurt him, but I need him to go away for a bit so I can get my bearings with Chloe.

"Can I talk to you?" he asks when he catches up to us.

"Can it wait?"

"Not really," he says, alternating his glance between Chloe

and me. I want to point out that I was right. That Chloe was alive all this time, but he takes my elbow.

What in the world could be so important right now?

"I'm sorry. Please don't go anywhere. This will only take a sec," I say to Chloe.

She nods and smiles. It looks forced. Her eyes have a scared animal quality to them that makes me a little nervous and also breaks my heart.

"What is it?" I ask Jensen when we're out of earshot.

He looks quickly at Chloe and then back at me. He says, "What's going on?"

"That's Chloe. She's back."

He juts his chin forward and his eyes widen in surprise. "Excuse me?"

"I know it sounds crazy. It *is* crazy. But that's my cousin, Chloe Webster. Don't you recognize her?"

He moves his head slightly as if to get a glimpse without her noticing even though he full-on gawked before. Does he not recognize her? Chloe has pulled out a black vape pen the size of a cigarette and has it to her lips.

"I'm sorry but that can't be her. You know Chloe is ..." He trails off.

"Dead," I answer. "I know everyone thinks that, but then why the hell is she standing right there?"

He shrugs like it's an actual question. "No idea, but don't you think it's kind of weird?"

"Yeah, it's fucking insane, so please let me go." I step toward Chloe, leaving him before he can argue again.

"Where are you going?"

I shrug. "No idea. I'll call you later."

"Fine," he says and then waves me off as he walks back into the music hall.

"Who was that?" Chloe asks when I reach where she's at.

"Jensen Ailor."

Her face doesn't change. She doesn't recognize him or his name.

"From school," I continue. "He was in your class. I think you might have dated him for a minute at some point."

"Oh, okay."

Her response is weird. Like even with the added information she doesn't know who he is. Jensen has gray strands and some wrinkles now, but he's recognizable.

"Forget him," I say because who cares about Jensen right now? Chloe is back. Something makes me feel a bit light-headed and my knees turn to jelly. I need to sit before I collapse. I think I might be in some state of shock. My body is trying to take all this in and it's too much.

I motion toward a nearby bench on the sidewalk, so we sit and I start right in.

"You sure you're okay? You look okay, but why were you gone so long? Where have you been? What happened?"

She puts the pen in her cardigan pocket. Then she tucks her hands between her knees and drops her head. Her body starts shaking. She's crying—pretty hard, actually.

"Hey, I'm so sorry," I say, rubbing her back. "I'm sure it's not easy to talk about."

She nods furiously, but keeps wiping her eyes and nose with her brown sweater sleeve.

"That's the worst part, Frankie. I hate it so much, and you're going to hate it too."

I'm not sure what she could tell me that would be worse than her kidnapping and disappearance for twenty-five years, but I close my mouth and listen when she says:

"I don't remember anything."

CHAPTER 16

FRANKIE

My reality bottoms out for the second time tonight.

"What?" I say, pulling my hand from her back and shifting my body to face her even though she's close. What does she mean she doesn't remember anything? How is that possible?

Chloe puts her elbows on her knees and drops her head into her hands, holding it like she has the worst headache in the world. She shakes with sobs again, saying, "I know, I know." Repeating it over and over, getting more worked up each time.

I need to try a different approach. As much as I want answers, and I want them like yesterday, it seems like the more I push, the more upset she becomes. No matter where she's been, or what happened the night she disappeared, and even if she can't give me all the details I want, I refuse to further her trauma. She needs to go at her own pace.

"It's okay. Shhh," I say, rubbing her back again. It feels mechanical, like I'm faking it, but I'm not. I just suck at this. I'm never in situations where I have to comfort someone. I avoid them.

After a moment, Chloe seems to regain composure and sits up, runs a finger under each eye to catch the last few tears, and bumps her glasses in the process. The frames are actually kind of cute, especially the way they perch on her tiny little nose. They've got a slight cat-eye shape. It's like they're trying to be stylish. I think they would be if not for those thick lenses.

People start exiting Treefort and I have the sudden urge to leave. To be anywhere other than downtown Boise, on the sidewalk.

"Let's go somewhere and talk. Does that sound good?" I ask.

"Yeah. I'm kind of hungry. Is there a restaurant around here?"

No. No restaurants. I don't want to be in public at all right now. But I don't have any real food at home either.

"You good with fast food? We can do a drive-thru and then go to my place."

I want to tell her that my place is actually her old place. But she doesn't seem very emotionally stable. Not that I blame her. I'm sure she experienced hell, but she just stopped crying, and I don't want to upset her again.

"Fast food is great. I'm not picky." Chloe smiles and it's like a weight drops off my shoulders.

"Great. My truck is this way," I say and we walk across the street to the parking garage. Chloe follows and reaches into her sweater pocket for the vape pen.

"Do you mind?" she asks.

"Not at all."

Whatever she needs to do to cope. I'm sure it's hard to even be functional after whatever she went through.

Which she doesn't remember.

This fact hits me and I try not to let the rush of discouragement show. What if having Chloe back doesn't mean I get to find out what happened that night? It's something I've never considered before. The two things always went hand in hand when I thought about finding Chloe.

But having her back is the main point, right?

Something in me says I'm still going to struggle with the unknown that's plagued me for almost my whole life. But that's a problem for a different day.

We reach my truck and once we're inside and I'm pulling out, it seems like Chloe is doing better. At least better than she was before, so I play the odds and ask another question.

"So, when you say you don't remember anything, do you mean you don't remember anything from the night you ... disappeared?"

I hope that last word doesn't set her off, and I glance over to check as I drive.

She has her hands between her knees again, and she stares down at them. "It means I don't remember anything at all. I didn't even know I was Chloe Webster until a couple days ago."

"What?" I practically shriek. "What does that mean?"

I don't want to be driving right now. I want to be sitting down across from Chloe and able to focus fully on her. But I'm not stopping the flow of information under any circumstances either.

She sighs and shakes her head. "Believe it or not, a coworker told me I looked identical to some missing girl from the nineties. He dated someone years ago who was obsessed with the case and he'd seen pictures of her. He searched the internet right then and there, and then found a picture of her and showed it to me. The resemblance was uncanny, so when I got home, I did my own digging online."

Chloe pauses as if that's the end of the story.

"And?" I prod.

She wipes her eyes and *shit*, she's crying again. "Sorry," she says.

"Chloe, it's not your fault. You have absolutely nothing to apologize for."

"I feel so bad that it all happened. That I don't remember

anything and now I'm back but I don't have any answers. It must be so hard for you."

"Please don't worry about me. I'm here and I'm not going anywhere. I want to support you and listen to whatever you can tell me."

I can't push her. That's one thing I just won't do.

"Well, when I saw the pictures online, I knew it was me right away," she says. "I recognized my eyes. I've stared at them in the mirror for decades, dying to know where I came from and what my life was like before I turned eighteen because I have no recollection of my childhood. Here was this girl who disappeared off the face of the earth in August 1999, two months shy of her eighteenth birthday. And here I was, someone who looks identical to her, and whose first memory is waking up next to an alley Dumpster in the winter of 1999."

CHAPTER 17

FRANKIE

WHAT THE FUCK. What the fuck.

Chloe has been living this whole time as a completely different person and unaware of her identity? That means all these years, what I've been sensing was real—she was alive. She just didn't know who she was.

I have so many questions. Was the Dumpster in Boise? What happened in the months between August and winter 1999? But we're almost to my house when I remember that I promised Chloe food. I whip into the drive thru at Jack in the Box by my house and ask what she wants. I place our order and my phone buzzes.

How's it going with Chloe?

It's from Jensen.

I told him I'd call him later, and he needs to be patient. I put the phone down and pull up to the window to receive the fastest fast-food order I've ever ordered. Bless you, Jack in the Box.

Then I step on it, hoping to burn the single block distance to my house and also not get pulled over.

I want to dive right back into this conversation with Chloe, but we'll have another interruption in two-point-five seconds when we get to the house. Her house.

It's not until I pull into my driveway that I realize I haven't yet told her this part. "Do you recognize this place?" I ask, turning the ignition off.

She shakes her head and clenches the top of the fast food bag tighter. "I'm sorry, I don't remember anything." She starts crying again.

I kick myself for making her repeat this, and I apologize.

"This used to be your house. The one you grew up in." Saying it makes me tear up. I still can't believe this is happening. All of it. Chloe's return. That she has no memories.

Chloe squints her eyes. "Why do you live here?"

"Oh, I bought it."

Does she even know about her mom, Aunt Bertie? Who she was, that she passed away. I don't want to go into all of this right now. I'd rather hear Chloe's story, so I decide I'm going to drop this unless she presses.

Chloe stares at the house like she's debating whether to say something, but she seems to decide against it and slides out of the truck. It strikes me that she looks like a child when she does it because of her height. Another gut punch to think about how much time has passed. How much of her life I've missed, and how odd it is that she can still just resemble her younger self in my mind. It feels like I'm seeing her frozen in time, the way she used to be. Despite the gray in her hair, despite the years that have passed. I still see her as my Chloe.

Once we're inside and sitting at the kitchen table with our food, I say, "Please go on. So, you woke up in an alley? Here in Boise?"

"No, Montana. Helena, actually. That's where I've been living all these years."

Montana. How did she get up there when she went missing here? I nod in acknowledgement and shove a few fries in my mouth, trying to act normal to encourage her to keep talking.

"Anyway, when I came to, I felt pain so strong I could barely stand up. My breasts, my abdomen, all over. This woman came out of a back door—a restaurant—to throw some trash away, and saw me. When she approached to help me up, her mouth fell open. My pants were blood-soaked."

I gasp.

"I know," Chloe says, her chin quivering like she's about to cry again. "It gets worse. Are you sure you want to hear?"

"Absolutely," I say and push my food away. I'm actually not that hungry and anxiety has my stomach in such knots that a burger is a bad idea right now.

"This woman took me to a hospital and after the doctor examined me, I found out I'd given birth only days prior."

I'm stunned. I can't do anything but stare at her in disbelief. *She was pregnant?*

"Chloe, what are you saying?"

"I had been pregnant, given birth, and lost the child, and I found all of this out in one fell swoop."

"Wait. Did you know you were pregnant the night you guys went up to Skinny Dipper? Who's the father?" I blurt.

Chloe's eyes well up with tears and she starts crying and wiping her face with her sweater again. I stand to grab a box of tissues off the kitchen counter.

Slow your roll, I remind myself. *Let her tell it at her own pace.*

"I'm so sorry," I say, placing the box next to her, and touching her shoulder in passing before I take my seat.

"I don't know the answers to those questions. All of that is filed in my brain under 'before Jane.'"

Who is Jane?

Chloe must read the question on my face because she says, "Jane was my name until a few days ago when I found out that I'm Chloe. You know, like Jane Doe. It was the hospital's doing, and I kind of kept it, but not the Doe part. That would be weird."

"So 'before Jane' is everything that happened in your life before the night at Skinny Dipper?"

"No, before that winter in 1999 when I woke up in the alley," she corrects, taking a bite of her burger.

"Right," I say. "Do you remember me?"

Chloe finishes chewing and then swallows. She reaches for a tissue and dabs under her eyes.

Shit. I did it again. If it were a sport, I'd win an Olympic gold medal in making Chloe cry. It's not that I'm bothered by her emotions, I just feel so damn bad that I'm bumbling onto all the things that seem to trigger her trauma. But of course I am, because those are where all my questions are.

"No," she whispers, looking down. "I found the event website and learned who you were from there. It means a lot that you kept my memory alive with the annual benefit."

So that's how she knew where to find me. I feel like tearing up again, at the fact that she doesn't remember me, but I clear my throat and prompt her. "So you woke up to the news you had a baby and you didn't remember any of it ..."

"Yeah. And the hospital had no record of a baby that could be mine. It would have had to be a days-old infant someone brought into the hospital, or perhaps dropped off. They put me on antibiotics and the police interviewed me. I was a girl who didn't know her age with a missing newborn, so the hospital had to report it. But I was no help in putting together my past, of course, and as a result, there wasn't much the police could do. They said they'd keep looking for my baby, but nothing came of that. The doctors used the information from my physical exam to determine I was most likely a young adult. Of course, now I know that I was barely eighteen, but back then they thought I could be in my early twenties. A kind nurse gave me some information about a women's shelter that had resources to get me on my feet, and the volunteers there helped me search for my baby. I called other hospitals—all over Montana, into Idaho and even Washington—but came up empty. I couldn't find my baby and I couldn't figure out who I was during the years 'before Jane.' But I couldn't stay at the shelter forever either, so I got a job working at a local grocery store, and then year after year, I slowly built a life and an identity. My unknown past became its own version of a past, if that makes sense."

I want to say that it doesn't. Not remembering your childhood, or that you were pregnant and delivered a child doesn't seem like something anyone could get used to.

When I don't respond or even nod to this, she adds, "When your life is full of trauma, you have to find ways to come to the surface for air. You can't live in those deep dark waters of fear, sadness, and shame every moment of every day or you'll drown. I had to make a life and move forward with as much normalcy as I could muster. You know, search for pockets of happiness for my own sanity."

I nod at this. It makes total sense.

"So, your child could still be out there?" I ask.

"Everyone who works with situations like mine says it's very unlikely, and the baby probably didn't make it. About ten years ago, I finally gave up and found a spot in a park I love back in Helena. I decided that was my memorial for my child. Every day I make the choice to move forward from that, too."

Tears streak Chloe's face and she reaches for the tissue.

So much trauma. I still have a lot of questions, but Chloe's eyes are puffy and red-rimmed. I feel an exhaustion that I can only pin on a long day—the benefit tonight already feels like ten years ago—along with all of this. I should probably call it a night, but I'm not ready yet, so I linger.

My phone buzzes with a text message again. I bet it's Jensen wondering why I haven't replied yet. Why is he being so impatient? I don't look at my phone.

"Chloe, please stay here at the house with me," I say. "I bet you're wiped out. I have a spare room with a bed. It's actually your old room."

"Are you sure? I don't want to intrude."

I can't help but chuckle at that. "Having you back is my dream come true. It's so far from an intrusion."

Chloe has gone through oceans of horrible experiences and I hate that I wasn't there for any of them. But I'm here now. And who knows? Maybe being back in Boise will dislodge something from her 'before Jane' memory. Maybe I'll get some answers after all.

THEN

CHAPTER 18
CHLOE

A SEX TRAFFICKING OPERATION.

I let the thought sink in and try not to freak out about it, but after my determination to escape, the panic has snuck back in. There's no way out of this room except through that locked door. The one that allows Bill to come and go as he likes. The one that's got more trapped girls on the other side of it. More men who want to hurt them. And I have no idea what's beyond that, or where this prison is even located.

I let out a soft cry. This is hopeless.

But then, no. There has to be a way. There always is.

What is it?

I move to the window again to see if I can recognize anything through the peephole. Something other than pine trees.

I groan in frustration when all I see is forest.

If I'm somewhere in Idaho, it's definitely not Boise. My city doesn't have pine trees this dense. So, north of Boise maybe? Perhaps somewhere close to Skinny Dipper.

I consider this for a minute, but then realize there's no way I can figure out my location with so little information. And even if I could, there's still the issue of needing to escape.

Why did Bill murder Amy and Kristi and not me? I'm assuming Bill did it, and that's a pretty safe bet.

Why hasn't he hurt me? At least not in a sexual way. Is it because of my broken ankle? Maybe he's waiting for it to heal.

One thing is for sure: He's trying to hide his identity because he never removes that mask.

It could be because he doesn't plan on killing me, so he's worried that when he lets me go, I'll turn him in. But he knew my name, my favorite kind of pizza, and that makes me wonder if Bill is someone from my life. I don't recognize his voice, and that's all I have to go off.

Footsteps approach and the door opens.

I shrink myself, leaning against the cold, concrete wall. Of course, it's Bill. He bends down and places a plate of something —looks like one of those mini pot pies from the grocery store freezer section—in front of me, along with a plastic fork and another bottle of water. Then he sits down without a word. He's directly across from me and with that mask on, I can't see his expression. Why is he staying? I don't get the feeling he's going to violate me. It's more like he wants to ... hang out.

I swallow down my fear and decide to go along with it.

"Thank you for such good food," I say, forcing a smile and picking up the fork to dig in.

He doesn't move. Doesn't speak. He keeps his face pointed at me.

Stupid first attempt at being friendly. I have to do better.

"I was thinking it might be nice to get to know each other a little since we both seem to be stuck here." I give a small chuckle.

He tilts his head to the side, but doesn't speak.

Shit, it's not working. My attempts at conversation are failing, but still, this feels like the right approach. I don't know what his plans are for me, but I'm not out there in the cell like the redhead, and I don't have duct tape on my mouth. I'm not being punched like one of the girls. In fact, compared to what I assume is going on out there, I've had it pretty good so far.

Again, I wonder why.

"Are you going to make me do what those other girls are doing?"

He stares.

This isn't working. I have to somehow win him over.

And what then? I ask myself. I'll still be stuck here even if I win Bill over. Do I really believe he'll let me go? After he killed Amy and Kristi? I feel the pinch of tears, but I stuff down thoughts about my friends.

"Shut up and eat your food," he growls as he stands and steps toward the door. He's going to leave, which normally I'd want. But I haven't gotten through to him yet. He can't go.

"Thank you for the meals," I blurt. "And the clean sweats. I appreciate what you're doing for me."

I cringe inwardly. It's so hard to pretend to be nice to him.

He doesn't face me when he says, "You don't have to worry about what's going on out there. I won't let anyone touch you." Then he leaves.

I sit completely still in numb silence trying to comprehend what that means. It's impossible to reconcile that the man who killed my friends and is holding me as a prisoner is going to protect me from anything at all.

In time, the words to my favorite song creep into my mind. Hot tears run down my cheeks. The lyrics to "These Are Days" are so hopeful. All about miracles and laughter and warm days, but the reason I love it is that it also feels sad. Haunting, almost.

I need to draw from the happiness in it, while in the midst of being in this scary situation.

My voice is froggy and quiet when I start singing, but soon it echoes loud off the concrete walls, and gives me a charge of courage.

I will get out of here or die trying.

NOW

CHAPTER 19

FRANKIE

FINALLY, I call it. Chloe and I are both zombies and I still have to get fresh sheets on the bed in the spare room. She goes into the bathroom and I head to my room to give Jensen a call.

It's not like me to prioritize Jensen's panic, but I left him with so little information earlier, that a quick update would be a good bone to throw. Maybe the shock is starting to wear off for him too, and he's concerned about Chloe.

Jensen picks up after the first ring.

"Hey, Frank. Everything good?"

"Yeah. It's so much to unpack it makes my head hurt, but I'm insanely grateful to have her back. So crazy."

"Your head probably hurts from all the crying."

"Okay, true," I agree and laugh softly, even though I didn't do nearly as much crying as Chloe.

"How is she? Where has she been? Did she go to the police to give a statement? Did you text your dad?"

Dad. Jensen's right, I should tell him.

"She seems fragile, but physically okay. The rest is a long story." Then I whisper, "She gets upset easily and I'm trying to let her tell the story without rushing her, but I still have so many questions too. I'll call you tomorrow."

"Okay. Take care of yourself."

For some reason this rubs me the wrong way.

"Why?" I ask.

"I don't know, I feel this urge to protect you or something. I know that's stupid, but I don't want you to get hurt."

I blink a few times while my mind plucks around for a response to this. I can't tell if he's being weird or if this is a normal thing to say considering the situation.

"You think I can't take care of myself."

It's an assumption and I know what they say about people who assume, but I feel like he's trying to manage me. Maybe I'm being sensitive, but one thing I'm good at is looking out for myself. Plus, Jensen is just a friend. He doesn't have any responsibility for me.

He clears his throat. "No. That's not what I'm saying."

"Okay, then tell me what you mean."

"Fine," he says, and I imagine his hands splaying as he speaks like they always do when he's making a point. "It's just so strange, her returning out of the blue."

"Tell me about it." I'm relieved that there wasn't more behind his comment and I was just overreacting.

"Just be careful."

"Of what? Chloe?"

Jensen sighs. "Look, Frank. I just care about you, that's all."

"I promise I'm good. This is all I've ever wanted."

Even if it's different from how I imagined it would be. I thought if Chloe returned, we'd pick up right where we left off. Instead, I need to accept that this isn't a continuation of a friendship. It's the beginning. At least for Chloe. She has no memories of us, so it's the construction of something new, not an add-on.

Jensen scoffs. "Trust me, I'm aware."

"I'll call you tomorrow," I repeat because I can hear the toilet flush and Chloe working the lock on the bathroom door. It often gets stuck. She jiggles the handle more aggressively and then it opens.

I hang up with Jensen and grab some fresh sheets out of an unpacked box in the third bedroom. At least I labeled everything with the last move. I thank Past-Me and get busy with my task. Chloe stands in the doorway of her old room with her arms crossed. She kind of hunches when she does this, as if she's trying to shrink herself.

"So you worked at a grocery store in Montana?" I ask. I imagine she's too tired for more questions, but I have to ease this awkward silence. She stands there, watching me make the bed.

"Yeah. I started as a bagger. But then I worked my way up and now I'm managing the bakery. Or I was ... before I came here."

I'm shoving a pillow into a case when a dark thought claws its way to the front of my mind.

What if she's not back for good? She had a life in Montana. Will she go back to it?

I toss the pillow onto the bed, and it's not worthy of a home-decor spread in a magazine or anything, but the bed looks put together and comfortable. I want to press her about her comment. Make sure she's planning to stay, but it doesn't feel like the right thing to bring up so late in the evening.

"I'll probably try to get on at a grocery store around Boise," Chloe says, and I feel my body deflate in relief.

"So you're planning to stay?"

"I think so. I want to see if being back here jogs my memory at all." And once again, it feels like Chloe has read my mind. Or at least, that we're on the exact same page. God, how I've missed her.

"Well, you can stay here as long as you want. My house is your house. Or rather, your house is your house." I laugh at my own stupid joke.

"Are you sure?"

"One-hundred percent."

CHAPTER 20

FRANKIE

I HAVE the first night of restful sleep in what feels like weeks, and when I wake I'm shocked to see that it's past nine in the morning. I never sleep this late.

A text from Jensen greets me.

Something pops up inside of me. This little feeling of *No*. I don't want to call him right now, and it makes me feel immediately guilty. But Chloe is my priority and I want to spend my day with her, so I'll call him later.

I wrap myself in a robe and step into the hallway, aiming for the bathroom. Chloe's door is closed, so she must still be asleep.

I make some coffee, do the dishes, and pick up a book that I've been reading for weeks. It's some fantasy romance novel that everyone is talking about, but I can't get into it, so I don't last more than a few chapters. I decide to jump into the shower, and maybe Chloe will be up by the time I get out.

But she's not.

Her door is still closed when I pass it on the way to my bedroom.

I dress in jeans and a pink tee and it's almost eleven now. I don't have Chloe's phone number yet, or else I'd text her. Would it be rude to knock?

Standing outside the door, I decide that yes, it would be kind of rude to knock. Especially since we were up late, and I could tell she was exhausted when we finally turned in. I need patience.

I could do something productive while I wait. Maybe swing into ReHome, a local store that sells used fixtures and appliances. They often get vintage and antique items as well. The shop owner knows I'm on the prowl for a pink sink, but I haven't heard anything from him in a while, so I'll remind him what I'm looking for. He can be forgetful.

I put my wet hair into a topknot and grab my keys.

It's a quick in and out at ReHome because there are no pink sinks, so after I remind the owner to call me if he gets one, I drive to my dad's to check on Sundown.

By that point, it's been an hour or so and the only thing I want to do is rush home and see Chloe again.

When I get there, she's not in the kitchen or the living room, so I go down the hall to see if she's in her bedroom—surely she's awake by now.

But her door is still closed. It's afternoon, so I decide it's probably safe to knock.

No answer.

I knock again and wait, but when there's still no answer or any movement on the other side, I slowly turn the knob and push the door open.

Her bed is made, and she's not in there.

THEN

CHAPTER 21
CHLOE

I TWIST one end of the 101 Dalmatians sheet, wringing as if I'm handwashing it. It's night again, and all this nervous energy keeps billowing inside of me, making me want to run around, to do something. But my leg hurts way too bad for that.

When I realize the sheet is damp from my clammy hands working it, I let go, rubbing my palms together. They feel almost itchy from how hard I was squeezing.

Think. Think.

I have to come up with a plan to get out of here, but every time I set my mind to it, I get overwhelmed by my situation. Trapped inside an execution room, inside a prison. I have no idea where—and even if I could get out of the prison, what then? I can barely walk. And even if I could walk, how would I get help if I'm in a forest?

I'm getting ahead of myself. First things first: I need to escape from this room.

Of course, I don't see any way out based on inspecting the room, which I've done. I'd have to either overpower Bill— impossible with him being so much bigger than me, and with my hurt leg. Or get him to let me out for some reason.

I let this idea simmer.

Bill said that I don't have to worry about what's happening outside my prison cell, but it doesn't relieve any of my worries. I can't trust someone who murdered my friends. Even so, it's all I have to work with, and I have to work fast. Before Bill finds out about the baby. Before he changes his mind about protecting me. Before … any number of things that could happen in this hellhole. How long is he planning to hold me here? What will he do when he finds out I'm pregnant? My instinct is to keep the baby a secret, but what if telling him would make him more sympathetic?

No. Don't tell him.

I don't know why, but that feels like a death sentence.

I groan in frustration. I hate feeling this helpless, and tears fill my eyes.

It's impossible to know what to do when I can't even figure out why he's keeping me here in the first place. We must know each other—but he's not going to elaborate on that. I already tried, and how can I possibly recognize him with that stupid mask hiding his face and muffling his voice?

One thought keeps resurfacing, but it seems so dumb. Like something a child might think, and I'm not a child. Not anymore. Still, the thought paces in my mind: What if he wants me for himself?

Worst-case scenario: To do unthinkable things with me.

Best-case scenario, if it can even be called that: Maybe he thinks he's in love with me.

Dumb. It's dumb. It makes me cringe to think about it.

But either way, it's something to consider, and one thing is certain: In his twisted brain, Bill thinks he's protecting me. And people only do that when they care.

Or when they're getting something from it.

Bill is an evil man, so if I assume the worst, it means he thinks he's going to get something from keeping me here. But what? And for how long? Surely there's an end point in his mind.

I feel a mini spark of hope inside. There has to be a reason I'm here, and the time will come for him to do something with me. This place isn't set up for long-term residence, and so maybe he'll move me. That's when I'll try to get away.

———

IT FEELS like a long time before Bill comes back to check on me, but I don't have any way of knowing. I can only tell if it's day or night. I shove the peephole of plywood back into its spot so he doesn't know I have a way to look outside. I try to sleep when it's dark, but sometimes, like right now, I lay on the mattress, awake anyway.

The first indication that he's coming is always the sound of the outer door—I picture the main prison door—clanging shut. Then his heavy footsteps down the hall, usually one girl crying, but this time I hear a few different voices. There must be more than one girl out there.

Bill doesn't come directly to my room, and that's when I picture him feeding or checking on the other girls like they're his caged pets. I shake my head to dislodge the thought because it's too evil, and I have to focus on my plan. I'm already dealing with my heart rate going ballistic, along with dry mouth, and shaky hands.

This time it's two sets of heavy footfalls. I picture a man with Bill.

As they get closer to my door, I can make out the tail end of a conversation.

"... where I'm keeping some girls I need to get rid of," Bill says. "Don't want you to get your hands dirty. As long as you don't see those faces, I figure you're safe. Plausible deniability."

The other man grunts in agreement, but doesn't speak.

It sounds like they're right outside my door.

And Bill is talking about getting rid of girls.

I inhale sharply and my pulse throbs at my temples. He's not only trafficking the girls. He's killing them too.

Bill goes on. "Here, got this new girl for you …"

Again, the man says nothing in response, but it sounds like a prison cell opens and then they walk past my door and farther down a hallway.

I can also hear a girl moaning and crying, but her mouth must be taped because she doesn't say any words.

I assume the other man is a customer, but Bill talks to him like he's also the boss. I feel like retching at the thought, but I'm distracted by the sound of footsteps returning. It's one set this time and my door cracks open, sending a patch of lantern light across the room. I shield my eyes.

Bill's boots strike the concrete floor as he approaches, and my pulse feels like it might explode out of my veins.

Breathe. Think. Focus.

He sets a small paper bag in front of me. Inside are three pieces of fried chicken—two legs and a breast, and I'm surprised at how my stomach churns with hunger. I didn't even notice it before.

Bill puts another paper bag full of something on the ground and sits across from me maybe five feet away. He pulls his knees up and rests his arms on them. "Enjoy that. Probably your last warm meal for a while."

I stop before taking a bite of the chicken. I feel like I might choke even though there's nothing in my mouth yet. What does he mean?

"Got some shit to take care of. There's food and water in here." He nudges the bag. "Should be enough until I get back."

Eat. Act normal, I remind myself. But this throws me off a little and I have to regroup quickly. He only ever stays for as long as it takes me to eat the meal.

"Okay," I reply softly. "Thank you for taking care of me."

It's what I said last time, and it seemed to work to make him a bit more open.

This time though, he doesn't respond, just watches me from behind that hideous mask with its exaggerated smile.

I swallow and say, "The mask is kind of creepy."

"Not taking it off."

I wasn't asking him to. I don't know if I'd even want that because it might take away any chances I have that he's planning to let me go eventually.

"Okay," I whisper. And then my mind goes blank. Anything I'd ask—where do you live? What's your name? Where do you work?—seems stupid. And it's unlikely he'll tell me anything based on how tight-lipped he is.

"Only thing you need to know about me is, I'm what's standing between you and certain death," he says.

This should probably frighten me, but instead I feel a little flame of anger. He's so dramatic, always saying these vaguely threatening things that zap my strength and determination to escape.

"You don't have to try to scare me all the time. I'm scared enough as it is," I say. My tone is firm, but not harsh. I don't want to trigger his anger, but if he's already told me he's not going to hurt me, I might as well stand up to him a bit. It's off-script from my original plan, but too late. The deed is done.

He doesn't say anything, so I go on. "I get that you can't tell me your name, or where you're from, or any normal get-to-know-you things, but surely there's something we can talk about. What do you like to do when you're not doing ... this?"

I want to say *when you're not hunting down teenage girls and keeping them in prison cells*, but I hold back.

"I hang out with my dog."

What? I'm so shocked that he gave me something, and that it's something normal. I take another bite of chicken, trying to hide my excitement. I can totally work with this.

NOW

CHAPTER 22
FRANKIE

I'VE BEEN HOME for about an hour, stressing about where Chloe might be. We haven't swapped phone numbers yet, and I've lathered myself into a full panic when the front door opens and a voice calls out. "Hey, Frank!"

It's her. My body releases a truckload of worry, and by the time she's made her way into the living room, my tears are streaming. I brush them away, hoping she doesn't see, but nope. She sees.

"Oh my god, are you okay?" Chloe sets down a backpack and a black suitcase and comes at me with arms out.

"Yes, I'm fine. Glad you're home."

"What happened?"

You left.

I don't say it out loud. Chloe is an adult. She can come and go as she pleases. It's just that opening that bedroom door and seeing it empty when I thought she would be in there—it sent me right back to being the teenager who lost her mom and then her best friend like a jab-cross punch.

"Nothing ... I had a little spat with Jensen," I lie. The words fall out of my mouth so easily. I swear, I'm incapable of vulnerability.

"I'm so sorry!" Chloe says. "Is there anything I can do?"

"No, it's fine." I pull away from the embrace and manage to gather myself, wiping my nose with the back of my hand like a toddler.

"Are you guys pretty serious?" Chloe asks.

Well, now I've opened a different can of worms. One that I'm not at all interested in diving into, so I wave the question off. "No, but relationships are tricky."

"True."

"Is that all your stuff?" I ask, hoping to change the subject.

"Yeah. It's not much, but I wanted to check out of my hotel as soon as possible, and get my car. I also went to the police station. That was a trip. I pretty much walked in and said, 'Ta-da! I'm back.' I mean, I didn't really say that, but that's what it felt like. They took my statement, which as you know isn't very helpful. Oh! They also took my DNA and they want you give a sample to compare it to. I have the detective's info here ..." she opens her phone and taps something out. "There I texted it to you. You're sure it's okay for me to stay with you for a few weeks?"

I'm trying to keep up with this firehose of information. The police. Right, of course she wanted to go in. My phone vibrates, and I assume it's the text she just sent.

"Why DNA?"

"Oh, just to make sure I am who I say I am, I guess? Pretty rare for someone to return after so long."

"Right. Of course. Oh, and stay as long as you like. Is it okay if I tell my Dad you're back?"

"Yeah, definitely." She smiles and goes back to the entryway for her stuff, adding, "Hey, I wondered if you have any old photos I could look through? Maybe I'll remember something."

I gasp. Great idea. Why didn't I think of it?

"Absolutely!"

Most of my boxes live in the third bedroom, so I head there, slide open the big old mahogany closet doors, and scan for the right one.

There's *Mom's stuff.*

Coats.

And then I see *Photo albums.*

I'll need to go through the albums individually because I have no clue which one has the pictures of Chloe and me. It's been years and years since I've cracked any of them open.

Before I reach for the box, I pull out my phone to text my dad. I can't help but notice I've sent five texts to him over the past few weeks and he's replied to exactly none of them. He's the one on summer break from his job, and he can't find time to even give one of my texts a thumbs up?

I decide to call him instead, but of course, he doesn't answer, so I leave a message. "Hey, Dad, I need to talk to you about something. Call me back."

I set my phone down on a random box and reach for the one labeled *Photo albums.* It's heavy for how small it is, and I set it on the hardwood floor before pulling out the first album and crossing my legs to sit. I thumb through the plastic-covered pages quickly, zipping past my childhood and all the pictures of my mom, like they hold some contagious disease. Until I get to the last page of the first album and one photo arrests me. It's of Mom and Dad on their honeymoon in Disneyland.

Mom was a total knockout. Thick, blonde hair that she wore permed with fluffed bangs, in traditional 80s fashion. Something loosens inside of me, and I'm surprised to find that I want to linger on this image. It's a completely new feeling, and so opposite from my usual tactic of ignoring and looking away. It's not long before the familiar little inkling inside is prodding at me to move along, though. Don't stay here in this place, because the feelings are too much. But still, I pull the image out of the plastic sleeve and stare at it more closely.

I actually do remember quite a bit about my mom, but wow, she looks so young here. Mom was so much fun—a bundle of energy always finding ways to make our time together sparkle. We'd have these dress-up lunches while Dad was at work. Mom would paint my nails and let me wear a little mascara, and then we'd sit at the table she set using a fancy tablecloth and the china she got from her grandma.

In this picture, Mom looks deliriously happy. Her toothy smile is huge, and she faces the camera while laying her head on Dad's chest, arms wrapped around his torso. Dad's smile is so big it creases his skin. They were happy. So goddamn happy, and I was too.

Tears warm my eyes, and that brings me back to now. My reality, where apparently, all I do is cry. But when was the last time I allowed myself to remember Mom? Maybe this is personal growth. Maybe something about having Chloe back is unlocking my heart. No time to analyze that right now with Chloe waiting on me, though.

I thumb through the other albums fast until I've got two down and three to go. That's when I hit pay dirt. A whole album that's full of pictures Chloe and I took with disposable cameras.

"Found it!" I shout and walk down the hall to Chloe's room.

CHAPTER 23
FRANKIE

CHLOE SITS cross-legged against the gray tufted headboard like she's waiting for me. When I walk in, she smiles and pats the spot next to her. It gives me a little flashback of how it used to be with us. No matter what was going on in the world, or even in the rest of the house, we were each other's safe spot.

A wave of warm affection drenches my heart and reminds me of happier days. Maybe I can get back there.

I open the album, and the first page is full of pictures of the two of us at camp in McCall: Paradise Point on Payette Lake. "This is where we went to summer camp," I say.

In the first picture, I was probably in about fifth grade, judging by the braces, which puts Chloe in seventh. Chloe's in shorts and a Barbie-pink bikini top, with one skinny arm draped around my shoulder.

"You were always so much prettier than me," Chloe says. There's no jealousy in her tone, which for some reason makes me even more uncomfortable.

"Whatever," I say. "We were two peas in a pod. People used to mistake us for sisters."

For some reason the mention of sisters brings Amy and

Kristi to mind. Now that Chloe is back, I can't help but wonder about them.

"I wish you could tell us more about what happened to Amy and Kristi."

Chloe immediately starts crying, and I scramble to make it better. "I'm so sorry. Please forget I said anything."

Stupid. Why in the world did I think that was worth mentioning? And I could have worded it better, too.

"I've thought about them so many times since learning my real identity," Chloe says, sniffing and dabbing her eyes with her brown sweater sleeve. It's the same one she was wearing last night. "I wish I remembered that night, if anything, for them. So we could know what happened. I hate being so unhelpful."

"It's not your fault." I try to be soothing, but I'm no good at it.

"But I'm the one who lived. I made it out somehow, and I don't know why or how. It's unfair that I'm here, and their lives were cut short.

"I understand why you'd feel that way, but it doesn't make it true," I whisper.

Chloe nods and the moment swells into a silent pause before she speaks again. "We really used to look like sisters, didn't we?"

"Yeah, but let's be honest, *used to* is the key word, because you aged so much better than me. You barely have a wrinkle," I say.

Chloe nudges me. "It's Botox. That and vaping are my guilty pleasures. Look, I have gray hair to make up for it."

"Whatever." I laugh and nudge her back because she's right about the gray. I color my hair brown all over to avoid seeing mine.

"Anyway, you're gorgeous, as always," Chloe says before returning to survey the pictures.

I watch her face, hoping one of the photos will spark some recognition, but there's nothing. Chloe looks up at me, as if waiting for audio captions for the images, so I narrate a picture where Chloe's angling a flashlight up toward her face in the dark.

"It used to be so freaky to walk to the bathroom at night when we were at camp. You always woke me up and made me go with you."

I point to another one where Chloe and I are on the dock. One of the lifeguards sits in a chair off to the right while Chloe poses in a red striped bikini with her arms making a huge Y. It was the summer before she disappeared. I remember because we bought matching suits that year.

"I took this picture of you so we could have one of him." I point to the lifeguard. "I don't remember his name, but he was always trying to talk to you even though he was so much older than us."

"I wonder what he's up to these days," Chloe says. "He wouldn't be too old for me now." She gives a wry smile, so I know she's joking. But even so, she's right. A seven-year age gap is a lot when you're a kid. Not so much when you're in your forties.

"Do you remember if he was from Boise too?" she asks.

"Oh, probably. Most of the counseling staff was from around here, but I'm not sure."

"Did I ever spend time with him?"

"No. He was like an adult, so he didn't really hang out with the kids. Why?"

"I was wondering if he'd remember me if I ran into him now."

She doesn't laugh or smile, so I can't tell if she's serious or not.

"Oh. I don't know. He could even be married. Hard to say."

"True."

My phone vibrates on the nightstand and I reach for it.

My dad is calling. Impressively responsive for old Jeff Oliver.

"Hey, I need to step out and take this really quick," I tell Chloe, who gives me a thumbs up.

I rush into my bedroom and close the door. "Hi, Dad."

"Hey, Moose." It's his usual greeting, which I hate. A nickname he gave me as a fat toddler that manages to feel patronizing instead of endearing. I let it slide in order to get to the point.

"Dad, Chloe is back."

"What do you mean?"

"I mean she's here. In Boise. She doesn't remember anything, really. She woke up in Montana. Dad, she had a *kid*. A baby, and she didn't know she was Chloe until a few days ago." It all gushes out.

There's silence on the other line.

"Dad?"

"Yeah, Moose, I'm here. I just don't know what to say. It's … shocking."

"Tell me about it. And hey, please don't call me that. You know I hate it."

He doesn't apologize. Instead, he goes on. "How did she find you?"

"She showed up at the memorial event." *Which you missed, like you always do*, I want to add, but I don't. "And now she's staying with me."

"Holy shit. Where has she been all these years?"

I give him a quick rundown—the few details she gave me about being Jane and living in Helena.

"So she doesn't remember a thing from her life before?" he asks. "That's really weird." Then I hear the beeping of microwave buttons, like he's warming something up.

"Are you busy?" I ask, trying not to let irritation cloud my voice.

"Oh, putting a Costco tamale on, but yeah, then I've got to run. Tell me she at least remembered *you*."

"She doesn't. But she's read everything online about her case, and I'm trying to fill in some blanks in her memory."

"That's good. Hey, meant to tell you. The camp wants me to stay on a bit longer than I planned."

"Why? It's almost the end of August. School starts soon."

"It's a long story, but let's just say I'm doing a lot of running between the camp and my cabin. Hey, how's Sundown?" He changes the subject.

"Fine. He misses his owner. That's you, in case you forgot."

My tone is clipped, and I'm reminded again of my anger toward my dad. But over what? I'm a grown-ass woman and don't need my dad around. Still, there's a little smolder of frustration that he always dismisses my attempts at conversation. That he's never interested in my life.

But I do make a mental note to check on the cat.

"I can't wait to see him," Dad says and then starts blowing on what must be a too-hot tamale that he's probably going to take a bite of.

"You always do that. Just wait three seconds for it to cool."

"I'm fine," he says around a mouthful of food, then swallows. "And Moose, keep me posted on Chloe. I'm so glad she's back. I can't believe it."

"I will."

CHAPTER 24

FRANKIE

"W as that Jensen?" Chloe asks when I return to the room.

"No. My dad. I told him you were back. I hope that's okay."

"Of course! How is Mr. Oliver doing?" Chloe asks. It's weird that she uses his school name instead of Uncle Jeff, but I'm not going to analyze it. This already feels like the longest 24 hours ever with Jensen last night, then Chloe being gone and my unnecessary worrying over it, and then my feelings about how distant my dad is. I'm suddenly limp with exhaustion even though I slept great last night.

"He's fine," I say, sitting beside her again.

"He still works at the school?"

"Yep. And he spends his summers at Paradise Point, actually," I point to the album we were looking at. "He volunteers up there with the ropes course, and whatever maintenance odds and ends they need."

"That's nice he does that. Giving back to the community."

I don't respond. It's a classic case of someone who gives their best to everyone around them, but won't offer the people close to them even a fraction of attention.

"Did he ever settle down with anyone?" Chloe asks.

My head throbs. The start of a headache. "Not really. He's had girlfriends on and off, but nothing sticks. He says my mom was his one great love and nobody can replace her."

"Does he ever talk about her?"

I wish I didn't bring the subject of Mom up. I don't want to discuss her and especially not right now.

"Not really," I say. "It was a long time ago."

I swear she's about to press further when my Ring doorbell chimes.

I'm so relieved to have an out that I practically jump off the bed to answer it.

Jensen stands on my porch with two reusable Whole Foods bags full of what must be groceries.

"Hi. What are you doing here?"

"Hey, I missed you too," he says in a way that's supposed to make me feel bad. But I don't. "Cooking you guys dinner. You know, so Chloe doesn't starve while she's here. I wasn't going to leave it up to your dysfunctional relationship with meal prep." He edges past me and moves into the kitchen to set the bags down on the counter.

It's thoughtful, yes, but also, I would have liked a little notice, and he's mad. I didn't call him this morning like he asked me to.

I join him in the kitchen and debate whether to apologize. But why should I? He's the one barging in. I don't have to do everything he tells me to, and he should understand that these aren't exactly normal circumstances in my life.

"I thought I'd hear from you today," he says, taking items out of the bag. Ricotta cheese. Noodles. Fresh tomatoes. Basil. Mozzarella.

He must be making lasagna, and all of a sudden my stomach growls.

"I've been a little busy the last twenty-four hours. My missing cousin came back, remember?"

"Are you mad at me?" he asks in surprise.

I clench my jaw because, yes, I am. But it seems stupid because what exactly am I mad about? That he's not being understanding about Chloe? It's not like he owes me anything. But do you have to be in a romantic relationship to offer support to someone in your life? I'm not asking for more than I would from a good friend, and he's not capable of even that.

As he makes me dinner.

I groan because it's so frustrating to feel angry with him, but also feel like I don't have any right to be.

When I don't answer, he says, "I'm not sure what you expect from me. I'm just your fuckboy. Isn't that how you want it?"

I can feel my face getting hot. It feels like he's withholding support in order to pay me back for not wanting to move our relationship forward.

Chloe joins us in the kitchen, standing at the entryway, holding her arms like she's cold. She doesn't say anything. Did she hear us arguing?

"Hi, Chloe," Jensen says, turning to offer her half a grin. "Do you remember me?"

He knows she doesn't remember anything, and I can tell by his tone that he's pushing buttons. His favorite thing to do.

"Hey, Jensen," she says. "No, I don't remember anything, unfortunately, but Frankie told me we went to school together. Are you cooking dinner? How can I help?"

"See?" Jensen says to me. "That's what you say to someone making you a meal."

Anger flares inside of me again. Has he been upset that I don't help him when he cooks us dinner? What the hell? This is the first I've heard of it.

"Can you chop the basil and parsley?" he answers.

I want to ask him to leave, but now Chloe is here and I can't cause a scene or make her feel uncomfortable.

"Sure." Chloe walks over to the knife block.

"So, Chloe, you don't even remember Frankie?"

My heart starts racing. I think I'm going to get into a fight with Jensen tonight. He's being a dick. It would be our first real fight because I always stuff my irritation instead of dealing with shit. But maybe it's time. My nerves mix with the frustration I feel toward him and the pit in my stomach grows.

The two of them stand side by side in the kitchen. Chloe opens the basil package, not making eye contact, and Jensen sets down a box of noodles, waiting for her to reply.

The tension balloons in the space until the only sound is water running, filling a pot to boil noodles. I pray this will be over soon and we can move on without me having to confront him.

Chloe tears basil leaves off the stems, then stacks and rolls them up, slicing them. "No," she finally answers. It's so totally obvious that she wants him to stop asking questions. Her throat bobs like she's trying hard not to cry.

He better knock it off.

Jensen pulls the pot of water from the sink before placing it on the stove.

"Wow. That's wild. What's it feel like to be Boise's very own Jason Bourne?"

I rush over to him. "Enough. You can either stop it or leave."

"What?" He spreads his hands in a defensive gesture. "I think it would be so strange to not remember entire phases of your life. Like, how common is that type of amnesia? What did the doctors say?" He looks at Chloe, but she keeps her eyes trained on the cutting board, working on the basil. She starts sniffing, and I'm sure it's because she's about to cry.

"Okay, leave."

"I'm making conversation. It doesn't seem that unreasonable of a thing to ask someone who moves into your not-girlfriend's house after being missing and presumed dead for twenty-five years."

Chloe sets down the knife and leaves the room, crying.

I want to scream at him, I'm so mad. And the anger is bigger than this. It's our whole relationship. All of it. I shove his chest and he stumbles back a little, throwing his hands up as if in surrender.

"Whoa. Where did that come from?"

"You're being a dick to her. And you pressure me all the time for more in our relationship when I'm not fucking ready! I don't know if I ever will be. If you really cared about me, you'd accept that. Or move on. But instead you stick around and push me. You don't even seem to care that the most important person in my life is back. You only care about yourself. I can't do this anymore."

I'm not sure I meant to break up with him, but once I say it, I know it's right. It feels right. Instantly, my body is more relaxed and I walk back over to the table and sit down. I turn to look down the hall, and wonder if Chloe is okay.

"The most important person in your life, huh? You mean her?" he throws a finger in the direction Chloe went. "She just now showed up on the scene. I've been here for you through thick and thin for months."

"Well, maybe you don't have to do that anymore."

Jensen's face falls. "You can't dump me. We aren't even in a relationship. You made sure of that."

"Jensen, leave."

"Frankie, please," he practically whispers. The desperation and sadness in his voice is a one-eighty from his attitude when he showed up tonight. I can't look at him. Despite everything, I feel bad for hurting him.

"I've made up my mind," I say.

"Fine," he snaps. "Make your own damn lasagna then."

Jensen storms out of the house and slams the door.

THEN

CHAPTER 25

CHLOE

I'M FEELING the baby move a lot now, and with it, my love grows. I find myself fantasizing about keeping it. But every time that thought comes around, I shut it down.

I can't keep it. Even having the baby would be the end of my life, but I'm past that point now. I'm definitely having the baby.

If Bill doesn't kill me first.

At least he hasn't found out I'm pregnant.

I have to win him over. I *have* to, but it's been much harder than I expected getting Bill to talk about his dog. Weeks have passed, and nothing has worked. He goes silent every time I ask questions about it. I did have one success. The last time he was here, he finally told me the dog's name is Nala.

Bill has a thing for Disney stuff. Based on the 101 Dalmatians sheet, and that he named his dog after a Lion King character. It's not like this will help me escape, but it's painting a picture of him. And I need to know him in order to get to him.

So, when the outer door clangs shut today, and the sound of Bill's heavy footfall follows, nervousness washes over me. This is the only idea I have, and it has to work.

He comes through my door, gives me a plate of food—

chicken nuggets—and some water, like always. Then he sets a grocery sack down near my mattress. He's going to leave me for days on end again. Like last time. That's what the grocery sack means. It strengthens my resolve to make progress today. Bill sits across from me and pulls his knees up to rest his arms on them. Then he watches me eat, like always.

A familiar shudder goes through me. It's so creepy how he does this. How it seems like he wants to spend time with me instead of simply giving me supplies and leaving.

"I've been thinking about Nala," I start. *God, please let this work*, I mentally pray. "What kind of dog is she?"

Bill doesn't move. He doesn't shift his body, he faces me in that freaky mask.

"Golden Retriever."

He answered. I want to fist pump, but instead, I channel my excitement into my reply so it seems genuine.

"I love Golden Retrievers! They're my favorite. What do you think about Goldendoodles? You know, that new breed—a cross between a Golden Retriever and a—"

"I know what a Goldendoodle is," he cuts me off. "It's not a new breed."

"Oh, really?" I say in a chipper tone. He wants to tell me more. I can feel it. I wait to see if he'll do it on his own because this conversation feels delicate. He could get up and walk out and who knows when he'll return or if he'll be willing to open up again.

I eat my food and wait, but he doesn't offer anything else.

"I'm sorry, I guess I thought Goldendoodles were new because I only recently learned about them. Do you know how long they've been around?"

"People have been cross-breeding dogs for centuries."

I know this, and it's not what I asked, but I keep going.

"That's true. I was curious about the Goldendoodles because I love them so much. A girl from school has one.

They're so happy and they don't shed. I want to get one as soon as I have my own place."

I don't tell him I'm actually scared of dogs. I got bit by a neighbor's Chihuahua when I was a kid and I've never gotten over the fear.

"I'm going to breed Golden Retrievers," he says. "My family has property where I plan to start a puppy farm."

I want to gasp at my luck. This is the most he's told me about himself. And I've been here a long time.

"Wow! That's so cool. A puppy farm sounds amazing. I would love to see that. A bunch of adorable puppies all around —it's practically my dream. If I lived on a puppy farm, I would work so hard to help take care of the dogs so they know how loved they are."

I stop abruptly and feel a shift in the room. I overdid it. My excitement came across as fake.

Like usual, Bill doesn't answer. He watches me, and even though I can't see his eyes at all through that mask, I can feel them.

"Why don't you see what's in the bag?" he says.

I brush crumbs off my hands and reach for the bag. When I look inside, my stomach drops.

Tampons.

No.

I swallow hard and look up at him.

"Why haven't you asked for those yet?" Bill says.

"What?" I whisper.

He raises his voice a little. "You haven't needed them yet and it's been way over a month."

"I'm really light." It's not true, but I'm scrambling to keep the baby a secret.

"Your pants are never stained."

My bikini bottoms. The makeshift underwear I've been in

all this time. He often asks to wash them. "You can't tell because they're black," I say.

"Bullshit. I could tell."

Gross. Oh god, so gross. I brush the repulsion away and try to stay focused. "I'm irregular. Sometimes I skip months at a time."

No way he can argue with this. He doesn't know my body.

He gets up and moves to sit next to me against the wall. I want to get away from him, but I don't dare to even flinch.

Seconds that feel like minutes pass until he speaks. "You're pregnant, Chloe. No sense in lying to me anymore."

My mouth goes dry the way he says it, and it makes the tiny hairs on my neck stand.

"Now," he continues, "I want to hear you say it." He reaches a hand out and pets my hair, feeling all the way to the nape of the neck where he grips it. My insides clamor at me to get away. Don't let him touch me. But I steel up because I don't know what he'll do if I try to move.

"What do you want me to say?" I let out a tiny sob.

His hand travels from the back of my neck to the front. He applies a bit of pressure to my throat, and I gasp.

"Tell me the truth about why you don't need tampons."

I can't. I cannot tell him about the baby. He's unpredictable. Sure, he hasn't hurt me too badly yet, but he's nearly cutting off my air. I remember how he forced me to swallow those pills on the first day. I have no guarantees he won't become violent toward me.

"I'm very light. Just started getting my period. Late bloomer," I lie again, barely able to push the words out.

He squeezes my neck harder so that even in the dim room, I can see blackness seeping around the edges of my vision. Tiny sparkles appear, like stars. I think I'm going to black out.

"Truth, Chloe. Don't disappoint me."

"It's yours—the baby," I blurt and my mind races for backup

to this declaration. Surely Bill has had his way with me at some point here. I was out cold a few times in the first days. Would he hurt the baby if he thought he was the father? It's a stupid attempt to appeal to humanity I don't think he has.

"I would never do that unless you wanted me to," he whispers, his face so close I can smell latex and sweat from the mask.

He lets go of my neck and I cough, touching the spot that's still warm from his stranglehold.

"You can't be pregnant."

I keep coughing, and my throat is raw and dry.

Bill stands to leave and I cry from the pain in my neck, and because I'm so glad he didn't hurt me worse than this.

But his words hang in the air and I'm afraid to ask what he means before he leaves the room. I curl up on the 101 Dalmatians bed and cry.

NOW

CHAPTER 26

FRANKIE

I WENT into the police and gave a DNA sample, but they won't have the results for weeks, most likely. For our part, Chloe and I have spent the past few days doing things around Boise, trying to jog her memory. We went to Camelback Park, followed by ice cream at Goody's in Hyde Park. Chloe loved it, but remembered nothing from her past even though we spent so many summer days in that part of town.

We rode bikes on the Greenbelt, which is a stretch of blacktop that parallels the Boise River, stopping for lunch and at multiple wineries along the way. This was another thing we did as kids, minus the wineries of course.

Today, we're hiking up the Boise Foothills to a plateau that overlooks the city. It's called Table Rock. But, when I park the truck at the trailhead, Chloe's attention gravitates to the right of the trail.

"What's *that*?" she asks.

"Oh, the Idaho State Pen. That's the old prison," I say, swinging my water bottle by its lid loop.

The facility was built in the 1800s. It's a museum now, and

definitely impressive, with its sandstone buildings and the turrets on the four corners of the prison wall. I can see why it grabs her. I went there once in elementary for a school tour. It's where I learned the meaning of the word "rape," actually. It was etched into the paint inside one of the cells, and the next day, I had asked Chloe what the word meant. She was in eighth grade by then, and she tried to change the subject like she didn't want to tell me, but I wouldn't drop it. She told me to ask my mom. But that made me more convinced to make her tell me, so she gave in. That was a mistake because when I found out, I started crying. I didn't even know what sex was beyond the vague notion of kissing that makes a baby. Chloe had to tell me that part first, and it was its own shock. Then to learn what rape is in the follow-up breath was traumatizing.

"It looks open. Can we go in?" Chloe's voice is laced with eager electricity.

"You don't want to hike?"

Because I'd way rather hike. I don't want to go into the old prison. Once in a lifetime is enough. It's creepy and sad, and this is such a perfect morning, the cool edge of the day still hanging on before August heat bullies its way in.

"Yeah, I want to hike, but I don't know," Chloe says. "Something about that place is begging to be explored. I can come back to it later by myself if you'd rather do Table Rock."

"No," I say, reminding myself that these outings are for Chloe, not me. "That's totally fine! Let's tour the prison."

We walk the sand pathway up to the main prison building and buy two tickets. Self-guided. Chloe insists.

"You sure? We have time for the guided tour," I say.

"Nah, I like to go at my own pace and feel these things out."

"What does that mean?"

"I want to experience it here"—she puts her hand on her chest. "Instead of only here"—her hand moves to her head.

"You want to experience a creepy prison with your heart," I repeat flatly as we walk through the building and into the prison courtyard.

Chloe laughs, then looks around and pulls out her pen, quickly taking a hit.

"Not sure that's allowed," I say and immediately feel dumb. It's not like I care if Chloe vapes. I'm just worked up from being here. I look around and notice the birds are singing and there's a slight breeze. It's a perfect day, but being here in this place of so much ... evil—to call it what it is—unnerves me to no end.

"The sign said no smoking and I'm not smoking. I'm vaping," Chloe says with a shrug. "That'll be the last one until we leave." She puts it away. "To answer your question, no, I don't want to feel it with my heart, not exactly. I want to *be* with it." She emphasizes the word "be," as if I should understand what she's saying. I still don't.

"It's what I've been doing the whole time I've been back. Trying to feel things out. I can't use my mind to remember, so I'm trying to lean on other methods. Our bodies process information too."

This makes me think about my crazy Chloe dreams and how it felt like I was somehow building a relationship with her in the dream world. I think she may be on to something.

Our feet crunch gravel as we make our way across the courtyard to the first building.

"Has anything come up yet? You know, since we've been touring Boise?" I ask.

Chloe sighs. "No. This truly feels like the first time I've ever been here. It's impossible to imagine this is where I grew up. Hey, I haven't wanted to ask, but what's going on with you and Jensen?"

I'm surprised it took her this long. The night Jensen left us with unmade lasagna, we ordered Uber Eats and Chloe acted like nothing had happened. I was relieved because I didn't have anything to say about it. Still don't. He hasn't called me and of course, I haven't reached out either. I think it's really over.

"Oh, we broke up. It's something I should have done a while ago. He's a good guy, just not what I need right now, you know?"

She nods as we walk and I take the opportunity to ask more about her life.

"I don't remember you dating anyone the summer you disappeared. It's so hard to believe you were pregnant."

She sighs, but doesn't answer. I don't full-on ask because I already know she has no idea who the father was.

"Did you ever find anything out about the baby? I know you struck out when you first started looking, and then you ended the search ten years ago. But in the middle were there any details that surfaced?"

We take a right turn into one of the prison buildings, and it immediately feels like suffocating. The ceiling at the entrance is low, but it opens up to four levels of cells, paint peeling in a rainbow of colors: pink, cream, turquoise, yellow. As somebody painted the metal bars all these happy colors over the course of a century.

"No. It was like it never happened. Then I made peace with the possibility that the baby didn't survive whatever we went through."

She sniffles and wipes her face. I think she's starting to cry, but I have to ask one more question before she shuts down.

"Have you had any romantic relationships over the years? I'm assuming if you had another kid, you would have told me."

She laughs. "For sure. No, I'm kind of a loner and I like being home. I bake even when I'm not working as a bakery manager."

I'm trying to remember if Chloe liked to bake when we were young. I guess we made cookies, but most kids do. It's not like baking was her thing. Then again, does anyone have their thing while in high school? I didn't learn I loved DIY construction and design until I was well out of college.

We mosey along and look into about every third cell as the conversation stalls. Then we exit and follow the path.

"What's that one?" Chloe points to a building running parallel to a dirt basketball court.

"I can't remember. Let me look." I pull out the pamphlet because it has a map. "Maximum security."

Chloe nods and crosses the court with confidence as if this is where she was hoping we'd end up. "I wonder if solitary confinement is there."

I hold up the paper to look again. "No, that's way on the other side." I point behind us.

So far Chloe has been more into this than anything else we've done in Boise. Is that weird?

Immediately when we step inside the building, there's a sign that says "Gallows upstairs."

My stomach drops. Once again, we're the only ones in the building, and the atmosphere is heavy and dark.

Chloe takes the metal stairs toward it as if she's being pulled by some invisible rope.

"Should we check out what's down here first?" I ask. I don't want to go up there, but I don't want to separate from her either.

"Come on, Frank. Let's look at the gallows and then we can leave this place. If it's not too hot, we'll do the hike."

I nod and follow her up the flight of stairs, where we come face-to-face with two door openings. One with a sign that says "Death Row," and the other, "Witness Room."

Chloe stops in her tracks, and all of her bravado and curiosity seem to wane.

"What's wrong?" I ask. The turn from curiously morbid Chloe to what seems like scared Chloe is sharp.

"Nothing, I just ..." She fades out, and I'm starting to worry about her.

"Let's go, Chlo. I feel like I need a shower after being here."

"No." She waves me away with a hand, but keeps her gaze on the two doors. Then she turns and walks toward the one labeled "Death Row."

CHAPTER 27
FRANKIE

INSIDE ARE A HANDFUL OF CELLS, and the one at the end has a sign saying it was Raymond Snowden's cell. The last man executed by hanging in Idaho. I read the sign on the prison bars about how he was known as Idaho's "Jack the Ripper" and how he spent his final days doing crossword puzzles and visiting with the chaplain.

"This is really disturbing," I say.

But even so, I can't make myself leave. It's like rubbernecking a car accident. Everyone does it even when they know there's no point and they're slowing traffic down.

Chloe doesn't say anything as she grips the bars of Snowden's cell and stares inside. She's feeling something out again, and I don't want to interfere.

"It's fascinating to think of what could bring someone to the point that they'd end up here," Chloe says. "Like, what goes on inside of a person that makes them so sure they can break the law —break the laws of nature, even—and get away with it? Do they all have a death wish? Don't they know they'll probably get caught?"

I've seen enough true crime shows to know that no, those

types of people are often driven by such narcissism or sociopathy that they don't think they'll get caught. They make a mistake, and that's when it happens.

"I don't think so," I say. "They see themselves as above it. Godlike even."

Chloe nods as if she's decided something and turns to walk out. Her stride is determined now.

Instead of taking the stairs back down to the exit, Chloe goes into the Witness Room next door to Death Row.

No. I want to leave.

Calm down, I coach myself. *Something is happening with Chloe. Pay attention.*

This is the first time she seems to be opening up and I don't want to spoil it or distract her. It doesn't matter that I feel like I have ants in my pants and want to run to my truck.

Inside the Witness Room, there's a big window with a small, white room on the other side. What looks like an oversized metal loop hangs from the ceiling. It's where Chloe's eyes go first. I follow her gaze as it travels down, and I lean in to get a closer look through the glass.

"Fuck. That's got to be the trapdoor," she says in a hushed tone.

She's right. It's a metal square nestled into the hardwood floor with a lever nearby.

"Jesus, look how the paint is worn, like the feet that scraped it off knew this would be their last stand. Imagine the desperation," Chloe says.

It sends a chill down my spine. Again, she's right. The whole metal plate is a primer-gray color except right in the middle. Precisely where accused men would have stood with a thick rope around their necks. That paint is chipped.

Chloe groans like she's physically uncomfortable.

"Are you okay?" I put my hand on her shoulder.

"Yeah, I just started feeling a little funny." She touches her stomach.

"We can go," I say. But what I really mean is *Please can we go?*

Then, Chloe bends over and puts her hands on her knees.

"Oh my god, are you sick?"

Her back is to me so I can't see her face, but she whispers, "No, I'm sorry. I just got so ... overwhelmed all of a sudden. I don't know what happened. My body freaked out and I got super dizzy. I feel better now." She straightens.

"Can we go?" I'm worried about her and so I take her elbow in an attempt to turn her toward the way we came up.

"Wait," Chloe says. "I need a minute. I don't know why, but I have to stay a bit longer."

"Do you think it's some sort of trauma response?" I ask. I can't think of any other reason for this physical reaction since she says she's not sick and we've eaten all the same things. I feel fine. "It seems like it's something to do with the prison."

"It's not only the prison though. I was fine until we came up here. It's this area specifically. Do you know if I came here before?"

"You came at least once. It's a sixth-grade field trip everyone takes." I don't tell her about my experience and the word I saw etched into a prison wall. It's not the time.

We stand there in silence and anxiety climbs inside me.

"Okay, let's go," she says finally, and I'm so relieved.

I start toward the stairs that lead to the way we came in.

"Hey," Chloe says. "Let's go that way instead."

It's another open door and it leads down a flight of stairs to bright daylight. It's an exit, sure, but the sign above the door says "Drop Room."

I take a deep breath. Almost done. I need to get through this part and then we can leave.

When we get down there, it's more freaky than the Witness

Room was. If the Witness Room was a home's foyer, the Drop Room would be its basement. Literally. It's directly below, with the metal trapdoor on its ceiling. The museum sign says it's where they'd retrieve the hanged bodies after an execution.

The room's floor is sunken, and there's a drain in the middle. Chloe points to it.

For the bodily fluids, I think but don't say. Instead I wince.

We follow the sunlight streaming in to find the exit, and once we're in the courtyard again, I exhale a loud sigh.

"Jesus, that place is …" I start, but can't think of the right word.

"Fucked up." Chloe finishes my sentence. "I think all the 'f' words are appropriate right now."

We walk toward the building that leads out of the courtyard and back through the gift shop to exit, and Chloe is quiet. She steps off to the side behind one of the buildings before we go in and pulls out her vape pen.

"Sorry, I have to after that," she says holding it up and then takes a big hit.

I reach for the pen and her eyes widen, but she hands it to me. I take a hit and start coughing. Not sure it helps my anxiety, but it's worth a try.

Back at my truck, Chloe says, "Can we go to the hot springs tomorrow?"

"You mean—"

"Skinny Dipper. Yeah."

Chloe is getting more serious about facing what happened that night. I'm trying not to get my hopes up, but maybe she's going to open up more. Maybe she'll even remember something.

"Of course," I say, pulling the truck out and making my way down Warm Springs Road and toward the house. If Chloe had this big of a reaction to a prison museum, what's going to happen at Skinny Dipper?

THEN

CHAPTER 28
CHLOE

HE KNOWS.

Bill knows I'm pregnant. And no matter what I've told myself about him in order to win him over, the bottom line is Bill is batshit crazy. He shot my friends. He's offering up girls for men to abuse and hurt in unthinkable ways. And a few days ago, he almost strangled me.

When he arrives today, it's with a pregnancy test.

I handle the box carefully as if it will bite me, but when I stall, he points to my waste bucket. He wants me to take it in front of him.

"Can you turn away?" I ask.

To my surprise, he does.

I take the test and hand it to him, not even caring to see the result. I already know.

He immediately growls under his breath. "Fuck."

Then he throws the test against the concrete wall so that it makes a tiny clatter. "We'll have to get rid of it," he says.

I furrow my brows. "I'm sorry, what?"

"The baby." He paces back and forth in front of the door.

Think. Fast.

Bill clearly doesn't have a plan right now, and it's my chance to take charge.

"Do you want to take me to a clinic?" I ask in a soft whisper. I doubt he will, but if he does, maybe I can escape at that point. I'm not getting an abortion.

The thought of truly losing the baby crushes me, and a little feeling rises up inside and I realize something.

I want to keep this child.

I don't care what it costs me.

"No clinics. No doctors," he barks.

How else would he get rid of it? I think of coat hangers and stories of back-alley abortions and fight back tears.

"You could help me ... raise it," I offer, seeing an opening to go back to my plan to win him over.

He charges toward me. "No! No kids. I don't even care if it was my own child, I would get rid of it!"

"Why?" I whisper, shrinking back from his huge frame, now so close I can smell body odor leaching off his skin.

"Doesn't matter. I can raise dogs. But no kids. Never kids." He pauses as if trying to calm himself.

"I would love to raise dogs," I say slowly, trying to insert myself into his future. Trying to get him to see a life with me in it. If I can accomplish that, I think he'll start to trust me. Maybe move me out of here. And then I can escape.

It's like he didn't hear me because he says, "There's a new pill out to get rid of unwanted babies."

"Are you talking about Plan B?" I remember hearing about it in Health class, but it wasn't available back then. Is it now?

"You'd need a prescription."

"I have my ways."

"I'm too far along. It won't work."

"Worth a try. Drugs, I can get." He moves closer, crouching to get into my face again. I want to turn away, but I don't. I can't cringe when he comes near or he won't believe me when it's time for me to say I want to build a life with him.

"And if it doesn't work, I'll tear the thing out of you," he adds.

Ice runs down my spine. Terror that makes me want to scream and cry and fight all at once. But instead, I take a steadying breath. "I thought you said you didn't want to hurt me?"

"I don't. But I will if it keeps you safe."

That makes no sense. He'll hurt me to keep me safe? I put it aside. Right now I need to stall. Buy some time to warm him up to my idea. The puppy farm. Me as his perfect little woman, there to serve and please. It has to work.

He puts his hand on my stomach and presses lightly. I can't help but gasp. "No, Bill, please."

"Who the fuck is Bill?" he yells.

Shit.

"Sorry, that's what I've been calling you in my mind because of the mask. You won't tell me your real name."

He doesn't answer, and he keeps his hand in place. I feel like I'm going to come out of my skin, but I clench my teeth and turn to face him, even though I'm repulsed. "Unless you're a doctor, you'll kill me trying to get rid of the baby. Are you a doctor?"

He grunts. "You can't have a baby. That's not how this goes with us." His tone is quieter, and there's almost a question mark in there, as if he's in the process of changing his mind.

But the one thing I latch onto is that he does see a future with us together. I pounce on it.

"Tell me how it goes then. Because I'm a good problem solver, and I can help you figure it out so we can be together without you becoming a baby killer."

The last two words make him flinch. "I'm not a baby killer. It's not a baby yet, just some cells."

"I can feel it moving, so that means it's alive inside of me, trusting me to protect it." I pause and swallow before saying the next part to be sure it comes across as genuine. "Exactly like you're protecting me."

"Fuck," he mutters to himself, then stands up and paces the room.

Is it possible that he truly believes he's protecting me by holding me hostage? He says he wants to keep me safe, but also that he'd hurt me to do it.

It's baffling.

"Fine," he says after a few minutes of silence. "But I'm getting rid of it after it's born."

"What does that mean?"

He doesn't answer, and while panic lights me up inside, I try to stuff it down. At least he's not going to abort my baby. That means I have time—a couple months—to come up with another plan to make sure he never gets his hands on my child.

My child.

The words linger in my mind and I find that it's absolutely true. I want this baby. I want to be a mother.

"I'll do anything, as long as you don't hurt the baby." As soon as the words spill out, I'm already praying he doesn't take me up on it.

But he approaches again and sits against the wall right next to me. Like he did the last time. The time he almost choked me to death. I want to inch away, but I don't. Instead, I breathe slowly to try to soften myself toward him when everything in me screams *Get away from him.*

"Anything?" he whispers.

He's going to violate me. Why did I offer this? Tears well up but I grit my teeth. "Yes."

He moves his hand to my leg and his touch is gentle, and yet it somehow feels so forceful that I want to hold my breath.

"I heard you singing earlier."

I have been singing a lot, but I tried to do it when I thought he wasn't around.

"I didn't know you could sing like that," he continues. It feels like he's asking for something and his hand is still on my leg. I want to shake it off, but instead, I focus on staying alert.

I clear my throat and speak as softly as I can. "Do you want me to sing to you?"

He doesn't answer. This moment is so full of contradictions. His hand on my leg tenderly as if we are a couple, yet the action is still so charged with aggression. The way he's asking me to sing to him—there's a vulnerability to it. Yet it's creepy as fuck.

"'Amazing Grace'," he says.

I never did go to church, but we sang a lot of hymns in choir, so luckily, I know it.

He seems to relax next to me, crossing his arms and sighing. The heat of his body presses against my side. The intimacy of the moment shocks me and it's terrifying in a different way than being violated would be. But I go along with it and sing.

When I'm halfway through the second verse, he puts his hand on my leg again and I flinch, but immediately try to calm myself down. I can't let him see how revolted I am by him.

"You telling me the truth about liking dogs?" he asks.

"Yes, of course. I love Golden Retrievers especially," I lie again.

He nods like he's considering something. Then he says, "Like I said, I'm going to start my puppy farm up in North Idaho—Pate. I want to breed a few dogs at the same time. Scale up fast. I could use some help with fixing the place up and when it comes time to take care of the pups."

I suppress a gasp and say, "I'd absolutely love to help you." My excitement is genuine, but it's not about the dogs. It's about the huge surge of hope that hits my heart. He's not going to kill me, and he's going to move me out of this room at some point. That's when I'll run.

NOW

CHAPTER 29
FRANKIE

CHLOE and I are almost to Banks-Lowman Road, where we'll turn off the highway toward Skinny Dipper. We've been in the car for about an hour, following the Payette River to our left, and I've answered more of her questions about our childhood. It's nice to talk about our shared history. Even if it's all new to her. So much of this is more like getting to know a new friend than reconnecting with an old one. Not that I ever dared to hope for Chloe's return, but the times I allowed myself to, it looked nothing like this in my imagination. But I don't hate this either. Mostly I'm just grateful.

Chloe looks past me and out the driver's side window at the people rafting. They're putting into the river at Banks, and it's all helmets and life jackets.

"You mentioned that I didn't have a boyfriend that summer. But somehow I was pregnant. It got me wondering about the guys in my life in general. Do you know if I had a crush on anyone?"

"I don't think you did. You were talking about holding off on dating until you got to college. It was the summer before your senior year and you were pretty done with the guys we'd gone to school with since kindergarten. I've racked my brain and I can't think of who you would have been seeing in secret. Honestly, we were so close, I think you would have told me."

"Maybe I didn't want to tell you."

"I mean it, Chlo. We talked about everything. That summer, you weren't with anyone."

Chloe doesn't reply, but I can feel her silently disagreeing. She thinks she must have had a boyfriend and kept it from me. But of the two of us, I think I know both her and me better than she does.

"Was I sexually active before that summer?" she asks.

"You mean …"

"I mean, was I a virgin as far as you knew?"

"No, you'd had a few boyfriends once you got to high school and you'd had sex with them. You dated Jensen when you were younger. I don't think you guys slept together though."

"Do you remember any of the guys I slept with?"

"Not their names, I'm sorry."

I could probably look them up in my yearbooks, if I had kept them. Old high school annuals aren't something I want to drag around with me as I remodel houses. Jensen probably has his, but I can't exactly reach out and ask him after what happened the other night. *Hey, I know I broke up with you and pissed you off but can I borrow your yearbook from 1998?*

"Okay, let's try this," Chloe says. "Was anyone interested in me even if I didn't return their feelings?"

"You mean maybe you were sleeping with someone you didn't like?"

"Yeah, like was anyone obsessed with me? It's a weird question to ask, but if you're right and I wasn't seeing anyone, it's possible someone forced themself on me."

"Fuck," I whisper. I hadn't considered that, but I don't know why. I'm certain I'm right that Chloe would have told me if she was seeing someone. So if she was pregnant, which obviously, she was, could it have happened non-consensually?

Now I start tearing up. The thought of her going through that kills me.

I want to reach over and hug her, but I can't because I'm driving. I wipe my eyes and say, "I'm so sorry for everything you went through. Even if you don't remember it. I'll try to think of possibilities."

"Thank you," Chloe says. I can hear her words catch in her throat and she looks out her side window.

I put on my blinker and turn right off Highway 55 toward Garden Valley and Skinny Dipper Hot Springs. We drive for a few more minutes before I pull over.

"We aren't to mile marker four yet," Chloe says, straining to look ahead and then down at her phone.

"I know, but this is the closest pull-out to the trailhead."

At least I think it is. I haven't been up here for at least a decade, and even then it wasn't super easy to find. The trail is a narrow path carved into the side of the mountain. This reminds me of the climb and I groan.

"What's wrong?"

"Oh, I'm dreading the hike."

She laughs. "You love to hike. I thought you were going to cry when we decided not to hike Table Rock."

"True. But this is next level."

It's scorching out, and the air smells like river mixed with hot dirt and pine needles. It makes me thirsty already, and I haven't even started sweating yet.

Chloe finds a tiny slip of a trail almost immediately. "This has to be it!" she calls out.

"Did you remember where it was?" I can't help the hope in my voice.

"Nope. I looked at pictures on Google Maps," she laughs,

then her eyes track up the mountainside. "Wow, you weren't kidding."

"Yeah. After you guys disappeared, people speculated about why you'd attempt it in the dark. But who can know teen logic?"

"I certainly don't know. After you," Chloe says, then waves me on to lead the way.

"You don't want to go first?"

"I think I'll slow you down. I'm not in great shape." She smiles, and elbows me in the ribs, which makes me laugh. I doubt she'll slow me down, but man, she's going to roast out here with her hair down and in those long joggers. She's still got the glasses on too, and I can imagine that would be uncomfortable while hiking, but chances are she's used to it.

After a few times of turning around and checking on her, and catching her holding her hair in a ponytail with her hand, I say, "It's hot, huh?"

She nods and drops her hair.

My hair is up, and I pretty much always have an extra hair tie around my wrist, so I offer it to her.

"No thanks. I like it down," she says.

Pretty soon we're taking the switchbacks in silence because we're both pretty damn winded.

I see steam rising from a crevice in the mountain ahead.

"There's Skinny Dipper," I say, pointing to it. "Up and over that small hill."

CHAPTER 30
FRANKIE

I STAND, staring at the site of the hot springs, and I know what to expect because I've been here before, but that doesn't lessen the soft thrum of anxiety I feel about it. It's so solemn. It's not as creepy as the prison, but it's definitely got a vibe to it.

Chloe catches up and gives a small gasp as we both take in what looks absolutely nothing like hot springs. More like a waterfall full of rocks, algae, and who knows what else. It's gross, but beautiful in a weird way too, because the forest-green and orange plumes of algae in the water are not a sign of decay. They're quite alive, actually. Billowing with the slow flow of water like mermaid hair.

The scorching hot liquid trickles down the mountainside, leaving trails of algae everywhere it touches. As if it's been doing this since the dawn of time.

"Hard to imagine where the actual pools were," Chloe says, breaking the silence.

"No kidding. I remember coming up here when I was in college. Of course it was closed because of what happened with you guys, so we didn't get in. But there were still actual pools. There was one there," I point. "And there, and there."

"Why are they full of rocks now?"

"Well, BLM shut the hot springs down after the murders, and then about ten years ago, it's like Mother Nature decided closing it wasn't good enough and a rockslide happened. After that, it was impossible for anyone to soak here even if they were willing to break the law to do it."

Chloe rock-hops over to what used to be the larger pool.

"Where did they find Amy and Kristi?" she asks.

"Kristi was still in this pool." I motion to the one we're right beside. "And Amy was …" I bend a little to point down below. "At the bottom."

"Jesus Christ," Chloe whispers. "It feels like a cemetery." Her face points down and she peeks over the edge as if she's searching for where they may have found Amy.

"It really does."

I watch her intently, trying not to show that I'm disturbed by this place.

Chloe moves to the other side of the pool that's opposite the trail. It used to be covered in trees, but now it's a bunch of burnt stumps. A wildfire out here laid the pine bare a couple years ago. She wipes at her eyes like she's trying to stifle tears.

"You okay?" I ask.

"Yeah, I'm feeling it out."

Right. Like she did at the prison.

"Look at that," Chloe says, pointing to where the burnt stumps are, and it resembles another path. I don't remember it being there the last time I came up, but then again, there were lots of trees back then. Pre-wildfire.

"I bet it's an animal path. Deer and elk," I say.

"Do you think it was there before? Like that night?"

"Not sure. It would have been hidden by trees and almost impossible to access because of the dense brush."

"Let's check it out," Chloe says, lunging toward a large rock to step on. It's a bit out of reach, but she manages it. I don't see a way to get to the path. It's up the mountain a bit, and there's not really a way to climb it.

"Why?" I ask. It looks dangerous and while I love this detective mode she's in, I don't want to go over there.

"Why not? We're here, so we might as well."

Chloe reaches to grab on to a bush branch growing out from the side of the mountain. There's a rock underneath, and she pulls herself to stand on it, inching closer to the wild game trail. "Come on!" she calls out.

I could stay here and wait. But curiosity flickers, and suddenly I don't want to.

Chloe manages to make her way safely, so I hop over to the first rock, retracing her steps. "Fine. Lead on," I say.

Chloe gets her footing along the brush and tall weeds and pulls herself up to the little game trail, turning to help me do the same.

From this vantage point, you can look back and see the hot springs, or what's left of them, and the trail on the other side. You can also see the road way below, along with my truck parked in the pull-out.

"They think the attacker was already up here when we arrived," Chloe says. "I don't remember any of it, of course. That's what I read online."

It's true. The best theory is that whoever hunted the girls was already in position because there's no way he could have followed them up to the pools and then gotten behind them, high up on the rocky perch where they think the attack came from. The girls would have seen him.

"But it doesn't make sense to me how he would have known we were coming up here. Was he hanging out in this craggy valley sprinkled with hot springs for fun, and then when we showed up, he decided to attack us?"

That's always bothered me too. And it feels like it's been supremely overlooked by everyone. The consensus is the person was up here hunting. But the type of arrow the police recovered from Amy and Kristi's bodies weren't the sort you'd use to hunt. They were heavier. Shorter. Crossbow arrows instead of archery arrows.

He wasn't there to hunt game.

The police guessed the attacker was up higher, where he could have had a clear shot at the pool. It would also work for the direction Amy fell off the cliff. Still, it's as if the gruesome scene made no sense, so when there were no new leads to follow in the case, they accepted this half-baked idea as truth.

"What if he was following us and actually came up this way instead?" Chloe points to the game trail, which is even thinner than the one they climbed up. And much more steep. Animals don't need switchbacks.

"I hadn't thought about it," I whisper. I've never even noticed that other trail before. My heart picks up at the idea. What if there's something to what Chloe is saying?

I don't remember whether the police knew about the animal trail or not. Did they even look on the other side of the hot springs? Have they been up here since the wildfire? Why would they come up? Until Chloe returned, the case was so cold it was practically ice.

Chloe lowers herself on the steep trail so that she's in a sort of crab-walk position, and she moves down, trying to control how much she slides on the dirt. No way you'd be able to walk down this path standing upright.

"Where are you going?" I ask.

"I have to see if there are any clues."

Chloe is already on her way, and I don't want to follow. I really don't. But I'm not letting her go off alone, either. Plus, the hope of finding something overwhelms any anxiety I felt before. I crouch down and move behind Chloe, mimicking her.

My palms are getting scraped, but so far there's no blood.

It's just very dirty, and I keep hitting my ass on the ground when I get too close.

Then Chloe stops and tries to stand. Gravity works against her and she loses her footing, but she catches herself. She reaches to the left of the path, even farther from the hot springs, and it seems like she's trying to go off road and into the knee-high brush.

"What are you doing now?"

"I think I saw something. It caught my eye in the sunlight."

It's probably a broken booze bottle, but I don't say that and instead try to catch up.

"Holy shit!" Chloe yells, her voice full of excitement.

My heart races. She found something.

Not possible.

But what if it is?

It feels like it takes me forever to get down to where Chloe has gone off-path, but I finally arrive, and she's brushing dirt off something small. She holds up a piece of gold jewelry.

CHAPTER 31

FRANKIE

It's Chloe's old locket. The one I gave her. I don't even have to see inside to know because it's an oval shape with a heart engraved on the front. It's tarnished from being out in the weather over the years, but that doesn't lessen my doubt.

"Don't touch it," I say, much too late. "What if it has prints on it?"

Chloe drops the locket like it's a hot potato and it falls back into the tall weeds.

I pull off my thin tank top. It's crazy hot out anyway, and I'm wearing a sports bra. I reach down and use the fabric to lift the locket again so as not to rub it. I don't want to do anything to remove fingerprints if there are some.

"This was yours," I say, starting to choke up because seeing the locket brings back memories.

For a moment, Chloe and I stare at each other and the air becomes almost electric with anticipation.

"We have to get this to the police," I say.

Chloe smiles big.

We look around at the same time as if we're both trying to decide the best way to take the rest of the hill down to the car.

"I don't think I can climb up this trail to get back over to the main one. It's way too goddamn steep," Chloe says.

"Yeah, I'm shocked we even got this far without pulling a Jack and Jill. I guess we'll have to slide on our asses all the way down this game trail."

I slip the locket wrapped in my tank top into my sports bra so I can use both hands in order to avoid falling to my death.

"I want ice cream after this," Chloe says, tossing her face backward so I can hear from behind.

I laugh. "Okay, random. But I guess a celebration is in order. There's that huckleberry soft serve in Horseshoe Bend. Let's stop there before we hit Boise."

"Yes, please."

Then we scoot in silence. Because it's straight down, the trail is shorter than the switchbacks on the way up, and finally, we're back at the truck.

Chloe can't stop talking about the locket the whole drive back to Boise. She's so convincing that I find myself agreeing with a lot of her points.

That the attacker probably used the game trail.

That he likely took her somewhere and maybe that's when she dropped the locket.

That the police may be able to use it to re-open the case.

As soon as we're back in cell range, my phone pings from the console. I fight the urge to check it while driving. From a glance I can tell it's a Reddit notification, and my first thought goes to Punkass99's cryptic messages.

I haven't thought about them since Chloe got back.

Fuck him. Finding that locket feels like a sign, like the whole world is open and anything could be possible. Like maybe we could discover who killed Amy and Kristi. Or learn what happened to Chloe all those years ago. Maybe we could even help put the psycho who did this behind bars.

We pull into the little market selling huckleberry ice cream on the side of the highway, and Chloe says, "I'll meet you inside. I have to pee like crazy."

I chuckle and nod. Looking at my phone, a message from Jensen banners across my home screen.

> Hey, sorry about the other night. Can we talk?

My gut reaction is no. There's nothing to talk about. He's going to try to come back into my life, but this time I feel like we're done. The past few days I've been more free than I have in a long time.

I don't reply and instead tap the Reddit message from Punkass99. The message says:

> DON'T TRUST CHLOE WEBSTER.

I roll my eyes. I want to type some version of *go pound sand*, but I hesitate, trying to think of something I could ask him to draw him out and get him to tell me who he is. Is he related to the murders? Another message comes through.

> SHE KNOWS MORE THAN SHE'S LETTING ON.

THEN

CHAPTER 32
CHLOE

Amazing Grace, how sweet the sound. That saved a wretch like me.

Wake up and check outside. If there's daylight, scratch a mark in the window plywood. There's snow on the ground now.

I once was lost but now I'm found.

Count the marks. Today is ninety-three. It's been ninety-three days since Bill said I'm going with him to the puppy farm. Ninety-three days of mind-numbing boredom filled with anxiety. How many days was it before I started keeping track?

Was blind but now I see.

Sleep. Eat. Call out to the other girls when Bill is gone. Get no response. Ever. I wonder if I'm the only one here now.

'Twas grace that taught my heart to fear.

Bill comes. Sing church songs to him. Find a way to bring up the puppies. Ask when we will go. He gets mad and says it's not time yet. Stop asking about it.

And grace my fears relieved.

Sing to the baby. Feel the baby move. How its feet shove up into my ribcage—that pocket of space right under the left rib. Let the aching remind me this is real. The baby is real and I'm going to be a mother. The baby is coming, and I must protect it.

How precious did that grace appear.

Walk around the room to strengthen my ankle. I'll need it when I run.

The hour I first believed.

Go to sleep and wonder if the puppy farm will ever happen. Maybe I'll end up dead in a cell after all. Shake off those thoughts and focus on the baby. My *child*. Think of escape. Come up with a backup plan in case Bill never moves me out of here.

I sit on my mattress with my legs crossed until it's too uncomfortable and I have to lay on my side. I'm very big now. But that means the baby is healthy, and I'm happy about that. I sing my song while I make a doll from strips of the 101 Dalmatians sheet. My fingers work fast, forming knot after knot, tying the strips together like a balloon animal. Right now it's only a long piece of knotted fabric. Loose strings fly everywhere as the ripping noise bounces off concrete walls, but I'm careful to keep the mess contained under the mattress so Bill doesn't catch me doing it. I pull so tightly because it must be strong enough that a toddler couldn't destroy it.

Because my baby *will* be a toddler someday. I won't let Bill get rid of it. He says he's not a baby killer.

I choke on a sob at that thought. Surely Bill has killed children before, though. Amy and Kristi were going into their senior year, but they weren't adults yet. And that redhead I saw in the cell when I first got here months ago—she was young too. I wonder what happened to her.

It's idiotic to believe Bill will spare my baby. I have to get out of here before it's born.

Despair floods in, but I push it back. "No," I say out loud.

I take inventory. My ankle is getting stronger. I'm not in perfect shape, and of course, I'm very pregnant, but I only need to be quick enough to get away. Quick is probably wishful thinking. I'm front heavy, and while maneuvering around is possible, there's no way I can outrun Bill. I have to subdue him long enough to get away. Take advantage of a moment of weakness.

Like I got away at the hot springs? Back when I wasn't hobbling, didn't have a baby bump, and was free to begin with? No, I froze up. Got myself and my child into this.

The harsh intrusive thoughts bring tears so that I have to blink to see what I'm doing with the fabric. My chest tightens at the memory of how paralyzed by fear I was the last time I could have gotten away. Back when I was stronger and had a better chance at escape. But that was weak Chloe. Scared Chloe.

This is lying, manipulating, willing-to-die-for-my-baby Chloe.

Maybe I'm capable of more.

That's when I stop and stare at the knotted strip of fabric. I pull it tight, and it makes a whipping sound. An idea blooms.

What if...?

I slowly wrap it around my own neck to test the length. Definitely long enough, even for his neck, which is thicker than mine.

Am I serious about this? My hands start to shake as I bring the makeshift rope down to look at it again. It's strong enough. I squeeze the fabric to ground myself in this idea. It could work, and it's the closest thing I have to a plan where I'm taking control instead of waiting for Bill to move me to North Idaho.

How would I do it? He's so much bigger and stronger than me.

He would have to be very distracted.

I only know of one way I can distract him for sure.

NOW

CHAPTER 33
FRANKIE

IT TOOK SOME CONVINCING, but I finally got Chloe to agree to come with me up to The Springs in Idaho City, which is a hot springs resort about forty-five minutes away from town. After being up at Skinny Dipper, I realized a soak would be nice, and this place is perfect. It's more like a big pool you make a reservation for, and they serve wine and appetizers. I scheduled us for massages, and tonight there's live music.

And kids. I don't have anything against kids, but damn I wish I chose an adults-only day. It's the difference between a quiet, relaxing soak and a pool-noodle-infested circus full of splashing and crying. At this spot, you can soak for two hours before your session is over and they kick you out, and this was the time slot available on this short notice. In the evening. With kids.

After our massages, we go into the small locker room to change into swimsuits. There's next to nobody inside, which is pretty rare. It's so tight that it's usually a struggle to get a spot near your locker to change.

"I'll be right back," Chloe says, grabbing her tote bag.

"Where are you going?"

"To change."

"Oh," is all I say. Of course if she wants privacy, that's absolutely fine. It's just that I don't recall her ever being that modest —at least not around me. We changed in front of each other all the time. If anything, I was the more modest one.

She comes out wearing a black swimsuit cover with embroidered white flowers. It's ankle-length and has bell sleeves. We grab our towels and walk outside into the dark. The pool is lit up, so the water glows a shade of light blue, and the string lights add a magical ambiance to the outdoor stage, where a woman with a pixie cut plays something that sounds like indie folk on her guitar.

I glide in until the warm mineral water is up to my neck, then I turn around to say something to Chloe, but she's not behind me.

When I scan the pool deck, I find her still back at the shallow end, by the locker room entrance, moving to sit on the edge. She pulls her coverup around her knees and dangles her feet in the water. Why isn't she getting in?

I swim over to her, and ask, "What's going on? Are you feeling okay?"

"Yeah, sorry, I realized I don't want to get wet."

"Oh," I say again. I'm disappointed, but it's okay. She can sit on the edge and we can head home sooner than I planned; no big deal.

A little girl who is about four or five dog-paddles by us wearing a life jacket, and splashes me in the process. I laugh to make light of it, but Chloe pulls her feet out of the water and hugs her knees. Is she annoyed about the kids?

Then, out of nowhere, a huge cannonball of water drenches me and sends a sheet of water directly into Chloe's face. A boy pops up from underneath and paddles his way to the little girl, who is holding the edge near Chloe. He splashes so much that I have to shield myself and look away for a minute. When I finally wipe my eyes and can see again, I catch a glimpse of Chloe's back before she disappears into the locker room.

I pull myself out of the pool and follow, feeling worried that she somehow got hurt, or—I don't know, honestly. I'm not sure why a splash would be an emergency.

I walk past the showers and toilet stalls, but I have to wait for a small group of women to cattle by before I can get to the lockers. They take up all the space and they're moving so slowly, stopping to adjust bikinis and chatting as they go, so I strain to see Chloe around the corner. She reaches into her locker for her bag, and when she quickly glimpses back, as if to check and see what's behind her, my mouth drops open. She doesn't see me, and I duck back into an empty shower and pull the curtain to hide because I need to process this for a minute without her knowing I'm here.

It's her face. That scatter of freckles across her nose.

Chloe didn't have a single freckle.

THEN

CHAPTER 34

CHLOE

MY FIRST CONTRACTIONS land as pure shock. Not the pain, necessarily—that's like strong cramps and nothing I can't manage, but it's too soon. Granted, my stomach is big, but not as big as I thought it would get right before birth, and I still don't know when I'm due. I don't even know what month it is. The last period I remember was in the spring. Maybe April? It was August when Bill kidnapped me. That means it would have to be December or January for me to have gone the whole nine months.

Have I really been at the prison for that long? The snow is piling up outside, so I guess it's possible. So far I've been able to stay quiet through the contractions, and I get long breaks in between. But when one strikes, I have to focus and breathe through it.

Even though some time has passed since I set my mind to using the 101 Dalmatians rope I made to strangle Bill, I haven't had a chance. His visits have been increasingly sporadic, and when he's here, he doesn't sit close to me. I get the sense he's disgusted by my pregnancy. Normally I'd be happy he stays away, but I need him within arm's reach to put my plan into action.

I hope when he does finally get close, it's not during a contraction. The thought of trying to strangle a huge man in the midst of such strong cramping feels impossible.

When Bill comes in with grocery sacks today, I know what it means. He's leaving for a few days again. I swallow hard, watching him pull out bottles of Gatorade and water along with boxes of crackers, some dried fruit, a jar of peanut butter, granola bars, and cans of tuna.

Cans? He's never given me cans of anything before. Those require an opener.

I watch as he stacks the tuna in columns three high, and sets a small, metal can opener next to them.

"Pretty sure you're not going to use this to hurt yourself, with that baby and all," he says. "Not only that, but it'd be hard to do any damage with this."

Incredible that he doesn't see me as a threat to himself. His worry is that I'd want to hurt myself. And he's right. The can opener has a guard protecting the sharp metal wheel.

"I'm going to be a bit longer this time. Figure we have a couple more months before the baby comes, and there are some things I have to do before that. Before we leave."

He's waiting until I have the baby to leave for the puppy farm. That's why there's been such a long delay. Dread prickles up my spine when I realize why. He wants to get rid of it before we go.

"What month is it?" I ask.

"December."

I can't believe he actually told me, but I'm elated that he has the timing of the baby's birth wrong. The fact is that the baby could be coming any day, and maybe I'm just small because I haven't had vitamins or any fruit or vegetables. The thought sends waves of fear through me. Will the baby be okay? No matter. I'll get out of here and get help.

"I don't expect the baby until February," I lie.

He approaches. It's the closest he's gotten in a while and my breath hitches as I realize this is it. This is my chance. I sneak my hand under the mattress for the rope.

"I'll be back well before then," Bill says. "And once the baby is gone, we can be together. Away from here."

A slow cramping starts in my pelvis, signaling a contraction, and Bill moves to sit next to me.

No. I can't attack him during a contraction. I know for a fact I won't have the strength, but at least he's next to me, and not sitting across, staring, like he often does. I don't want him to see that I'm in pain and find out how close I actually am to having this baby.

I should ask a question and maybe he'll get frustrated, wave it off, and leave like usual. "Why are you doing this? Holding me and the other girls here?"

Leave. I need you to leave.

I grind my molars together in order to avoid showing the anticipation of pain on my face.

"I got tricked," he says, then turns to look at me. "You okay? You're acting funny."

I nod, holding back the urge to wince as the pain increases to what feels like bad period cramps, and I hate that he can read it. I also hate that bringing up this topic didn't do the thing it's always done in the past: make Bill run away. It's done the opposite—he's actually engaging.

"I'm fine," I say. "What do you mean 'tricked'?"

Leave. Just leave.

And yet, if the situation was different and I wasn't trying to hide that this baby is coming sooner than he thinks, I'd be dying to know anything he wants to tell me.

"I had a problem. Told somebody a secret and they used it against me."

Keep pressing. Make him mad and he'll leave.

"What problem?" I ask, smiling to hide the building pressure in my abdomen. This one feels worse than usual.

He clears his throat. The bastard is hanging around to answer my questions the one time I don't want him to. I need to stop asking.

"I'm afraid if I tell you it'll change the way you see me."

Nope, you'll still be a murdering motherfucker. Nothing can change that.

This is my chance, and I'm missing it. I want to cry in frustration with my body for not cooperating. For making the timing so wrong.

"That's not possible, you know. I love you."

He stands and moves away from me, toward the door just as the edge of pain from the cramping subsides, and I want to cry in relief.

But now that I could put my plan into action, Bill is on the other side of the room.

He puts a hand on the door but turns toward me. His cold eyes stare through that damn mask. He isn't buying my declaration of love.

"I do love you," I say. "You're the man for me, and nothing will change that. I can't wait until we're out of here and I can see your face and learn your name."

"Just us two," he adds, after a pause.

I glance down at my belly and nod, pushing down every dark emotion in order to focus on the life inside of me.

"Just us two," I say, but inside I'm thinking, *You and me, my little baby.*

NOW

CHAPTER 35
FRANKIE

DAYS HAVE PASSED and I can't stop thinking about that night when Chloe got splashed at the pool.

After I saw her face, I hid in the shower and moved the curtain to watch her go into a bathroom stall. I heard makeup clattering. I imagined her putting on foundation to hide the freckles, then I ran outside and got into the pool before she came out so she wouldn't know I was watching her.

As the night went on, and we drove back home, I began to feel like a real idiot. Was I really creeping her and then getting all worked up over a few freckles?

I looked it up online and it's possible to develop freckles later in life. Although it's more common for them to fade as someone ages. But maybe she spent a lot of years in the sun without protection.

And then there's the big question: Why is she hiding them with makeup?

This brings to mind the cryptic message from Punkass, which I readily dismissed:

She knows more than she's letting on.

I hate the skepticism that's inching its way into my mind.

Why would Chloe keep information from me? Why would she hide and lie?

This is the mental seesawing I do as I tail Chloe's little white Kia in my truck.

I want to know where she goes when she leaves the house, that's all. At first, I didn't think much of it because she went to the police station. Then she did a news interview. One time she went grocery shopping for us. I imagine she spent time around Boise, trying to jog her memory without me too. But after the freckle incident, I need more information so I know whether to confront her, or reach out to Punkass. Because I need to do something. I can feel my heart closing toward her in distrust, and that is unbearable.

We've been driving toward downtown, but when we get there, Chloe passes through and keeps going toward East Boise.

I don't even have a guess about her destination. Out here it's suburbia, with some industrial areas. But mostly, it's yoga studios, schools, and grocery stores.

I hang back farther once we start driving up the road that overlooks downtown. It's more open here, and I'm worried she'll see me.

Finally, she pulls into the parking lot of the Ralfroy Motel.

What the hell?

While the Ralfroy is cute with a seventies vibe, it's not a first choice place to stay for most visitors. And certainly not visitors who are already staying with a relative like Chloe is. It's an extended stay motel, but cheaper than say, a Residence Inn. It's tiny—less than ten rooms—with exterior doors, and Chloe parks in front of room number four. I park on the side of the building where I can see her, but she can't see me.

Chloe goes inside, and I wait.

And wait.

And wait.

It's been an hour and thirteen minutes by the time she

comes out. I know because I'm bored out of my mind and getting more keyed up with anxiety wondering why she has this room and what she's doing in there.

She drives away and I wait another couple minutes to be sure she doesn't come back, having forgotten something.

I feel so exposed because the motel faces Federal Way, which isn't insanely busy, but it's a four-lane road and it gets a fair share of traffic.

"It's now or never," I say to myself and walk over to room number four.

Of course, the door is locked. And of course, I don't know how to break into a motel, even if I had the guts to do it.

The curtains are drawn, but there's a tiny slit where they don't quite meet in the middle and I cup my hands around my face to block out the sun and see inside. It's dim, but I can make out a bed, a TV, multiple suitcases, open with clothes and other items falling out of them. There's evidence of takeout every-where. McDonald's bags and Taco Bell cups. The bed has linens that don't look like they came with the room. As if someone brought their own pillows to the Ralfroy.

Chloe.

This is all Chloe's stuff. It has to be, and it looks like she's been here for a long time.

My eyes travel to the walls and I see a bunch of things that certainly don't belong to the hotel. News article clippings, tons of pictures of Chloe when she was young.

Then I notice a picture of Jensen.

And next to it, is one of me.

THEN

CHAPTER 36
CHLOE

I WAKE up in the middle of the night and my sweatpants are wet and warm. The bed is wet too. I smell the sheets and it's not urine.

I think my water has broken.

Cramping begins like a bad period, but quickly progresses into a contraction unlike any I've had before.

It's time.

My body seizes up in pain as my abdomen clenches so all I can do is lie on my side and cry. My thoughts transform into sheer panic.

I'm not ready.

I don't know how to give birth. What little I know is from health class years ago, and the movies.

"God, please make it stop," I cry out. But then I inhale sharply, realizing I should be quiet. I don't think Bill is here, but something inside says to save my energy and strength for later.

Because it's going to get so much worse.

I can't do this. I can't.

I want my mom.

This thought makes me cry even more. I'm completely

alone, doing one of the hardest things any woman will ever do in her life. But I'm in high school. I'm not a woman yet. I can't do it.

Moving at all feels like a bad idea, but it hurts so bad I can't be still. I rub my feet together, writhing and begging for this to be over.

Please, please, please.

The contraction eases up and I let myself weep. I'm already exhausted. How am I going to do this?

I should try to sleep, but I barely drop off into slumber when the next contraction comes.

This keeps happening over and over, time feels irrelevant as I become a slave to my body, allowing it to take control and do whatever it wants. I'm so exhausted that eventually, I force myself to relax, even if I can't sleep, and even during a contraction.

I find that I don't need to tense up as much as I have been, and this helps a bit. It's the opposite of what I want to do, which is tighten up and scream. But if I breathe deeply and even hum my song a little, it helps.

But then I lose focus, crying because I can't do this alone. I don't know what I'm doing.

My body knows.

It's already starting the process of giving birth and all I've done is cry and go haywire. I think of my mom again, and how she gave birth to me. She must have experienced this exact same thing. The pain, the fear, the sense of being alone. I'm not the first one to give birth to a child and that bolsters me for a second.

My mom did this. I can do it too.

But my mom was in the hospital. She had a doctor. Medication for the pain. She was safe. She had her sister there—Frankie's mom.

I'm tempted to lose heart again, but that does no good. The

contractions are happening fast now, and I have to get a hold of myself.

I'm not the first one to give birth to a child, I think again, breathing and groaning through the pain.

Women have been doing this for centuries. Forever, in fact.

I force myself to picture them, all the women who have done this before me, who brought life into the world.

My mom's time—the eighties.

My grandma, who I never knew. She did this too. That would have been the sixties.

Then farther back to all the faceless mothers. I see them frozen in time periods.

World War II era—surely those women felt all alone giving birth. Their men were overseas, and the world was dark and uncertain.

The Great Depression. I picture women giving birth when they had no money, sometimes no home, no hope for the future.

I keep going backward in time, breathing through my contractions, imagining all the women across the world who have been in this exact same position as me. All the way back to cave dweller days when there were no hospitals. No medication to numb the pain. There was constant danger all around from the environment and predators, yet women labored and brought life into the world.

That's me. I'm one of them now, giving birth in the face of danger and predators, knowing my future is uncertain. If those women did it, I can do it too.

Suddenly, I feel so much pressure in my rectal area, like I have to go to the bathroom. I move over to the drain and find that it feels good to squat. But I can't give birth over a drain.

Why not? It's perfect. It'll hide the mess better than if I did it in my bed. I don't know if I can fully hide from Bill the fact that I've given birth, but I'm sure as hell going to try.

I need to push. I reach down and feel what's happening, and I'm shocked to find that my fingers touch the baby's head.

I cry again, but this time, it's because it's close to being over. My baby will be here and we'll be together.

I scream and push as hard as I possibly can.

CHAPTER 37
CHLOE

IT'S A GIRL. She's pink and perfect, but she's very small. My hair is soaking wet from sweat, and it was all worth it because here she is.

Natalie.

My very own baby girl, named after the woman who sings my favorite song.

I hold her up to inspect every square inch of this miracle, and as Natalie squirms, her crying signals that nothing else in the world matters. Not to me at least.

Warmth rushes throughout my body and I hold her close. How is it possible to love her as much as I do?

Even though she looks like *him* with her mop of black hair.

My insides tense up at the thought. How will he react when I return with a baby that resembles him? What will he do?

I can't think about that. Need to think about cleaning up and putting the plan into action. First step is to get out of here.

I use a few bottles of water to wash the mess down the drain and to clean myself up. After I gave birth, something else came out. I think it's the placenta, but I'm not sure. I tried using the can opener to cut the cord, but it wasn't sharp enough. After putting it off until I was afraid it'd be bad for Natalie to leave it, I chewed through the cord, crying the whole time. Eventually, it was done, and I put all of it in my waste bucket underneath a pile of toilet paper since it doesn't fit down the drain. Bill might notice it when he goes to clean out my bucket. But that won't happen because the plan is to strangle him as soon as he shows his face.

I have been thinking about that can opener though. It's no good for cutting, but could it stab? I don't think so because while one of the metal handles is thin enough to puncture something, it's got a tiny ball on the end. No sharp points.

Even so, I put it under the covers on my mattress as a backup plan.

Natalie's warm skin presses against me, and when she moves her mouth around, it's like she's looking for something. I try to give her my breast and I'm shocked at how natural it all feels, even though breastfeeding is more challenging than I expected. Even with those road bumps, I'm certain this is meant to be. Natalie and I are meant to be. Natalie fusses, trying and failing to nurse, so I sing my song—our song—to help calm her.

She finally latches on, and it hurts like hell, but all of that fizzles away as I take in the adorable little grunts she makes while she nurses. I keep humming quietly, trying to give Natalie as much comfort as possible. I don't know what the next days, hours, even minutes hold. But right now, right here, with my baby, I feel happy for the first time in forever.

That said, the pain in my body hasn't stopped. It's hard to sit at all, and I'm bleeding a lot, which surprises me. It's like I'm having a period. I hope that's normal, but mostly I don't let myself worry because there's nothing I can do but manage it and try to push through the discomfort by thinking about Natalie and anticipating what she needs next.

I do wonder how I'll hide all the blood from Bill though.

I think of the box of tampons.

They would stop the bleeding, and I could bury the soiled ones in the waste bucket. But my body is so torn up down there that the thought of inserting one makes me gag.

That doesn't feel like an option.

I'll have to sit near the drain and keep rinsing the mess down if I want to hide it. When I hear Bill coming, I'll move back to the bed. I'll be bleeding, yes, but I'll make sure to attack quickly before he notices. Then I'll run. I can't think past that part because it's terrifying. Where will I go? How will I find help?

No, think about Natalie. About strangling Bill.

As the hours pass, I notice Natalie isn't crying as much, and she's falling asleep a lot. I want her to get stronger and that means she needs to nurse, so I start waking her, but she's almost impossible to rouse. She isn't interested in feeding.

Is that normal?

Natalie's coloring seems a little off too, and that worries me.

I transform what's left of the Dalmatians sheet into a makeshift diaper. I still have plenty of water, so I can clean her when she messes. We're fine. As long as Bill returns soon, we'll be fine.

NOW

CHAPTER 38

FRANKIE

Before I'm even back to my truck, I've got my phone in hand and I'm navigating to Reddit to send a message Punkass99:

LET'S TALK.

When I get in, my body is shaking and my teeth are chattering as if I'm freezing cold, but I'm not. It's over ninety degrees out today. I hug myself while sitting in the driver's seat and then I start sobbing.

It's the kind of crying that feels less like something I'm doing, and more like something that's happening to me. I can't control it. Soon, I'm practically howling, and I can't see because my eyes keep filling with tears faster than I can blink them away.

Chloe must have been in Boise longer than what she told me.

She didn't check out of her hotel room, like she said.

What else has she lied to me about?

And why does she have pictures of me up on her wall? Of Jensen? Of herself? It looks like something a detective from a TV show would do if he was obsessed with solving a case.

I check my phone, and there's no movement in my Reddit inbox.

Please don't make me wait this time, Punkass, I silently beg.

I have to talk to someone. To make sure I'm not reading into things and being paranoid. Jensen comes to mind first, but I can't call him. Not with this. If I break my silence it'd have to be in order to deal with our situation, and then maybe I could bring this up, but no way I have bandwidth for all of that right now.

I could call my dad. But chances are low he'd answer. And he'd just encourage me to let it go, like he always does. I want someone who will listen to my concerns and tell me I'm not crazy.

I don't have anyone like that in my life. Except Chloe.

I cry harder, realizing how isolated and incapable I am of relationships, and how when Chloe returned, I felt like that was starting to heal.

But the lies and hiding make her feel a solar system away.

I don't want to go home. I don't want to face Chloe yet. Especially since I've been crying and I don't want her to ask me any questions about why.

Dad's house comes to mind. I could hide out there for a while until I get my shit together. I'll go home when I'm ready to pull off acting like nothing happened. Hopefully by then I'll have heard something from Punkass too.

Before I even reach my dad's neighborhood, I have a message from Punkass. I check it at the next red light.

WE CAN'T TALK HERE. HAS TO BE IN PERSON.

Is he crazy? I'm not meeting him in person. I don't reply yet, because the light turns green and I'm almost at Dad's.

Plus what if nothing is going on? Maybe Chloe simply doesn't like the freckles she developed later in life and wants to cover them.

I already know she's trying to figure out what happened in her past. So what if she's keeping a secret motel room with a detective spread on the wall?

Again, it's the lying and hiding. That's the real issue. Chloe knows I want to figure out what happened too, so why wouldn't she include me in her search if that's all she's doing?

Maybe she doesn't fully trust me yet, which I could understand. But it's been weeks and I feel like I've earned her trust enough for her to be honest that she's kept her motel room.

She's traumatized. I have to remember that. Even if she doesn't recall what happened in the past, it still happened, whatever horrible thing it may have been. Our bodies carry that information even when we don't remember.

Still. Something presses me to find out more.

I pull into my dad's driveway and grab my phone to type out a response to Punkass.

> DO YOU THINK I'M STUPID? I'M NOT MEETING
> SOMEONE IN PERSON THAT I DON'T KNOW.
>
> FINE, THEN GOODBYE.

An immediate response.

Shit. This is the farthest I've gotten in conversation with him, but I don't want to meet up in person. That feels idiotic. I type:

> WAIT. YOU REALLY EXPECT ME TO MEET UP WITH
> YOU WHEN I DON'T EVEN KNOW WHO YOU ARE?
> YOU MIGHT BE A SERIAL KILLER.
>
> YEAH, I MIGHT BE. BUT I HAVE ANSWERS
> FOR YOU.

Well, that's not the response I expected. Something more along the lines of "I'm definitely not a serial killer" would have been better. Then again, maybe if he said that, I'd think he was being too defensive and it would act as proof that he is a serial killer.

Ugh. So many brain circles. I don't know what to think except that if there are answers about Chloe, I absolutely need them.

I'M BRINGING MY BOYFRIEND

I type this even though I have no boyfriend, and the closest thing to it was Jensen. Who is, of course, not in the picture.

NO. JUST YOU.

I groan. Is there any other way? My fingers hesitate over the keypad while I think of options. I could forget this whole thing and go on with life. Decide I'm being paranoid. So what if Chloe has a weird secret motel room where she keeps pictures of herself and Jensen and me on the wall? So what if she has freckles she hates?

Let it go.

Dad's voice is in my mind. I groan louder because I can't. Maybe I could have eventually gotten to where I was fine not knowing what happened the night Chloe went missing. But with this new development? No way. I have to know more and I can't ask her. Considering she's already bent the truth with me, I think she'll do that again.

Not only that, but what about this distance in my heart? I don't even want to be in the same room as Chloe. I feel betrayed. Every fiber of my being is screaming to clam up, batten down the hatches and close off. And what if I'm stuck in this shut-down emotional space for the rest of my life? Not able to be open with anyone ever again because of this.

No. That's not how I want to live, so I type:

FINE. WHEN AND WHERE?

CHAPTER 39
FRANKIE

At a coffee shop in McCall that's two hours away from Boise. That's where this asshole wanted to meet. Plus, he insisted on seven in the morning. Since it's a trek from Boise, my options were to either leave at five a.m. or drive here the night before. All the hotels are booked because McCall is a tourist spot and summer is the high season. There weren't even any vacation rentals—at least none that I could afford. I have no choice but to crash at Dad's cabin for the night, and then meet up with Punkass at the coffee shop in the morning.

I texted Dad to tell him I was coming up, but like always, he didn't reply.

I texted Chloe to say I'm going out of town to look at a pink sink, but I didn't tell her where or for how long.

When I pull up to my dad's cabin, I'm annoyed all over again that I couldn't get a hotel room. This is going to be some seriously tight quarters, and I can't talk to him about any of this. I swore to Punkass that our meet up would remain a secret, and since it's going to happen in public, I feel safe keeping it under wraps.

Dad's truck is gone, so I assume he's at the camp. He may

not even have service up there, so of course he's not answering. I think there's only a landline.

Whatever. As long as the door is unlocked, which it should be. I shoulder the strap of my backpack and head toward the front door.

A couple acres of meadow surround the place and then it's pine trees as far as you can see. I've only been up here a handful of times, and not since I was a kid, and even then only the night before summer camp. Chloe and I would stay here with Dad and the next day, he'd drive us to Paradise Point.

When I push the heavy door open, a wave of stink hits my nose. Smells like garbage that's been out too long in the summer heat. There's a bag of frozen tamales out on the kitchen counter, and they've gone bad.

That's what Dad was making the last time we spoke on the phone.

It doesn't mean anything even though it's weird that he left the bag out. He only does a Costco run once at the start of summer before he comes up here, so there's no way he'd be lazy and let them all thaw like that. I can feel my radar going up. Something is off.

I survey the rest of the place. It's an open studio area with a twin bed across from the front door, a wood stove for winter warmth off to the right. Kitchen on the left. Everything else seems to be in place.

"Dad?" I call out, peeking into the tiny bathroom, half-expecting to see him curled on the floor after a heart-attack. I don't know why—worst-case scenario, I guess. But his truck isn't here. That means he's not home.

When I open our message thread, my last five texts to him stare back at me. He hasn't replied to any of them. Has it truly been that long since I heard from him? The last one was something about Sundown.

Eight days ago. I send him a text.

> I'm at your cabin. Where are you?

Jesus Christ, this is my life now. Being on high alert and staring at screens, waiting for people to reply to my messages.

Calm down, he's probably over at Paradise Point.

It takes a second, but right when the word "Delivered" appears on the screen, I hear a ding in the cabin. A text message notification. And it didn't come from my phone, it came from over by the bed, but I can't find anything when I feel around the blue-and-white quilt.

I send another text.

Ding.

Under the bed. That's where the sound came from, so I duck down to peek, and there, plugged into the wall on the ground, is a bright screen. Dad's iPhone.

Why the hell is Dad's phone here when he and his truck aren't?

The thought sends a spike of anxiety through my whole body. I can't think of a good reason because while he might suck at replying to text messages, I know he keeps his phone on him.

He's in trouble. That has to be it.

I don't want to go there in my mind, but there's no other explanation.

I stand next to the twin bed, feeling jacked up from adrenaline. What should I do? I can't even get into his phone to see who the last person he talked to was, because it's locked.

Paradise Point. That's it! I'll call the camp. Surely that's where he is and maybe he forgot his phone.

It rings and rings until I get voicemail. "You have reached Paradise Point Camp. Please leave a message."

"Hi, this is Frankie Oliver. My dad, Jeff Oliver, works up there in the summer and I was wondering if he's there? If so, could you have him call me back?" I leave my number and hang up, turning my phone ringer on so I'm sure to hear it when they call back.

Right as I think about getting into my truck and driving around the property to look for him, the screen door slams.

I let out a startled yelp as I whirl around to see that there's nobody there.

What the actual fuck?

No way that happened on its own. There's not enough wind right now, and anyway, it wouldn't have slammed that hard even if the wind did pick it up.

Suddenly, I realize I'm out in the middle of nowhere, at least twenty minutes from town, back roads the whole way.

Seclusion isn't always safe for a woman who is alone.

It's dark out now, and I can hear the crickets chirping, but I can't see anything from inside the cabin. Maybe it's Dad. Maybe he made the screen door slam, although I dismiss the thought as soon as it comes. Why on earth would he do that instead of coming inside?

I step toward the front window to see out into the gravel area where I parked my truck, but there's nothing else here. Only one truck. Mine.

Dad didn't slam the door.

Then who was it?

And where is Dad?

Nothing in me wants to investigate this. But I have to know one way or another what I'm dealing with. I'll probably find that it's nothing and be able to relax.

I walk to the screen door and try to peer out before opening it. I don't see anyone out there. It's dark, but the lights from inside the cabin illuminate the porch and the area beyond that.

I have to be sure though, or I won't get any sleep tonight, so I push open the screen door and step into the night. I walk along the front porch, straining to see out into the line of trees beyond the meadow.

My phone rings and the words "Paradise Point Camp" flash on the screen.

I answer immediately. "Hello?"

"Is this Frankie?" a woman's voice asks.

"Yes. You got my message about my dad?"

Hesitation on the other line. "I did."

"Please tell me he's there."

"I'm sorry, I can't. I didn't recognize his name, so I asked around, and our cook, who has been here the longest, said Mr. Oliver hasn't been up to the camp in at least a decade."

My stomach bottoms out, and I don't know what to say to this. It makes no sense. He goes up to the camp to volunteer every summer, and has for as long as I can remember. I hang up and my arm drops to my side, but I squeeze my phone.

Now I'm fucking terrified. Where is my dad?

I'm about to turn to go back inside when there's a painful burst at my head, and everything goes dark.

THEN

CHAPTER 40
CHLOE

Natalie isn't the only one who needs a doctor. I'm feverish. A couple days have gone by, or at least I think it's been a couple days. I don't want to move over to the window to check because I'm bleeding and it would be an extra mess to clean up. I'm tired and can't imagine corralling the blood back toward the drain with water. That and I'm running low on water; even down to my last bottle of Gatorade.

I don't know how long it's been since Bill left. Since Natalie was born. The days mesh into each other.

Natalie doesn't mess the fabric diaper I made as much now that she's refusing to nurse. I worry my milk is bad, or that maybe there's not enough. My breasts hurt like hell. They're hot to the touch and huge, but that makes me think there's plenty of milk in there. I don't know why Natalie won't eat.

I feel so woozy at times that I worry I'll drop Natalie if I accidentally fall asleep. I moved the mattress near the drain and I pretty much stay lying down, wrapping my arm around this sweet baby like a barrier from the world.

The worries don't stop there. What if I'm too sick to go after

Bill when he finally gets here? What if he finds Natalie and … I can't think about that one.

Then there's the other fear: What if Bill never returns and I die in this room with Natalie?

I can't let my mind go there either—it's too excruciating.

Bill will come back. He knows I'm about to have a baby, and he wants to be here for it.

So he can get rid of her.

But he thinks the baby isn't coming until February, so he won't be in any hurry. Why did I tell him that?

It's not like I had a lot of options. I haven't had any options this entire time.

Natalie roots around, and my heart flies. She wants to nurse!

"You're tiny, baby girl. But you're tough. We're getting out of here and I'm going to show you how beautiful life can be."

She falls asleep nursing and that's when I hear it.

The outer door clanging shut.

He's here.

I have a few minutes while he does his rounds and so I quickly make a little nest out of blankets in the far corner of the room. Bill will bring his lantern, but that corner is the one spot the light doesn't totally reach. If I put Natalie there, I'd be closer to her than Bill would be if things go sideways. I've already thought all of that through. I gently set her down and pray she sleeps through this.

Then I rush to rinse any leftover blood down the drain, and pull the mattress so it's back against the wall.

I pause to brace myself against the dizziness.

Bill won't immediately know I gave birth. My swollen belly is almost as large as it was before Natalie was born and I look pregnant. I pull the blanket over my lower half so he can't see the blood-soiled bed in the dim room. I squeeze the knotted sheet-rope in my shaking hands under the covers.

Bill walks in.

"It smells in here," he says.

"Sorry. You left for so long, I think my bucket is more full than normal."

Don't look in the bucket, don't look in the bucket.

Why did I mention the bucket?

I need to get him to come over here. Nice and close so I can catch him by surprise before Natalie wakes.

"It's not that," he says. "Smells like a locker room. What have you been doing? Running laps?"

"I'm too big to do that now, so no, but can you come here? I missed you so much. I was thinking I'd like to hold you."

He tilts his head. This is the first time I've initiated physical contact, but based on how he said he wouldn't do anything intimate to me unless I wanted him to, I think he'll go for it. I push back the urge to cringe at the thought of touching him. That doesn't matter right now. I'm so close to escaping.

When he steps toward me, I grip the rope again, reminding myself of the stakes so I don't chicken out. *It's now or never.*

He sets the lantern down.

"Come sit," I say. "I was so worried you weren't coming back for me. I need to feel you close."

He does what I ask, and excitement flares inside.

"Let me sing to you," I say, dipping my head to indicate that he should lie on my lap. He's never done that before, but again, he seems to take it as a signal that maybe I do love him. He's eager. I am too. I can barely keep myself contained.

As he shifts to lay, I slide my hands out from underneath the blanket. He's not looking at my hands anyway; he's already got his eyes closed in anticipation of a song.

With his head heavy against my thighs, I rest an elbow on his shoulder, and gripping the rope with both hands, I start singing "Jesus Loves Me."

Before I get to "little ones to him belong," I whip the rope around his neck and twist it fast.

CHAPTER 41

CHLOE

BILL STRUGGLES and I pull with all my strength so the thin rope seems to cut into him below the mask. There's a necklace of blood wetting his flannel shirt. It's working. I pull harder and get an overwhelming urge to tear the mask off. Find out who the hell this is, and stare into his eyes to watch his light go out, but his fist reels up against my shoulder and a spike of pain makes me cry out.

It's enough for him to pull himself free, and he grabs my wrist, throwing me back toward the wall. My head ricochets off the concrete, and for a second all I see is black. Bill coughs hard.

"You little bitch," he pushes out through clenched teeth. My vision clears. He's holding his neck with one hand.

I want to laugh in his face. But when I move even a bit, the headache fills my skull and I spiral in dizziness. "You shot my friends! You want to kill my baby!" I scream.

And then, as if she heard me talking about her, Natalie cries out. A piercing wail that sounds like she's in pain.

No. No, this can't happen. Bill isn't hurt enough for me to escape. He's standing there, just as strong as ever, like I gave him a paper cut or something.

"What the fuck? You had the baby?" he shouts. I can hear the disorientation in his voice. The disbelief that I could trick him.

I scramble to scoop Natalie up in my arms, then stand in front of my mattress, facing him again. Tears blur my dizzy vision, and I'm shocked Bill isn't tackling me right now.

This is horrible; nothing is going as planned. But I hold Natalie close and kiss her little forehead as I stand, swaying, trying to stabilize myself. I must keep fighting. Even if Bill catches me, I have to try again.

"You lied to me about your due date," he says, then laughs so loud it startles me. "Like I wouldn't figure it out! Give me the baby."

There's no way in hell I'm ever handing Natalie over to him, so I don't move. My mind is fast at work trying to come up with another plan.

I remember the can opener. It doesn't have a sharp end, but if I go at him with enough force it might cause a wound.

Bill walks slowly toward me, but he's still very much in the way of the one exit.

"Get away from us!" I shout, surprising myself with how forceful it comes out.

Every step he takes feels like the charge before a storm electrifying the air. It's his anger toward me, and it's a different sense than when he choked me, or when he wrestled me into swallowing the pills. This feels like a black hole.

"Give me the baby," Bill says the words slowly, rage simmering at the edges of his tone.

"Wait," I say, turning to set Natalie on the mattress behind me, and palming the can opener in the process.

I breathe as my back is to him, turning my head slightly to keep him in my peripheral vision. Natalie screams, kicking and punching the air, wriggling her blankets off so she's naked on her back.

"You set this all up. You don't care about the farm. About me. You ... you fucking tricked me!" Bill's voice climbs in pitch. I can feel his fury.

Adrenaline lights up my body and I spin, charging toward him in a lunge, aiming the can opener at his neck. It lands and somehow cuts him. He screams and staggers to the side, falling to his ass.

I rush back for Natalie, ignoring him. Hoping, praying he's wounded enough to let me slip by, but the fact that he can still speak isn't good.

Bill grips his neck and is trying to stand, but failing. He staggers and moans as blood rushes from his neck. Still, he's gathering composure.

Now. Go now.

I fly past him, out the door and into the prison hallway.

The redhead is in her cell, passed out, and the key hangs on the wall next to it, out of her reach. Without thinking, I grab it and unlock her cell so the door creaks open a centimeter or two. Enough so Bill won't notice. The girl stirs, and we make eye contact.

"Run," I whisper, and toss the key into the dark hallway behind and sprint toward the door.

It's snowing like a blizzard outside. Not nighttime yet, but the clouds make it dim, and I push open the main door. Fresh air strikes me and I gasp. It's the first time I've felt moving air in months. It's freezing cold against my hot skin. Winter, yes, but it cuts through me to the core and my body doesn't even bother to shiver. It goes right to shaking. Maybe it's been shaking this whole time and I'm only now noticing. Everything feels surreal.

I look down and my feet are bare. How will I run in the snow? I only wrapped Natalie in a blanket, but it doesn't matter now. I have to find shelter, so I run.

Every step is liquid fire on my feet. I hurry as fast as I can in knee-deep snow, thinking *shelter shelter shelter*. We need to get out of the cold, but this is the middle of nowhere. There's no road. Just forest.

My eyes scan as the distance bounces in my vision from running.

Snow all around. Piles of it on the ground, and jumbo flakes feather downward all around me. Trees as far as I can see.

Then, up ahead, peeking through the pine is a small lean-to.

CHAPTER 42
CHLOE

I CAN'T FEEL my feet. My lungs burn from gasping the icy air. I hold Natalie close to me while she wails. It's about a hundred feet until I get to the lean-to. I can do it.

Then I'm falling.

Natalie flies out of my arms and lands in the deep snow a couple feet in front of me.

I move forward, trying to get to her, but I can't.

My leg.

I turn and see dyed-red snow.

There's a small arrow jutting out of my hamstring.

Pain flashes and I scream.

He shot me. Bill shot me like he shot my friends.

Natalie screeches and it's the most horrible sound I've ever heard. I crawl through the snow, dragging my limp leg behind me.

I have to get to her.

I'm almost within reach when someone grips my arm and pulls me up.

It's him.

My knees buckle and I try to be dead weight so he can't carry me. But he's huge. And I'm so weak.

"No!" I scream and throw fists with every bit of strength I have. It does nothing. He lifts me up and over one of his shoulders easily.

I pound his back and scream, "No! I can't leave Natalie! She'll freeze!"

He turns and walks back toward the prison without a word. I lift my head to see my baby. She's still wailing loudly in the snow where I dropped her, and I feel like someone is tearing my heart out, inch by inch. I thrash hard trying to wiggle out of Bill's grip, but it's no use. I can't get free and he's not going back for her.

"You're not only a baby killer!" I yell. "You're a fucking monster!"

No answer. He keeps walking and then, from my upside-down viewpoint, I see tires on the road. A parked vehicle. We're not going back into the prison, he's going to put me in a truck. He opens the back door.

I try to resist, but my body moves into the truck against my will. His grip hurts my arms as he shoves me backward.

Natalie.

"No!" I scream and kick even though I can't move my shot leg. I put all of my energy into fighting back. This is it. This is my last chance to get away from Bill and save Natalie.

She's running out of time.

He punches my face and it stuns me into stillness. He takes advantage of it and wrestles me into the backseat, zip tying my hands, then my feet. I stare at the upholstery on the ceiling and sob.

"Please," I yell even though he's right there. "Please, her name is Natalie. Please take her to a hospital. Drop her off. Don't let my baby die in the cold. I don't care what you do to me. Please just save her."

Snot and tears drain down my face and wet the back of my neck. I can't see Bill from this angle, but I feel him there.

"You're the one who dropped her in the snow, Chloe. She's dead and you're the one who killed her," he says, and his voice sounds like it's underwater.

No. I didn't kill her. I loved her. She knows that. She has to know that.

"Don't let her die!"

"She's fucking gone. She was always going to die," he shouts but again, it sounds muted.

A drop of agony wracks my body when I realize I can't hear her crying anymore. He must be right. She's gone. I scream, but I know it won't do anything.

Hands spread around my neck and there's pressure.

So much pressure.

I want to push them away, but I can't.

My vision fuzzes in and out of darkness. The pull to fall asleep is so strong.

I can't see much. Everything is dark and blurry.

"This isn't how I wanted things to go," Bill says, but I can barely hear him.

Tension builds in my head.

He squeezes harder and grunts.

I try to jerk my body out of his grip, but it does nothing.

I can't breathe.

The surrounding light grows more dim.

This is it. It's over. I'm dying.

I crank my neck backward, trying to see Natalie but all I can see is this man, my killer.

All I can hear is his ragged breath.

No.

I manage to squeeze my eyes shut. An act of defiance, my very last one.

Instead of him, I picture Natalie's little pink face, warm against my chest.

Instead of his grunts, I hear the sounds Natalie made nursing.

Everything dims until I can't even picture her anymore. Mounting pressure builds inside and then it's bright. So bright that I'm blinded. And Natalie's song is all there is, reminding me of warmth. Of hope. Of love.

Then nothing.

PART II

NOW

CHAPTER 43

NATALIE

FRANKIE SUSPECTS SOMETHING, I'm sure of it.

I don't know if she's figured out who I am, but I think she's caught on that I'm not Chloe. She texted to say she's out of town looking at a pink sink for the house. But the fact is that otherwise, she hasn't come home or been in contact with me all day.

I'm not worried about her, nothing like that. It's just so different from her usual mode, which is wanting to be together all the time.

I sit on the bed inside my motel room, holding the gun I bought before I came to Boise. It's not loaded, but for some reason squeezing the grip is a source of comfort. I look at Frankie's picture on the wall while the TV blares *Shark Tank*. I take a hit from my pen because it helps me think. And right now, I need to figure out what my next steps are going to be.

I still haven't accomplished what I came to Boise for because I got sidetracked running around town with Frankie. She sucked me into this illusion that I could belong some-where. That I could somehow use Chloe's life in order to cobble together my own happiness.

But happiness isn't in the cards for me. It never has been.

The best I can hope for is revenge.

I take another drag of my pen and set it on the bed next to me.

I tried so hard to keep Natalie and "Chloe" separate in my mind, and to distance myself from Frankie. What a monumental fail that was.

Maybe it's good that Frankie is out of town because it forces me to refocus on my goal. I shouldn't get too attached anyway, because when she finds out who I am, and how I've hoodwinked her, she'll hate me.

I would deserve that for fucking with her emotions like I have been. And to top it off, I'm actually getting something from it. As if it's me, Natalie, Frankie cares about instead of her cousin, Chloe.

If I close my eyes, I can imagine Frankie smiling at me, and I can feel her tender love in every hug. Her affection in every laugh.

But none of it is for me. And it'll all go away when Frankie finds out the truth.

I should have told her once I got past the police and the news. Once I saw that nobody was going to call me out or even be suspicious that I'm not Chloe. Well, except Jensen. But he's out of Frankie's life now.

My gut says maybe Frankie would eventually accept me for me. Natalie. After all, I am still family. But that's wishful thinking after I've been lying to her for so long.

Family isn't in the cards for me either. Not after losing my mom a few months ago. Or, I should say, the woman I thought was my mom. But Rachel never was. My mom was Chloe Webster and she's been dead for over twenty years. The only other person alive who knows this, is the one who killed her.

Which is why I came back.

How to Pass as Your Dead Mother and Hunt the Motherfucker Who Murdered Her
by Natalie Smith

Step One: Discover that your entire life has been a lie.

When I see my mom, Rachel, lying in bed this morning, I have the thought: *It's time to say goodbye.*

At barely forty years old, she's too young to die. But I don't make the rules, and ovarian cancer is unforgiving and brutal. I've been trying not to think about it, or about how I'll manage my life without her. She's all I've ever had.

"Natalie?" she calls out when I walk past her bedroom. Her voice is weak, and I'm surprised she's even awake since she sleeps most days.

When I walk through the door, she motions with her hand like she wants me to help her sit. I get more pillows from the chair next to the bed and shove them behind to prop her up.

"Are you hungry? I can make some breakfast," I say.

"No. Sit down."

I do it without hesitation even though I don't know what she could want to talk about. We've discussed everything already. That she doesn't want a funeral at all. No fuss. That I'll inherit the house and her savings account, which isn't huge, but will support me while I try to find work. I've been taking care of her for the past couple of years and had to give up my job as a dog groomer. All of my clients have gone to other people.

The doctor gave her weeks to live a few months ago, and she's getting close. The past couple of days have been a waiting game.

"This is a long story," she starts. "And maybe I should have told you years ago, but I worried it would cause more harm than good."

I have no idea what she's talking about. Her watery eyes search mine, and I can't read her expression, but now I'm very curious. Also quite surprised at this sudden strength she seems to have.

"Please hear me out," she goes on. "You'll be mad at first, but you need to listen to the whole thing. I'm sorry I've been so stubborn and scared." She glances away from me and out the window, then mutters to herself, "So much fear."

"Whatever you have to tell me, I'm here," I say with a smile, trying to lighten the mood.

She smiles back and reaches up in a motion that looks like trying to brush a strand of hair from her face. But she lost her red hair a long time ago, and now she wears a purple floral bandanna.

"Nat, I'm not your biological mom. But your mom saved my life and so I saved yours."

CHAPTER 44

NATALIE

I START LAUGHING, and move to stand, saying, "Okay, sure. Whatever." She's always had a teasing sense of humor.

She grabs my hand faster than I thought she could move at this point.

"Sit. I'm being serious."

The intensity in her eyes says that she means business. But what the fuck?

"I'm not your biological mom."

I can't compute those words.

I sit down, but don't say anything.

"You look exactly like her, Nat. And I mean, identical. You could be twins, except she was blonde."

I feel like I got shoved off a cliff. Mom—Rachel, or I don't know what to call her now—watches for my reaction again.

I touch my brown hair mindlessly, and then anger lights up inside.

"Why are you telling me this now?"

"To save you from yourself. Your rage."

"What?" I blurt. Sure, I'm not a happy-go-lucky person, but I've never thought of myself as having *rage*.

"I couldn't let you continue down this path of increasing anger. It's eating you alive, and I think it's because of your past and what happened. Everything you're in the dark about. I kept it from you because at first, I was afraid he would find us and kill us like he did your mother. But years passed and I realized we were probably safe. He either didn't care to find us or he'd stopped looking. Truth is, I liked our life together out here in the woods. It was peaceful and that was something I'd never had for myself. I don't remember a childhood outside of being abused daily by my parents."

Tears form in her eyes, but it's hard to keep up with what she's saying. She's never once spoken about her childhood. This is all new information and I'm still stuck back at the original revelation: This isn't my mom. This woman lying in bed and about to die, this woman who raised me—she didn't give birth to me.

Rachel squeezes her eyes shut and says, "I don't want to talk about that part of my life though. I want to use my energy to tell you about who you are. That's what matters."

"Okay," I whisper.

"I ran away from home when I was fourteen. Originally, I was from Denver, but I slowly made my way west. Hitchhiking mostly. I was aiming for Seattle because I always wanted to visit there and see the Space Needle. When I got as far as Boise, I met a girl at the shelter and we immediately clicked. She invited me to a house party. I thought it was strange that she lived at the shelter if she had friends with a house. If I had even one friend with a home like that, I'd be doing everything in my power to stay with them. It was a red flag that I should have listened to, but I didn't. The next thing I knew, I was waking up in a dark and cold room with a concrete floor. It was a prison cell."

"Oh my god," I whisper.

"It was hell," she continues with a sigh. "I thought my home life was bad, but this was worse. The abuse was—"

Tears streak her face and I reach over to her bedside table for a tissue. I should comfort her, but I'm still angry.

"Why didn't you try to find my family members? Why would you keep me all these years and not tell me?" I ask.

"Told you that you'd be mad," she says, wiping her eyes slowly. It takes so much effort.

She's right. I'm pissed, but I also see how slowly she's blinking, how her hands shake, and I shelve my anger. No way I'm unleashing it on her right now.

"I'm sorry, please go on. I want to hear," I say.

"In the prison, he kept me drugged, in and out of consciousness, but I remember snippets. I remember the girl across the hall from me. I don't know her name, but she was your real mom, and she loved you. She tried to escape with you. That girl sang all the time. Had a beautiful voice."

Rachel chokes up and starts to cry. She uses the balled-up tissue to wipe her nose instead of getting a fresh one, and I sit there, in stunned silence.

"I guess you didn't get that from her." A little glint in her eye tells me she's teasing me about having a shitty singing voice. This is more like the woman I know. I haven't seen this side of her much since she's been sick, and it makes me swallow hard. I don't want to cry.

"Very funny," I say.

She gives a weak smile and goes on. "At some point I realized the girl had had a baby because I heard you crying from time to time. It was shortly after that when he returned and everything happened."

"She had me in a prison?" I blurt.

"Yes. I was only fifteen, and she had to have been around the same age. I've thought a lot about it over the years. This young girl, isolated and giving birth totally alone. The strength it must have taken to do that. Your mom was a powerhouse."

Now I start to tear up, but I don't want anything to keep her from telling the story and I know the clock is ticking on her strength, so I swallow it down again.

She gazes down at her hands, folded around the tissue, and speaks again. "Usually the man in the Clinton mask would give us girls drugs before he went into your mom's room. But by this point, the other girls were gone and it was just me and your mom left. I don't know where he took the rest, or if they were even alive by the time he moved them. But on this day, the man was so eager to see your mom that he didn't bother with drugging me. He gave me food and water and disappeared into that room across from mine."

"Wait," I interrupt even though I know she doesn't want me to. "What do you mean man in the Clinton mask? Is that ... my dad?"

"I don't know. He was our kidnapper and he wore this President Clinton mask all the time. I don't remember seeing your mom when she arrived, so I don't know when she got pregnant. Plus, the drugs made everything dreamlike."

Holy shit. I don't even know how to process all of this, but I must try to keep up.

"There was an argument," Rachel goes on. "I heard your mom and the man yelling at each other. You were wailing in that high-pitched cry, you know, like newborns do when they're in distress?"

I don't know. I've never been around newborns, and she knows this, but I let it go.

"Anyway, next thing I know, she's standing outside my cell, holding you against her with one arm, and you were crying. She used her free hand to unlock my door."

Rachel breaks down and tries to reach for another tissue, but it's like she can barely move her body. My instinct is to tell her to rest, that this much exertion isn't good for her. But I so desperately want to hear the rest of the story. I get her a tissue and then wait.

"After unlocking my cell, your mom propped it open a sliver. She made quick eye contact, and told me to run. Then she ran out of the prison. The man came out of that room a moment later, bleeding from the neck. She had gotten a piece of him somehow, but it wasn't enough. He was still strong and very angry and he ran after her. A few minutes passed where they must have both been outside, and I didn't hear his car leave. I thought maybe she had gotten away and he was looking for her. But she was barefoot, carrying a baby, postpartum and bleeding through her clothes.

"I debated about whether to wait in my cell or to run like she told me to. Unlike your mom, I had shoes. I could sneak out while the man was distracted with her. Or I could wait for him to leave and then go, which seemed safer. But how did I know if he would leave? Maybe he'd come back into the prison and even though I hoped and prayed she'd get away, the reality was he'd probably catch her and bring her back. Or worse. And what if he noticed my cell door open? What if I missed my chance? I was weighing my options when suddenly you started shrieking outside. It was an ear-piercing cry, stronger than any I'd heard you do so far. I decided I couldn't wait, so I slipped out of my cell and crept quietly down the hall to the main door."

CHAPTER 45
NATALIE

RACHEL'S FACE isn't pale like usual. Her cheeks are flushed, and her eyes are bright, almost fiery. It's like she's channeling any strength she has left to tell me this. It feels final and I'm conflicted because of that instinct to take care of her, the one that's been my role for so long, but I also know this might be my last chance to find out who I really am. Luckily, I don't think anything could stop her from finishing the story.

"The big door was open, so I peeked outside and the snow was coming down so hard, I could barely make out your mom lying in the snow about fifty feet away," Rachel says. "She had an arrow in her leg, and he was pacing toward her holding a crossbow. I couldn't see you, but there was a spot in front of your mom in the snow, an indent, where your screaming was coming from. I imagined you, a tiny thing wrapped in a sheet lying in the deep snow alone, and I could barely keep my feet in place because everything in me said *Go. Run to that baby. Get her out of the cold.*

"But I couldn't. Not while he was still right there, and I expected him to catch your mom and take both of you back into the prison. If that happened, this would be my only opportunity to escape, so I waited until he was looking away and snuck out of the building to hide behind the far wall. This way I could dash to the forest when his back was turned. But then, the most unexplainable thing happened. The man lifted your mom, but left you in the snow. He took her to his truck, and she started shouting. I'll never forget her words or the despair in her voice. How she pleaded instead of demanding. 'Please, her name is Natalie. Please, don't let her die. Please save her.'"

She cries and wipes her eyes with the tissue. "I felt like she was talking to me."

Rachel stops to gather herself.

Tears stream down my face and collect at my chin, but I let them drop. Emotion rampages inside of me and pushes to get out but I don't know what form it would take. Whether it's sadness or anger. It feels stronger than both of those and I'm afraid if I move, I'll start ugly crying, and Rachel will exert energy she doesn't have in order to comfort me. If I fall apart, and that happens, I may not hear the rest of the story.

Rachel gathers herself and says, "They wrestled for a minute there in the truck, but he overpowered her. Your crying died down at one point, and I prayed you were okay, but couldn't check until he was gone. Seconds later, he pulled out and drove away. You started crying again, although softer. I remember waiting and watching his taillights, my eyes alternating between them and the spot in the snow where you lay. You see, I was the oldest of seven, and since my parents were so neglectful, by the time I left home, I'd raised a sibling or two. So your crying to me was a good sign. You were still fighting. It was torture waiting until that truck was gone, but finally, it was, and I ran to you, scooped you up and pulled you close to me. Your skin was sheer ice to the touch. I had to get you shelter, but the prison wasn't an option. That's when I saw a small shed in the forest. I trudged through the knee-high snow as fast as I could, cradling you underneath my sweatshirt, skin-to-skin, trying to give you as much warmth as possible.

"When I got there, I noticed something big underneath a snow-covered tarp, but otherwise, it was just a utility shed. I knew right away we couldn't stay there because it was too close to the prison, and most likely the first place that bastard would search when he realized I was missing. I knew he would either kill me or put me back in the cell, and either way I was dead. Even if I escaped, it wasn't only him I was afraid of, Nat. It was the man who visited me in the prison too. He was evil, and I don't want to give you those details, but I'll say this: He couldn't get hard unless I was in pain. And he would threaten me saying things like, 'You're mine and you'll never leave this place. If you do, I'll hunt you down and kill you.'

"This is the fear that has driven me for decades." She breaks down and cries again, gasping between sobs because she's so weak.

Something snaps into place inside of me and it all makes sense. Rachel's extreme paranoia. Her insistence that we live in isolation. No Wi-Fi. Nothing but a landline. Her determination to homeschool me. Her hatred for men. I was planning to run away before she got her cancer diagnosis. I couldn't take it anymore. I had to see what was outside of this bubble she'd kept me in for decades. My mind was overrun with messages like "Never trust a man" and "Don't rely on anyone but yourself." She constantly quizzed me from the time I was a small child about what to do in the presence of a man. The answer was pretty much always "get away from him."

All of it was in response to her trauma.

Rachel takes a deep breath and starts talking again. "I found some old blankets in that shed and made a sling so I could tie you against my chest, keeping you touching my skin. You were so exhausted that you fell asleep as soon as you were warm. I worried about not having food for you. You needed a doctor too. We had to find a town. I went out to see what was under the tarp, and it was a snowmobile. I couldn't believe my luck. Finally something had gone right for me. Because I was raised in the mountains, I knew how to drive one. The keys were in the ignition, but as I went to turn it, I thought about the tracks it'd leave in the snow. They'd point him right to us. But again, taking the snowmobile and getting help felt like my only option. The snow was coming down so hard I just prayed there'd be a fresh layer to cover the tracks a bit.

"I found a town and learned we were in McCall, Idaho. I met an older woman—a trucker. She was headed to Montana and said she'd take us that far. We ended up staying and I found a women's shelter. They helped me get on my feet, and I got a job at a grocery store in Helena and moved my way up to managing the bakery. Eventually, I bought this little place, and you know the rest."

She swallows, and I stare at her in disbelief. She lied to me about who I am my whole life, and yet, I can't fault her. I still love her. She was fierce but I understand now a little more about why that is.

"Do you think my mom is still alive?" I ask.

She looks down. "No, honey. He killed her in the truck that day."

I don't know why, but this makes me tear up again. It's not like I thought she'd be alive, but still.

"Do you know who my dad is?" I say, and my voice cracks.

"No. I don't even know what your mom's name was."

"Do you think the men are still looking for you?" I ask.

"No. I realized a long time ago that they'd probably given up, if they ever even were looking."

"Why didn't you tell me this before?" I ask again. It's dumb. She's told me her reasons, but it's like I can't accept them. My throat constricts and I sob.

Rachel moves a hand slowly and places it on mine again.

"I'm so sorry, Nat. Forgive me." She's wheezing now, as if it's painful to speak. "I thought if you didn't know, you wouldn't have to carry the burden. The truth of how violent your first weeks were. And as time passed, I was afraid of losing you. But your anger. It's magnified over time and I had to face the truth: You needed to know. Like I said, I was worried it would eat you alive, and you'd never understand why."

That very anger swells inside of me alongside the sadness right now, pushing my pulse faster until I can't stop crying. It's not directed at Rachel, who raised me and has loved me as best as she could. The white-hot rage is for whoever did this to her. To my mom. To me.

CHAPTER 46

NATALIE

Step Two: **Research, research, research**

A day later, Rachel is gone and I am alone. I find comfort in vodka as the truth of where I came from churns inside of me. I have questions that nobody can answer. But maybe there's another way to get information.

I dig out my laptop from a desk drawer in my room, but we don't have internet out here, so I pull on a pair of Hunter Boots. It's the end of May in Montana and it's raining outside, but I have to find somewhere with internet access, so I drive to a coffee shop in town and order a dirty chai latte. When I get my laptop set up, I type "Missing girl Denver Colorado" into the search bar.

Everything that comes up is current news, but this would have been decades ago. I do quick math in my mind based on Rachel's age. She was fourteen when she ran away. Fifteen when she escaped the prison with me. I'm twenty-four.

I type, "Missing Girl Denver Colorado 1998."

There are cases of missing girls, yes, but none of them are

Rachel. When the realization hits me that her shitty parents may not have even reported her missing, I feel my nostrils flare and my cheeks grow hot. I hate how girls can disappear and it seems like nobody cares. I hate Rachel's parents and I hate everyone who hurt her. I fucking hate the world for the way it treats anyone who isn't a man.

That last one is Rachel talking.

I close my eyes and make sure I notice it.

I don't have any experience with men. Not really. Maybe it's time to figure out who I am and what I believe about them. Maybe I'll come to the same conclusions as her, but I should arrive at them on my own.

Next, I type "Missing Girl Boise Idaho 1999," still looking for news of Rachel's disappearance. I'm not hopeful, but maybe I'll luck out and someone from the shelter would have reported her missing a year after she left Denver.

One headline immediately stands out: "Two Boise Girls Dead, One Missing, Police Say." The date is August 1999.

I click the link and when the article fills my screen I gasp.

That face. She looks exactly like me, but with dishwater blonde hair. Rachel was right about that. Her name is Chloe Webster, and she's from Boise.

I'm looking at my biological mom.

Tears sting my eyes as I study the picture for a minute. She's standing right next to a flowering bush, her head tilts so her long, straight hair drapes down one side. I read the article, but it's short. Seems like the first reporting of this incident, back when they didn't know much of anything. Still, I learn that she went missing at a place called Skinny Dipper Hot Springs. The other two girls were found, and they had been shot with arrows.

My blood runs cold.

Arrows. Rachel said the man in the Clinton Mask had shot my mom in the leg with a bow and arrow. I know it's a leap, but

I learned from Rachel to trust my gut and I've hardly been wrong when I get this feeling, like a tugging inside me. Whoever killed my mom killed these other two girls too—Amy and Kristi.

I open another tab and type "Skinny Dipper Hot Springs Murders August 1999" in the search bar.

The whole first page is full of articles about this incident, and I comb through each one, spending time taking notes. I order another dirty chai latte because hours have passed.

Amy and Kristi's cases are unsolved. The police never found their killer.

Clinton Mask.

That's who killed them. I'm sure of it even though of course, it doesn't do a lot of good since I don't know who that man is.

People still think Chloe Webster is missing. Nobody knows she's dead; her body was never found.

Not only that, but nobody seems to even know she was pregnant. That's a detail that would have been reported, and there's nothing.

Rachel went missing and nobody batted an eye, but not so with Chloe.

People cared about her enough to start an investigation.

I read one name in particular over and over in the most recent articles about the Hot Springs Murders: Frankie Oliver, Chloe's cousin. Frankie seems to be obsessed with Chloe's disappearance, even holding yearly benefits in her memory despite decades having gone by.

I sip my latte and consider what I should do next as I look out the window and stare at Mount Helena in the distance. It's covered with trees but there's a tiny bit of snow leftover at the summit. It reminds me of spring and new beginnings.

I should probably go to the police. Coming forward with new information on the case seems like the obvious move under normal circumstances.

But these aren't normal circumstances.

This man fucking murdered my mom and left me to die. He allowed Rachel to be tortured. Killed Amy and Kristi and probably whoever else was in the prison.

Rachel basically raised me to be a ghost because we have no close connections. I haven't been out in public other than quick runs to the store for months because of her illness. I could take advantage of all of this.

I type, "McCall, Idaho prison" in the search bar. There's a whole history of the small jail, and how it's been abandoned since 1973.

An idea comes into view in my mind's eye. It's a little out there, but I'm going to follow it and see where it leads.

I've had this anger my whole life, and now I finally know what to do with it. I'm going to find the man who killed my mom, who terrorized Rachel, who left me for dead, and I'm going to fucking murder him.

CHAPTER 47

NATALIE

Step Three: **Walk a mile in your mom's shoes**

I use some money from my small inheritance to drive to Idaho and stay in a Super 8 in McCall. The next day, I trek out to the prison, which is honestly fucking hard to find. Once I'm off the main drag, it's all muddy back roads, and my Maps app doesn't seem to know much more than I do.

The trees here remind me of Montana, and I'm pretty good at navigating a forest because our property was surrounded by one, so eventually I stumble upon an abandoned two-story building that seems like it could be a prison.

I park Rachel's white Kia and sit in silence. The car ticks as it cools down, and I stare out the front windshield at this place. It's haunting, being here. My skin crawls even at the sight of it, but I force myself to take it in. I need to find clues if there are any.

I let my eyes track some distance from the main door toward the forest, searching for the shed Rachel mentioned. I don't see it, so I grab my canvas messenger bag and get out of the car, planting a boot in the mud and splashing my skinny jeans. It seems like the snow may have just melted out here. I get a few steps away from the car and a shiver runs through me. It's not only the cold, it's something about this place—a presence, or I don't know—some type of leftover residue. I don't believe in ghosts, but I do believe that the stuff we're made of, our soul, or whatever, has to go somewhere when we die. It's energy that must get put back into the world in some form. I've never thought about whether that energy can get stuck in one place, but that's exactly what this feels like.

It's as if Chloe is still here. Still trapped, and unable to move on.

"I'm so sorry this happened to you," I whisper as my eyes fill with tears. I clear my throat and swallow them down.

It happened to you too, comes to me immediately.

It's true. I was here and there's a part of me that might be stuck as well, even though I'm still living. It explains a lot about the feelings I've had of not belonging anywhere, or with anyone. I loved Rachel, but I never understood her until a few days ago. I always felt a disconnect.

I reach into my bag for my vape and take a hit.

My original plan was to go inside the prison and investigate, but I find that I don't want to be anywhere near it. Against all reason, I'm scared.

Doesn't matter. I have to, and so I will eventually. But I let myself warm up to the idea by walking the grounds first.

That's when I see it.

The shed.

I track the distance from it back to the front prison yard and I shake my head in disbelief. Rachel ran that far in deep snow, carrying an infant. Carrying me.

I would have died if she didn't.

I would have died if Chloe hadn't unlocked Rachel's cell.

I should be dead.

But I'm not. I'm here, while both of them are gone. In fact, this may have been the area where Chloe fell in the snow and dropped me. Where he captured her for the last time, all the while she could have been thinking I was going to die too.

I didn't die, Mom. I'm here now.

The pinch of tears constricts my throat, but I clench my teeth and a ripple of determination goes through me. I need to make this count. Balance the scales. Make him fucking pay.

Fury sparks at the thought of him, still walking the earth free, and that possibility makes me change my mind and I turn toward the prison. Fuck my feelings, I'm going in there.

A rusted chain holds the metal door closed. Luckily, it's loose enough that I can hold it open as far as it'll go and squeeze in underneath.

Inside, it's dark. I reach into my bag and pull out a small flashlight, then flick it on.

The beam illuminates a hallway leading to the back of the building.

On the right are three prison cells, one after another with concrete walls separating them, and bars on the front.

I step down the hall slowly, feeling the horror grow inside my body, but shoving down the urge to run away. To the left is what seems to have once been a huge office. It takes up half of this side of the prison. There's an old metal desk, but nothing else. The desk is probably too heavy to bother moving. Metal stairs lead from the office to the second floor. I shine my light up there and it's all prison cells.

Next to the office is a closed door, surrounded by concrete walls. No way to see inside at all. It's the only door across from the cells, and it's exactly like Rachel described it. This has to be where he kept Chloe.

On the right, before the row of cells, is an open door. I make my way there first, again putting off what feels the most difficult to face.

Inside, a window allows for some light, and there's an old clawfoot bathtub. Also probably too heavy to move, but otherwise, the room is empty.

When I return to the hallway, my stomach starts to churn. I ignore it and make my way until I'm staring at the closed metal door. Waves of nausea wash over my body, and I feel like I'm getting sick, but even so, I turn the knob.

I can't believe it's unlocked, but then again, why wouldn't it be? There's nothing of value out here. But I think of all the time Chloe must have spent watching this door from the other side, knowing it was locked. That she was trapped. And now, I simply push it open on the first try. As I stand there in the hall, and the door opens, I suddenly feel dizzy. I brace a hand against the door frame and debate if I should leave. Surely I've seen enough.

But I can't leave. I just can't. There might be something here that leads me to Chloe's killer.

When I step inside, the air feels thin. There's a drain on the ground and a trap door on the ceiling.

I swallow hard, trying to focus, trying to ignore the expanding nausea. They must have done hangings in this room when the prison was in use.

Sickness pummels me and I sit down on the concrete to gather my composure. I don't want to faint. But I start shaking. Bile rises and I vomit.

Afterward, I sob hard, and it feels like I can't control myself. I can't stop crying. I can't make my body calm down. It's telling me to go. Get the hell out of here. I don't want to, but I can't stay either.

I scramble to my feet and run out of the prison as if someone is chasing me.

CHAPTER 48

NATALIE

Step Four: Get mistaken for your mom

When I check out of my hotel the next day, the man behind the desk asks me what I thought about the continental breakfast. I skipped it because I'm not a cold cereal person, which inspires him to tell me all about this local breakfast spot. It's called Pancake Palace and I guess it's been a McCall treasure (he actually uses the word treasure) for over forty years. I am hungry and it's a long drive back to Helena, so I decide to check it out.

The restaurant looks like a massive log cabin and when I swing the door open, the fresh coffee and bacon scent of breakfast greets me. Dishes clink in the direction of the kitchen and all the bustle makes me feel a little anonymous, which I like.

I order coffee and orange juice when the hostess seats me in a booth, and then I open my phone and read over some notes I jotted down about my experience at the prison yesterday because it's still clinging to me like a film I can't scrub off.

Someone stands at my table, and I look up, expecting to see the server with my drinks. But this man doesn't appear to work here. He's in a pair of Carhartt pants and a green flannel shirt. He's shaved bald, the way men do when their hairline starts to recede. His skin is leathery, and I guess he's probably in his fifties.

"What's your name?" he asks before I can say anything.

His tone is gruff and even though this is a question, he phrases it like a statement.

"Excuse me?"

"Is your name Chloe?"

"Yes," I blurt, then follow it up with "Is your name Douchebag?"

He doesn't even flinch, just stares at me in silence and I start questioning why in the world I said I was Chloe. Regret floods my system and I feel a twinge of alarm even though we're in public. It's not like I'm in danger, but what the fuck am I doing? I can hear Rachel's voice in my mind, "Don't be bitchy to them, that'll only make it worse."

He tilts his head and the silence becomes its own gravity. He's not leaving, and he's in the way so I can't leave. Whatever, I'll just go to the restroom and I'm sure he'll be gone by the time I'm back. I move to squeeze by him, offering a firm, but not rude, "Excuse me, please."

He shifts his weight to further block me from getting by.

It's so aggressive that my adrenaline spikes. I glance around for someone—another customer, or maybe my server—who might be seeing this. My adrenaline surges and fight sparks inside me.

"Please move," I say.

"Chloe Webster, huh?" His gaze lasers me and it's intense. He has purple bags under bloodshot eyes like maybe he's on drugs. "What brought you back after all these years?" He pushes the words out fast like he can tell I'm about to bolt.

"What?"

"Sorry. Excuse me," a guy who looks like a teenager says. "I've got coffee with creamer and orange juice." He sets my drinks down and inches back again like he's trying to be invisible. But then he straightens and looks at the man. "Can I get you something?"

"Actually, I'm leaving," I say, fishing a couple dollars out of my messenger bag. I need to take advantage of this disruption to get the hell out of here.

"Are you sure? I'm sorry if the service was slow. We're so busy."

"It's not that." I look directly at the other man, and the server leaves.

Then I'm sliding out of the booth, fully prepared to collide with this asshole if he doesn't step aside, but he does.

"Well, welcome back, Chloe. Everyone will be excited to see that you're alive," he says.

I look him over once more. Now that I'm out of the booth, I feel less trapped and more confident.

"And what's your name?"

"You don't recognize me?"

"No, I'm sorry. I have a lot of memory loss from the trauma." I feel like I'm on autopilot and I have no idea where these words are coming from, but at the same time, an idea seeds in my mind.

"Oh, I bet," he says. "It was a horrible thing that happened to your friends all those years ago."

The girls who died. That's who he's talking about but even though I read all about them, I don't remember their names.

Shit. This idea may work, but I can't be convincing until I memorize the details of Chloe's past better.

I need to get out of here before he sees through me. Get home and come up with a real strategy because as I walk out of Pancake Palace, I know for sure what my next step in finding

Clinton Mask will be. I'm going to return to Boise as Chloe Webster.

CHAPTER 49

NATALIE

Step Five: **Become your mom**

I'VE BEEN in Boise for about three weeks now, getting the lay of the land and trying to uncover any information I can.

I've done more research, branching out to investigate Frankie and her family too. I have copies of birth and death certificates for Chloe's parents, Frankie, and her parents. I have marriage certificates for them as well. Chloe's dad doesn't seem to have ever been in the picture, and I couldn't find a death certificate for him, but I also couldn't track him down.

I check the mirror while sitting in my car on Frankie's street. I found out online where she lived and I've been following her to figure out her daily routine. I want to know what to expect from her when I break the ice at the memorial benefit in a few days. She's the one person I have to sell this to. I think if she believes me, other people will too.

I fluff my new bangs to keep them from laying over the thick frames of my glasses. The bangs are an attempt to hide that my forehead has no wrinkles. Wrinkles are the reason for these horrible glasses, too. The optometrist full-on gawked when I told her that I didn't want the thinner polycarbonate lenses. I've been going to her for years and she didn't understand why I was abandoning contacts for glasses in the first place, let alone Coke-bottle lenses. But I need them to be as thick as my prescription says in order to obscure my eyes. It was either that, or do some intense contouring to make it seem like I had eye wrinkles. I'm already using heavy foundation to cover my few freckles and I didn't want the maintenance of more makeup. Once I had that settled, I went shopping for clothes that would scream "sloppy." Maybe it's rude, but it seems to me that nothing dates a person's style more than ill-fitting clothes. If they're too baggy and hide my body, all the better.

I had my hair highlighted and then asked for a few gray streaks so I appear older. Again, I got a strange look. The stylist tried to talk me out of it, but I insisted.

I don't know if I'm going to be able to pull this off, and I'm pretty much banking on Frankie's obsession with Chloe to carry me through, hoping that she sees what she wants to see and doesn't push too hard beyond that. Based on what I've learned online and by watching her, she very much wants to believe Chloe is still out there somewhere.

Working for me I have:

The fact that nobody has seen what Chloe looks like as an adult. They can't compare me directly to her, making it so even though I'm much younger, they may believe me.

The fact that I already look so much like Chloe in specific ways that matter. Same nose, same eye color, and we're both short.

The fact that forty is the new twenty. I scoff at this last one because while it's true that forty-year-old women look much younger than in prior decades, it doesn't mean I'll pass easily.

Working against me, I have:

No ability to sing, freckles, and no memory of Chloe's child-hood beyond what I've read online. Stuff everyone knows.

None of this stops me though. I'm going to set the world straight by hunting down the man who ruined everything.

Frankie's charcoal-colored truck turns the corner, heading toward her house. I duck to hide behind my steering wheel even though I'm totally out of view.

There was a close call in the grocery store the other day, and I could tell she was a little spooked. She stopped and looked around, so I'm upping my surveillance game. No more risks.

Watching her get out of her truck, I feel something like affection for Frankie. Of course, I don't know her, but she's like me—a loner. She has one man in her life—Jensen Ailor. I did enough digging to know he was in Chloe's class at school, so I've got my eye on him. But it doesn't seem like Frankie is as into him as he is into her.

Frankie checks her mail before going inside the house. She's got her hair up, which seems like a pattern for her. It's very long and I'm gathering that she's kind of a no-fuss person, and wouldn't want to deal with it in her face. Frankie is a little taller than me, but not much. We're both short. I'd put her at about five-foot-two, and I'm five-feet even, like my mom.

I hate that I'm pretty much planning on lying to Frankie, getting her hopes up that Chloe is back, and then ... I haven't thought much about what happens after, honestly. I assume I won't have an "after." If I'm able to take care of the man who killed my mom and I don't get caught, I'll have to move away to be safe. Start over again. I wonder how many times one person can live a lie. It would be my third time. On the other hand, if it all goes to shit, I'll end up in prison.

Kind of ironic considering what happened with my mom.

But I'm not going to prison. I'll pull this off one way or another.

CHAPTER 50

NATALIE

STEP SIX: Return to the world as Chloe Webster

I CHOOSE the annual event to make my appearance because I can't show up as Chloe Webster quietly. It has to be public. Visible. I want to catch attention because the more people who know I'm—I mean Chloe—is back, the more likely I am to suss out anyone who knows Chloe is actually dead. Which is only one person, and he's the one I need to find. I don't know what he will think exactly, but I'm sure he'll want to silence me. I mean, Chloe.

I'm Chloe. I'm Chloe. I'm Chloe.

I repeat this to drive it deeper. It'll be easier to stay in character once I'm actually interacting with people, at least that's what I'm banking on.

Maybe I'll even make the news when I show up at the event tonight.

But no, it turns out not only do I not make the news, but Frankie whisks me away so fast I don't even get to meet anyone else. Except Jensen. And he's more interested in why Frankie is leaving the event early than he is in me.

Frankie drives me to her house, and I make sure to fall apart every time she asks a question in order to discourage her from questioning. I give her a few morsels which are a combination of my imagination and Rachel's true story, but for everything else, I claim that I don't remember anything from before. Crying when she presses me too much is perfect. She always backs off.

Frankie buys my Jane Doe story.

When she offers to let me stay at her house, I agree because it's perfect. It'll allow me to get to know her more. I'll get Frankie to tell me what happened in the years before Chloe went missing. Maybe it'll give me some suspects to check out.

I need to keep my motel room because it's the one place I can fully relax. I can't be in character twenty-four-seven because I'm afraid I'll crack.

I go to the police station with my fake ID and they comment on how young I look, but I take it as a compliment and tease them about feeding my ego. *Forty is the new twenty, you know.* When the detective says he wants to get DNA samples from close relatives, I'm a little worried. It's just Frankie, but will the DNA show that we are first cousins? When I ask this, he says no, just that you're related.

Frankie seems unfazed and has nothing to report after going in to give her sample. All of this makes me realize that I really don't want my return to be as public as I initially thought. It's a huge misstep that I hope doesn't blow up all over me.

To make it worse, days pass and I'm not making progress on my goal.

I get caught up in the feeling of belonging, which I've never had before. Frankie treats me like family, and I start to question whether I really want to keep searching for my mom's killer. If the cops couldn't find him, what makes me think I can?

And I'm pretty damn good at acting like a forty-something. Maybe this can just be my life now.

I have to keep searching, I remind myself as we drive up to Skinny Dipper. It feels like something I'm meant to do.

But Frankie is such an unexpected surprise. Who knew I could care so much about someone? The way she looks at me —nobody has looked at me like that in my entire life. Rachel loved me, yes. But Frankie adores me. Granted, she thinks she's looking at Chloe. But I can't help but bask in the total acceptance she offers anyway.

To my shame, I pretend she means it for me.

When Frankie floats the idea of going to the fancy hot springs the next day, I resist. I don't want to get into the water in front of her because my makeup may run. I also don't want her to see my body—my stomach specifically—which has no stretch marks or any indication of a past pregnancy. But she doesn't understand why I wouldn't want to go, and it seems like pushing my way will cause her to ask questions. Maybe it wouldn't, but she believes I'm Chloe, and I don't want anything to make her suspicious because as soon as that happens, my clock starts ticking, and the race between exposure as not being Chloe and finding out who killed my mom starts. It's nothing that refusing to get into the pool and a good swimsuit cover can't handle.

Wouldn't you know it though, even with me not getting in the water, I still get drenched sitting on the side of the pool. I hurry to fix my makeup, and I think I'm quick enough. Frankie is in the water when I leave for the locker room, and I take my bag into a bathroom stall to reapply.

When I come out, the locker room is still empty and Frankie is where I left her in the pool. But that's another close call. I can't allow any more of those. And it reminds me of another fact: I have to get more serious about finding Chloe's killer since that's why I'm here in the first place.

CHAPTER 51
NATALIE

I SHOVE the gun into my messenger bag and lock my motel room door. I need to get back to Frankie's house. It's dark out now, and I'm starting to worry because she hasn't replied to any of my texts. I hope she's home from looking at the pink sink, but honestly, something feels off. That's why I think she's starting to suspect me.

When I pull up to her house, the truck isn't in the driveway, and the lights are all off. Frankie's still not here.

My body flushes with heat and I'm full-on worried now, so I pull out my phone and text her:

Everything okay?

She left yesterday afternoon. I think she'd be home by now. Although maybe she's staying another night. Why, though? It doesn't seem like it would take that long to look at a sink and I didn't get the impression it was that far away. She made it sound like it was a day-trip, but left me no details, which is another tally in the column of "She's on to you, Nat."

I shove the phone in my cardigan pocket and walk into the house, but it pings with a text.

God, I hope it's from Frankie.

I tap my phone and see it's not a text at all. Frankie shared her location with me and she's somewhere near McCall.

"What the fuck?" I whisper. Why McCall of all places? I mean, it's a popular place to go if you live in Boise, but there are other cities all around. What are the chances the sink she's looking at happens to be in McCall where Chloe was murdered? That and I can't figure out why she'd share her location instead of just saying she's in McCall.

Then a dark thought snakes around my mind.

Someone else lives in McCall, presumably. The dude who confronted me at Pancake Palace a few months ago. I didn't think much of it at first because I was so distracted by the fact that he mistook me for Chloe. But there was that undercurrent of aggression I felt from him.

I don't know for sure he lives there, and it doesn't mean he's involved in this, but that doesn't stop my brain from pole-vaulting from one possibility to the next. I start pacing Frankie's living room.

Chloe Webster was so fresh in his mind that he recognized me immediately as her. How common is it for someone to so easily recall a missing person from decades ago?

At the very least, it points at obsession.

Maybe Frankie's in trouble and didn't have time to text me, so she sent her location hoping I'd come and help. Or call the police.

Or maybe this is me just being paranoid.

But then, that tugging inside happens. My intuition says she's in trouble.

I have to go. I have to drive there and help her.

Slow down. Make a plan.

I reach into my pocket for my vape and take a hit. Then another. I have to calm down and think this through.

If I'm right and she's in trouble, it could be that she's not alone.

Someone could have taken her.

I can't drive to this location by myself, that would be idiotic.

But will the police move on it fast enough?

Jensen.

I could bring him along with me. He's a dick, but I think he would want to help Frankie. At first I wondered if he could have been involved in Chloe's disappearance. I still don't know for sure, and that's a reason not to invite him on a road trip at night to a city I already know holds all kinds of dark history for Chloe. Honestly though, I think if he was Clinton Mask, he would have made a much bigger deal about my return. He would know I'm not Chloe, and further, that I could be Natalie. He displayed some skepticism, but not near the level I'd expect from someone who thinks they're in danger of getting exposed as a murderer.

Call the police.

Again, it seems like the smart thing to do. But it's doubtful the police would be very helpful, considering Frankie has only been gone for a little over a day. And I know where she's at. Her location is right here, so it's not like she's been kidnapped. All I have to go on is my own gut feeling that something is very wrong, which I absolutely trust, but I don't think for one second the police will.

The option of Jensen comes to mind again while I stare at the location icon on my phone. It's surrounded by a flaring green circle saying this is a live location. Wherever this is in McCall, Frankie is there *right now*.

Wait, could it be Jensen who kidnapped her?

I can't think of why he would do that, but statistically, it's usually the boyfriend or husband responsible for violence toward a woman. That's facts too, not merely Rachel in my head.

This snag is solvable. If it's Jensen, he won't be home.

But he could also be at the gym or the store or any number of places that don't have anything to do with kidnapping Frankie and holding her hostage in McCall.

I shake my head. It's the other way around. If Jensen is home, it means he's *not* holding Frankie in McCall and I'm safe to bring him.

Safe.

I replay that word. *No man is safe. Even if he seems like a nice guy, push him too hard and you'll find out what he's made of. Men hate being questioned by a woman. They think they're better than us.*

I groan because this is definitely Rachel in my brain, and it's not helpful right now.

All I have to work with is what I can sense, and if Jensen is home, it means he's likely, at the very least, not Frankie's kidnapper. I have to trust him to some degree.

I don't have his number, but I don't want to call him anyway. I need to see that he's at his house to test my theory, so I push open Frankie's front door and walk down the sidewalk, all the way to the end of the street, and then turn right to approach Jensen's house.

His truck isn't in the driveway, but maybe he parked it in the garage.

I ring the doorbell, and don't wait for a response before I call out. "Jensen? Are you there?" I knock impatiently, as if making enough of a ruckus will cause him to be home and answer the door.

Nothing. I walk to the front picture window—a ginormous single glass square set in red brick—and cup my hands to peek inside. The living room lights are off. I could tell that before staring into the glass, but it seems like there might be a light on somewhere in there. The back hallway, maybe?

I walk around and open the wooden side gate to see if Jensen is in the back of the house. Maybe he has earbuds in, or he's asleep.

Before I get to the backyard, I pull out my phone to check Frankie's location again to see if there's any movement toward Boise. It's a weak hope that maybe she shared her location with me to say she's on her way home.

"What are you doing?"

A man's voice from behind startles me so much that I almost drop my phone on the pavement when I turn around.

I put a palm against my chest. "Fuck, Jensen. You scared me."

He shoves his hands into his pockets. "Huh. No kidding. Well, imagine how I felt seeing someone creeping around outside my house in the dark."

"Sorry about that. You didn't answer the door and I needed to know if you were home."

He is home. I mentally rule him out of being involved with what's happening to Frankie.

"I need your help," I start. "I haven't heard from Frankie all day. Have you?"

"I haven't heard from Frankie in *days*. Ever since she broke up with me the night I tried to cook you guys dinner. Why? What's going on?"

"She went out of town to look at a sink last night and hasn't replied to any of my texts today."

"Okay?" he says.

"Something feels off. Then, after no communication from her, I got this." I hold my phone out so he can see her location.

He shrugs. "Okay, so she's in McCall."

"But she didn't tell me where she was going and sent her location out of the blue instead of texting 'Hey, I'm in McCall.'"

I wish he would catch up faster.

"So, I want you to come to McCall with me," I add.

"What?" He taps his Apple Watch. "It's like ten at night."

"Yeah, but I have a feeling she's in trouble."

He gives me a look that says I'm stupid for trusting my feelings.

My phone pings, and it's from Frankie again. This time it's a text that says:

> Come alone or I'll kill her.

I gasp and turn the phone to shove it in his face. "See?"

"Jesus fuck," he whispers. "You're right. We have to call the cops."

"I don't think they'll do anything. She hasn't been missing for much more than twenty-four hours and she's not lost." My voice climbs in frustration. He needs to get on board right now.

His eyes widen and he says, "This is a threat. The cops will respond to it."

My phone pings again. This time it's a picture. Frankie bound and lying on the ground. The message says:

> If you call the cops, they'll make it here before you do and I'll put a gun to her head before they can do a single fucking thing to save her.

"No cops," I say.

Jensen nods. "I'm driving."

CHAPTER 52

FRANKIE

THE FIRST THING I notice when I come to is a dank and musty smell. It brings to mind a cellar, and the air is cool.

I'm on my side, and it's not total darkness, but it's dim and I'm facing a concrete wall. The floor is dirt. I blink to clear my vision, and my brain comes online faster. My hands are tied behind my back, and my feet are bound too.

Oh god.

My heart hammers, so my breathing comes in short and fast bursts until I'm lightheaded. I have to calm down, try to do the in-through-the-nose-and-out-through-the-mouth thing, but my pulse is going wild and my body flashes with heat so it feels impossible. I roll over slowly and my body is sluggish, like coming out of sedation.

"Welcome back," a low voice says, but I can't see anyone.

Heavy footsteps pace closer, and I search for words to speak but there's nothing but cold, hard fear. It blanks out my mind.

Then I see him.

A man, crouching a little because of the low ceiling. He's wearing a Bill Clinton mask as if it's Halloween or something.

"What in the world?" comes out of my mouth in a low whisper.

He bends over me and tilts his head in a way that really only looks creepy when someone wears a mask. He doesn't speak at first, just watches me.

All the usual questions born out of shock come to mind, and in a split second I sort through them, trying to determine which is best for this situation.

Who are you?

Why am I here?

Where is here?

What do you want from me?

Then I see the phone in his grip. My pink sparkly case. He has my phone, and he shoves it at my face and then pulls it away. It clicks, unlocking, and now he's typing something on it.

"What are you doing?"

"Texting Chloe," he says. Then he shoves it into his pocket.

"What? Why?"

No answer.

Behind him and across the room from me, a low moan cuts the silence.

It sounds like another man.

I strain to see who it is over there by the stairs. The man with the mask follows my gaze, then mutters, "Good, everyone's up."

"Fuck you, asshole," the man across the room replies.

I recognize that voice.

"Dad!" Tears fly and I can't wipe my already-runny nose because my wrists are bound. Dad's here—I can't fully see him, but that's definitely him.

"Frankie? What are you doing here?" I don't like the panic I hear in his tone.

"I was wondering the same about you. I came to meet with

someone who knows more about Chloe. Then I got here and couldn't find you. I was so worried."

"Fuuuuuck," Dad groans.

Now I can see that he's against the wall in the dark. His black-booted feet are visible in a sliver of lantern light, but that's really all.

The asshole in the mask is sitting in a chair. Letting this happen like he wants Dad and I to talk. Why?

"Let her go, Punkass," Dad says. "She has nothing to do with this."

"You," I say to the man. "You're the one who was messaging me about Chloe." He has to be. That isn't a common name to call someone.

He doesn't move, and I can't see the expression on his face because of the stupid mask.

If this is Punkass, why would he want me? Then, my mind slowly plays with the idea that maybe he doesn't know anything about Chloe after all. Maybe he said that to lure me here. But why? Why does he want me and my dad?

"Dad, are you okay?" I ask. "Do you know what's going on?"

He coughs for a few seconds, then clears his throat. "No, Moose. I have no clue. Are you hurt?"

The most irrational thing comes alive inside me, and I speak before thinking. "Don't fucking call me Moose! I've told you so many times not to do that, and you never listen."

Stupid. Childish. Why does it matter right now? I'm losing my cool.

"God, sorry, *Francesca*."

He sounds more childish than I do. Like a cranky kid who got his toy taken away. I almost feel like I don't recognize him.

IT'S BEEN an hour and a half driving with Jensen in silence and so many winding roads that I feel like I may puke. But what keeps circling my mind is the fact that this is happening to Frankie because I showed up. I always knew there was a risk of danger to me, but I was willing to chance it if it meant finding out who killed Chloe.

My stomach drops. How could I let this happen to her? I did this. It's my fault.

And yet, I can't help but think that if I'm right and this has something to do with me—or Chloe, rather—that I could be closer to finding her killer.

"Drive faster!" I shout, leaning over Jensen's shoulder to see the speedometer. It's tipping over seventy miles an hour, and the signs say fifty-five is the limit.

"I'm going as fast as I can without flying off the road and into the river," he says. "Did she really go up to McCall for a sink? It seems odd for her to take off and leave you behind. She's been attached to you at the hip ever since you returned."

"I don't know," I whisper. "I think she's mad at me too."

"What? Why?"

Because she's on to me.

"I don't know. Maybe she's getting sick of me," I try to joke, but it lands flat and he doesn't even smile.

"You know, I don't believe you're Chloe Webster," he says.

"I know."

He flinches, straightening his back and tossing me a look of disbelief.

"You're not going to argue with me? Try to convince me I'm wrong?"

"I'm not really interested in what you think, honestly."

"Wow, thanks."

"You're welcome," I say, then switch gears. "So, we were friends in high school, I guess?"

He raises his eyebrows and I don't know how to interpret it.

"I'm trying to piece together my past and figure out what happened that night," I add.

He laughs. "I tell you I don't believe you're Chloe and your response is to quiz me about Chloe's past as if it's your own?"

"Like I said, I don't care what you think. Whether you believe something about me doesn't have anything to do with the truth. Newsflash: The world doesn't revolve around a man's opinion of a woman."

Oh, hello, Rachel. Not that I disagree with my answer, but it's definitely something she'd say, and it comes out of my mouth before I can vet it.

"Whoa," he says. "Newsflash: Not all men are assholes."

But you are.

I don't say that even though I want to.

"Here's an olive branch," Jensen starts. "I don't know who you really are or why you're fucking with Frankie's life like this, but I think you should come clean. It'll be better if you do it before she finds out on her own."

For a moment, I consider telling Jensen my identity. There's no reason to keep the act up, especially since Frankie may be in danger. I feel like I can trust him to some degree. He might be an asshole, but I don't think he's dangerous. I decide against it though because I don't want to distract us from what we're doing or from what we may come across when we get to this location in McCall.

It's a lame excuse. Maybe I'm just chicken shit.

But another thought is Frankie should be the first to hear it.

Fuck. None of this even matters if Frankie is in danger.

"Let's focus on finding out what's going on with Frankie, okay?" I say.

"Couldn't agree more. Pull up her location again. We're passing through Donnelly, which means McCall is next."

I open my phone and check our distance from Frankie. "We're thirty-two minutes away."

CHAPTER 54

FRANKIE

DAD SHIFTS, but it's clear he's not very mobile. He comes into view and his gray hair hangs over one eye. Unlike me, his hands are bound in front of him, and there's a rope around his chest keeping him strapped to something. I don't know what because I can't see that clearly. I start sobbing as if my body is giving up trying to make sense of this. The slow, creeping tiredness I've felt for weeks on end, mixed with the horror of our situation sinks into my bones. It suddenly feels like forty years of exhaustion, where every time I turn around there's a new trauma. Every time I get an answer, a new hard question presents itself.

"Don't cry, Moo—I mean, Frankie," Dad says from across the short distance. "I'm going to straighten this out. You're fine."

Why the hell is Dad acting so chill right now? We're both tied up! I feel more like we're in huge danger, and he doesn't seem worried. All I can hear is what he always tells me to do: Let it go. Get over it. *You're fine, Frankie.*

Something is fishy here, and it doesn't help that I'm pissed at him once again.

"What's going on, Dad?" I demand.

"I think she's probably close, so let's get started," the guy in the mask—Punkass, I'm sure of it—says.

"Who is close? Get started on what?" I ask even though I worry that he means Chloe. I'm pretty sure she's involved in this somehow, but is she coming here to help him? Is she involved in kidnapping us? Or is he drawing her here like he did me? I think it's probably the second one because why else would he use my phone except to pretend to be me while texting her?

She can't come here. I don't know why she has freckles and a weird motel room, but I don't want her to walk into this.

Punkass doesn't answer me, of course, and instead says, "Round one goes like this: Jeff, you come clean about everything from your past and Frankie gets to live."

I gasp at the mention of my fate, and Dad says, "Come on, man, let us go. You've made your point."

Again, he doesn't sound as freaked out as I think he should be. This guy just threatened to kill me.

"Have I?" Punkass says. "Then tell me, Jeff, what is my point?"

"You're some student I couldn't help years ago and you want an apology. This is kind of extreme though, don't you think?"

One of Dad's students. Is that true that this guy is just getting revenge? It doesn't ring true. I don't know why, but I don't think that's what's going on. If so, what does Chloe have to do with it?

The man scoffs and ignores Dad. "Round one," he repeats. "I ask a question and if you don't answer it truthfully, Frankie loses a body part. We'll start with her fingers."

"What?" I yell, then I try to wiggle out of my ties. I have more feeling and control over my body, but the thrashing does nothing for me. I'm stuck. Tears wet my face as I sob uncontrollably. I scan around, trying to search for something, anything to give me an idea to escape. Ice seizes in my veins and for the first time I have the thought: I'm going to die down here.

"Come on. Leave her out of this," Dad says. "We haven't seen your face. We don't know your name. Just let us go."

The man laughs. "Nice try. We both know that you absolutely know who I am. You already gave that away."

Because Dad called him Punkass.

"I don't know for sure."

But I don't believe him. I think Dad absolutely does know this guy.

I pull at my bound hands again, but that makes my wrists hurt because the zip ties are so tight.

"So, for starters," the man says, "tell the story of how you and I met."

"Let us fucking go!" Dad yells.

I swear, he acts more annoyed than scared, and for some reason that absolutely terrifies me. He's not taking this seriously. Then Dad starts laughing and the man stiffens.

My blood freezes and I don't move a muscle. Dad is laughing like this is the most hilarious thing he's ever seen. I flick my gaze from him to the man to try to figure out what the fuck is going on, but I can't determine anything. This feels like an episode of *The Twilight Zone*.

What is Dad doing? Nothing about this situation says this guy is joking around. This feels real. It is real. And Dad doesn't see it.

I am not safe here. I am in danger, and my dad is making it worse.

"You're not going to hurt my daughter. If you were, you wouldn't be hiding behind that mask."

The man pulls his mask off and I get the sense that it's just to prove Dad wrong. He is planning to hurt us.

CHAPTER 55
NATALIE

WHEN WE REACH a small cabin surrounded by pine, it's creeping up on midnight. "This is it," I say, looking at my phone.

The cabin is completely dark. Not a single light on inside, but Frankie's truck is right there. That seed of a feeling that something is wrong expands inside of me so the little hairs on my neck stand up.

"Maybe she's asleep," Jensen says.

"Her truck is here. Her phone is here. She's here, or someone took her to another spot and it's just the fucker who is doing all of this here. With her phone. Any way we look at it, it's bad. Do you not remember the picture he sent?"

"I remember." Jensen runs a hand through his hair. He's scared. Which I understand because he's a high school teacher and probably not used to threats like this. I was literally born into assuming everyone around me—especially men—wanted to hurt me. Rachel taught me that threats weren't possibilities. They were eventualities.

I reach inside my messenger bag and pull out my gun.

"What the fuck?" Jensen jumps like he found a spider on his lap. "Why do you have that?"

"Why *don't* you have one? We're coming out to confront someone holding our friend. Seems appropriate."

"I have guns. But they're rifles. For hunting." He talks like he's on trial and this is his defense.

I don't reply, instead I check that my magazine is full and I've got one in the chamber.

Must be nice to live on your own and not have to even think about your own safety. Rachel made me take self-defense classes until I could practically teach them. That and shooting at the range were my only hobbies growing up. Also my only opportunities to be around other people as a kid.

"You know how to use it?" he asks. "Because I know how to shoot handguns. I'm pretty good. I just don't own one."

I roll my eyes even though now the truck is off, so it's dark and I doubt he can see.

We get out and slink over to the cabin. By the time we get up to the front window, I've got an idea of the layout here. The cabin is in the middle of fucking nowhere, and there's a meadow that stretches about twenty-five feet between it and the treeline. Otherwise, it's all pine trees.

"Let's see her location again," Jensen whispers.

No idea why, but I pull out my phone and show him the green circle. It's here. Exactly where we're standing.

"I wonder if this is her dad's cabin," Jensen mutters, taking the phone from me and zooming around the map. "I've never been there, but I know he stays out here sometimes when he comes up to volunteer at the summer camp. The property fits what Frankie has described in the past."

"You think her dad kidnapped her?"

"No," he laughs. "Just saying that's where I think we are."

"I'm going around the back to check it out," I say.

"No, I will."

"I know it's hard to believe because I have tits, but I can handle myself."

"Great, so handle yourself right here on the porch." He holds up my phone, which he's now using as a flashlight and I try to grab it, but he's too far away. In a few steps, he's around the back and I'm loitering outside the tiny cabin in total darkness.

He didn't even take a weapon. Hell, a piece of wood would be better than nothing.

Jensen is right about one thing: It does seem like nobody is here. Very strange that a kidnapper would tell us exactly where to find him.

It's a trap.

"Fuck," I whisper, standing up. Why didn't I see it before? I was so preoccupied with getting to Frankie.

Something else: Jensen should be back by now. It would be stupid to call out his name, since I'm pretty sure the kidnapper lured us here.

That's it. I'm calling the police.

No phone! Jensen took it. Why the fuck did he take mine when he has his own?

And he has the truck keys too.

Fuck. Fuck. Fuck.

For all the attitude and claims that I can *handle myself*, I'm here in the middle of the woods at a cabin, waiting to be grabbed like some stupid girl.

I turn and run toward the treeline as fast as possible. I'll hide behind one of them at the edge of the mini meadow. The tall grass and weeds whip my legs, but at least I wore leggings instead of the stupid long skirts I've spent my days in, posing as Chloe.

There's a rustling coming from behind the cabin, and then I swear, I hear Jensen yelp. It's brief. Maybe a second before the silence returns.

Fuck.

They took Jensen. Or worse.

My heart thunders in my chest, narrowing all of my senses down to these facts that make up my reality, all of which I hate:

I'm alone.

Frankie is in trouble.

I have to get inside.

CHAPTER 56
FRANKIE

I GASP when I see this man's face. It's not full light, but the fact that he's not trying to hide his identity is the point. He doesn't care because we aren't going to live to tell.

"Fucking hell, Brian, what are you doing?" Dad asks. Again, he sounds annoyed more than worried.

A surge of fear rises when I realize that this isn't a mistake. Whatever is happening, this guy—Brian—has abducted Dad and me on purpose.

Before Brian can answer, a thump outside makes us all hold perfectly still. It sounds like it's coming from the side of the building. Brian strains to hear. Then he smiles.

"I'll be right back."

He goes up the stairs and there's some sort of trap door on the ceiling. He uses it to exit. When it opens, I see lights upstairs. This is definitely a basement of some sort. Next, I hear his heavy footsteps walking around overhead.

"We need to escape," I say.

"One way out, and that's the way he just took," Dad replies, his voice full of defeat now.

"How do you know that?"

"Because it's my basement."

"Your basement? But ... how...?"

My brain slogs along, trying to keep up with everything that's happening. Does he mean the cabin has a basement? Because I don't think I was out long enough for this Brian guy to drive us back to Boise, where Dad lives.

"Yes, the cabin has a basement."

Oh. How did I not know this all these years?

"Dad, this guy has been messaging me about Chloe. What does he want?"

Dad sighs. "Don't worry about it. Stay calm and I'll get us out of here."

Before I can give him hell about being so la ti da, the ceiling door opens and light-gray OluKai shoes come into view. No socks. The man wears shorts, and there's a tattoo of a vintage pinup girl on the outside of his lower right leg.

"Jensen!" I say. "What are you doing here?"

But then I see his face, and it's swollen like he got into a bar fight, and he seems out of it. Brian dabs his own bloody nose with his fingers, and he's got a gun to Jensen's back, guiding him down the steps.

Jensen's hands are up, and he says, "Are you okay, Frankie?"

No, I'm not okay, I want to say. *I'm fucking terrified.*

But all I can do is nod and cry.

At the bottom of the stairs, Brian pulls out a needle and stabs it into Jensen's shoulder. Jensen ragdolls to the floor.

Brian zip ties his wrists and ankles.

"Fuck. That was Chloe's dose. Now I'm out of sedatives." He throws a cell phone so hard against the dirt floor that it breaks apart. But I can tell by the case it's Chloe's.

Why does he have her phone?

Please let Chloe be safe.

But then I realize that this isn't going according to his plan, which is good.

"Brian, come on, let's talk about this," Dad says.

He doesn't answer, but sits in the chair and reaches into a backpack on the floor to pull out a pair of handheld pruners. Like you'd use to cut rose stems.

My fingers. That's what he brought in case my dad wouldn't talk. I want to retch but I try to hold still and be as invisible as possible.

"Okay, Jeff. Talk about how we met," Brian says.

"Fine." Dad lifts his zip tied hands in a giving-up gesture. "We met at school."

Dad's face is smug and it makes me so nervous.

"The story, Jeff. Tell the whole damn story. And tell it to your daughter."

Dad sighs and closes his eyes. "Fine. Brian came into my office his junior year because he was having trouble at home and with his grades. The usual things. I wasn't able to help him course-correct and he didn't graduate on time."

Brian stares at Dad, with his back to me. But I don't need to see his face to know Dad is making him more angry. Dad doesn't see how dangerous this guy is. He took his mask off, basically announcing he doesn't have plans to free us.

I might be on my own here.

I start looking around again to get information. Note every-thing. One escape—up the stairs. Under the stairs I see some boxes and things. I can move my body now. I'm bound but not tied to anything. If Brian leaves us again, I can try to get into those boxes and find something to cut us free. Jensen is passed out, but Brian doesn't seem too worried about him. I'll get free first and then come back and help Jensen.

"What's the real reason I came to see you, Jeff?" Brian asks. He keeps using my dad's name, which makes everything feel even creepier. "You've been threatening to tell people about it for over twenty years. So, let's go. Tell your daughter about my problem."

Dad's face screws up in confusion. "Really?"

"Really. And then tell her about yours too."

"No. No fucking way." Dad shakes his head.

What is my dad doing? Why is he arguing with this guy? He needs to say whatever Brian wants to hear right now.

"Dad, tell me," I say. "I won't be mad. Just—do what he says."

"Brian, stop this right now!" Dad yells and again it reminds me of a child's tantrum.

Brian turns toward me, holding the pruners up where Dad can see.

"Please. Please don't," I beg. "I have no idea what my dad did to you, but I know he can be an asshole sometimes. Please let us go."

"Okay fine!" Dad shouts. "Brian likes little girls. He came to me when he was in high school looking for help."

"Very good. Now tell her your problem."

"Never," Dad says, shaking his head.

What the fuck? My mind presses this thought, and it feels like something is there. A realization that I could simply allow if I wanted to. As if all the clues are present and accounted for.

"Tell your daughter about my problem."

"Then tell her about yours too."

Brian likes little girls.

I start gagging and sobbing all at once, because like a switch being flicked on in my brain, I know.

CHAPTER 57
FRANKIE

DAD'S FACE IS SET. His eyes look empty, and his mouth is a thin line. He's not going to confess to it, and I'm going to lose a finger.

"You like little girls too," I blurt.

Dad looks down, silently confirming my accusation.

Brian steps back as if he's impressed. "Very good, Frankie. She's done the hard part for you. Now tell the whole thing, Jeff. From start to finish."

At this, Dad starts crying. He wails. Tears and snot course down his face like he's finally seeing the danger we're in, but in an instant, his eyes flash and I don't recognize him. His face turns red and he screams. "No. I'll never, ever do what you tell me to."

Brian comes at me fast and grabs my bound hands. I try to pull away, but I'm sitting on my ass and my ankles are bound too. I have no leverage. I scream and yell at my dad. "Tell me, just tell me! Please!"

"Fine! Fine," he says. "I told Brian I would keep his secret if he helped me with a project."

Brian moves the pruning shears so I can feel cold metal on both sides of my left pinky. He's going to do it. I can feel it.

"No! Please!" All I can do is beg.

"Keep going," Brian demands. "Tell her what the *project* was."

Dad starts crying. "I can't, Brian. I can't."

"You can't?" Brian mocks him. "What was it you told me when I said I can't murder innocent girls for you? Oh yeah, I remember. 'You have no choice.'"

Snip.

Blinding pain sears my body. Then wet warmth in my left pinky.

I scream and Brian lets go of my hands and I feel for the wound. It's slippery everywhere from blood and I'm dizzy. Brian tosses a small towel at me and I scurry to use it to put pressure on my finger.

Breathe.

Breathe.

"Murder innocent girls for you."

Breathe.

I sob harder. I want to think about all of this, try to figure it out, but the pain in my finger is center stage and I'm sweating and I feel like I'm going to pass out, so I move to lie down on my side again.

Keep it together. As best as possible, Frankie, keep your shit together.

We have to get out of here.

I have to get out of here.

I feel a shift happening inside of me, a separation from my dad. I'm the only one looking out for me. Maybe that's the way it's always been, but at this moment, it's more real than anything else. My dad just chose to let this man mutilate me over complying and exposing himself.

"Are you still with us, Frankie?" Brian asks, bending down

as if to look me in the eye. "You should know I wasn't always like this. In fact, your dad shaped me. Little by little, he broke down my conscience."

I have to keep my mind straight. I can't freak out any more than I already am. This is it. This is the end of the freak-out line. Now I need to problem-solve. Mind over matter and shit.

"Why did he ask you to ..." I cough. " ... murder girls?"

"Well, I think we should let him tell it," Brian says. "Did you hear your daughter, Jeff? She wants to know why you made me kill the girls."

"They were nobodies," Dad says in a low voice. "No-name girls. Homeless, runaways. We were putting them out of their misery."

"What?" I shriek.

I stare at him and then at Brian, and I don't know who is more of a monster right now. I'm stuck down here with both of them, and I start gasping, feeling like I can't catch my breath.

"I'm not proud of it, okay?" Dad says. "But yeah, for a few years I ran a side business providing girls to men who couldn't get access any other way. When they were used up, we got rid of them."

"But that wasn't the case with Amy and Kristi, was it?" Brian asks. "They weren't homeless. They weren't runaways. The media circus proved they certainly weren't nobodies."

No. I start shaking my head as another bomb explodes in my mind. It can't be true.

CHAPTER 58
FRANKIE

"What do Amy and Kristi have to do with this?" I whisper, fighting back the disbelief that my dad could be involved in their murders.

"They found out your dad's second biggest secret, so he made me take care of them. Of course, by then, he'd been grooming me to do worse and worse things. At first, threatening to expose my *problem* to the school and my family, which would have ruined my chances at college, and in effect, my entire life. But as I did what he asked in order to avoid that, my situation got worse. Soon the rumors of liking little girls seemed like no big deal compared to the kidnapping, human trafficking, and murder he forced me into. By the time Amy and Kristi happened, I was numb to it. I had to be. It was a matter of survival for me because I had to do what your dad said or he would turn me in."

"Why didn't you turn him in?" I ask.

"Yeah, like anyone would believe a delinquent kid over a beloved teacher with standing in the community for his volunteer work. This was the nineties."

I close my eyes and my throat hurts from crying so much. Then a wave of anger.

"And you did it? You murdered girls because you were afraid of a rumor getting out?"

"You're not listening, Frankie. He held the rumor over me in the beginning. Your dad started manipulating me when I was seventeen. A kid myself. All I knew was if my dad found out about my problem, he would murder me. So, in a way, it was like I was choosing between my own survival and committing a crime. Your dad said all I had to do was get a girl into my car and drop her off at a certain location. I didn't even know why. I found out later that I had kidnapped her."

"You had no idea that asking a child to go somewhere with you might be kidnapping?" I yell, and immediately wish I had toned it down. I'm completely helpless and in pain, and the last thing I should do is piss Brian off.

"I didn't have a choice," he screams.

I flinch and decide not to do that again. Just go along with whatever he says. Don't argue.

Dad hasn't spoken for a while. He's staring at his bound hands on his lap. He doesn't even seem upset or concerned that his daughter got her finger cut off.

Brian reaches into his pocket and pulls out two pills and a small bottle of water. "Ibuprofen. For the pain. Open up," he says, and I obey.

It's a one-eighty from his screaming fit just seconds before. Why is he even bothering with my pain if he's going to kill me?

I swallow the water and remember Amy and Kristi.

"Dad, why would you want Amy and Kristi dead?" I whisper, trying to make my voice soft when nothing in me wants to be nice.

He doesn't answer. Doesn't even acknowledge me.

"They found out your dad's second biggest secret."

"What was the secret? The second biggest one?" I ask because I have to know.

"Jeff?" Brian says, "Your daughter is talking to you."

Dad's head hangs and he shakes it back and forth, repeating, "No, no, no" as if he's begging.

"Tell Frankie what secret Amy and Kristi found out about. The one that got them killed."

Dad doesn't look up or respond.

"You know, something just occurred to me, Frankie," Brian says. "I don't think he cares about you as much as he cares about himself."

Brian paces across the room and grabs Dad's bound hands, holds them up in the air. He takes one of Dad's fingers between the pruner blades.

"Stop! No!" Dad comes alive again, yelling and whipping his body around, trying to resist. But it's pointless. He's tied up.

Brian places his foot on Dad's crotch, and applies pressure.

"Maybe we should cut this off instead of a finger. It's kind of what got this whole thing started, in a way."

"No! I'll do it. I'll tell her."

Brian removes his foot.

Dad groans this hopeless growl, like he's giving up. "Chloe was pregnant. I overheard Amy and Kristi talking about it at their locker one day. They didn't say her name, but immediately I knew it was Chloe because she'd been so sick recently and I already suspected pregnancy. I remembered when your mom first started getting morning sickness with you."

He stops talking and I don't need him to keep going. I can connect the dots. I start crying and a little worm of despair tries to push to the surface of my mind, and I can't help but resist it. It's too horrendous to entertain.

"Tell her why you cared that Chloe was pregnant," Brian prods.

"Because the baby was mine, okay? And I couldn't have that come to light."

"What?" I scream, my finger throbs, my throat is raw. Hearing the confirmation of what I suspected just seconds before still feels as shocking as learning it for the first time. How can this be true? How could he do that to little girls? To *Chloe*? Snot flies and mixes with spit, and I don't care. How can this person I grew up with—this person I share DNA with—be such a devil?

"You're a fucking monster. I hate you," I sob.

A moment passes where nobody speaks, and I sit up and look right at Brian. "Please, Brian. Let me go. I don't care what you do to him. I agree with you that he deserves whatever is coming his way."

"Afraid I can't do that. There's one more big secret your dad has to tell you. It's secret number one."

Brian is back in position, with his foot on Dad's crotch and his shears rounding Dad's index finger.

Dad refuses to talk again, and Brian doesn't hesitate.

Snip.

Dad screams in pain.

I have to get out of here. He's going to kill us both. I've seen his face. I know his name.

Brian.

Oh my god. Realization wraps around my mind and I suddenly think I know who he is. "You're the lifeguard from Paradise Point," I say. "I remember you from summer camp."

"Yeah, Jeff made sure I was available for him in McCall all summer long. That's where he had his operation. His time at Paradise Point ended a long time ago, but Jeff still brings girls out here to his cabin in the summer. Don't you, Jeff?"

I cry out again, because it's so horrific and I can't bear the thought of it.

"In fact, this very cabin is where I brought the girls who

were at the end of their tenure at the prison. It's where I buried their remains." He stomps the dirt and laughs.

Dad gasps like he didn't know that, but all I can think is that's why I'm here. He's definitely planning to kill me.

He was always going to kill me.

I knew it from the moment I woke up down here. There was never a scenario where I would survive this. But something about that thought lights up another part of me. A will to fight. To live through this. I just have to figure out how.

"Up at Paradise Point is where I fell in love with Chloe," Brian adds. "And I tried to help her. I tried to overcome my problem and I wanted to start a life over again with her even though she was too old for me." He shakes his head.

"It's time, Jeff," Brian growls. "Tell Frankie about her mom. Or it won't only be your finger next time."

My mom? I swallow hard, and dizziness washes over me again.

Brian puts more pressure on Dad with his foot. "Your mom's accident wasn't an accident," Dad pushes out fast.

Total numbness clouds over me. It's so much shock, pain, and exhaustion. I drop my head and cry. I can't hear anymore.

"Stop," I say quietly.

But Brian is standing right by Dad and he pulls out a knife. It's huge, with jagged edges. He puts it up to Dad's throat. "Keep going," he says through clenched teeth.

"No, please, I don't want to hear it," I cry.

"Too fucking bad!" Brian screams at me.

I wail louder.

"It looked like a hit and run while she was on her long Sunday walk. But it was Brian driving."

"Tell her why, motherfucker."

"Because your mom found out about ... me. She realized that she was my first ... one. She was going to take you and leave me."

It's too much. It's too fucking much. My chest tightens and my mouth goes dry.

He murdered Mom.

I don't want to believe it, and everything in me rallies in an effort toward denial. Dad is saying that to appease Brian, right? He's finally cooperating and maybe he's even making up stories in order to get Brian to back off.

But then, Brian does back off. If Dad is lying, Brian sure believed him quickly. He removes the knife from Dad's neck and steps back.

"You have to understand, Moose. You were the one good thing in my life. The only proof I had that I could change. That I could resist my urges. Because I never touched you, right, Moose?"

He murdered Mom.

It's all true. Dad hurt girls. He had them killed. Amy and Kristi. He assaulted Chloe and got her pregnant. He's the reason she went missing.

He murdered Mom.

I keep thinking those words as my body shakes. I touch my pinky and wonder how much blood I've lost. I'm lightheaded and it feels hard to breathe.

"Now you see why I set all this up?" Brian asks. His voice is more gentle, almost compassionate. "He deserves all of this and more, and he'll get it. But first, let's talk about Chloe. I wanted her to be here when this part happens, but—"

A loud crash upstairs interrupts him. "Talk about timing," he says. "It's her. Has to be." He shoves the pruners into his cargo pants pocket, bends down for the Clinton mask and the lantern, then pulls the mask on and picks up the gun. He pads up the stairs, obviously trying to be quiet. He's going to sneak up on her. I have to do something. So when he lifts the door to leave the basement, I cry out, "He has a gun!"

Brian comes back down the stairs and stomps toward me, and I shrink back from him, petrified of what he might do.

He slaps my face and points a finger centimeters from my eyes. "Keep your fucking mouth shut or I'll come back down here and take another finger."

Then he goes upstairs again, this time trying to be even more quiet, and closes the door so gently I can barely hear it. And he's gone.

CHAPTER 59
FRANKIE

I SIT in the pitch darkness, and my face stings hot. I have to get free and help Chloe.

I hope she heard me because I can't yell again. I don't think for one second that Brian is bluffing.

"Jensen?" I shout-whisper, knowing he's probably still unconscious.

No answer, so I guess I'm on my own again, which isn't going to be easy. Imagining even cutting myself free with a wounded finger and my hands behind my back makes me want to cry all over again.

But there's no time for that. I have to get the fuck out of here.

"Chloe being back is the reason I haven't returned to Boise." Dad's voice cuts through the darkness. "I was trying to figure out where to go so that she couldn't find me and turn me in."

I wrap the towel around my finger as best as possible and hope my hand is useful to some degree.

My body has been cold, clammy, and shivering for so long tonight that when I feel the burn of anger start from the inside, it catches me off guard. It also seems to light up my senses and offer some energy.

Conserve it.

I need to save this strength to confront Brian—the thought makes me whimper—so I bottle up all the things I want to say to the man I used to call Dad.

All of this and your biggest worry is getting exposed?

No apology for all the lies.

No apology for raping Chloe. For killing her friends.

No apology for murdering my mom.

You're a psychopath, and you're dead to me.

I clench my teeth and start moving across the room on my side in a contracting and expanding motion in order to find out if there's anything under the stairs in those boxes that I could use to get free. That's the most important thing right now.

"What are you doing?" Dad asks. His voice is weak, and because it's dark now that Brian took the lantern upstairs, he has no idea, which I like.

I don't want to talk to him at all, ever again. But this is his basement. Maybe he knows where to look. "Need to find something to cut these zip ties."

"There's a metal toolbox under the stairs. Inside, you'll find a knife."

I don't acknowledge him as I make my way toward where I think the stairs are. It's hard to move because I'm shaking as if I were naked outside in the winter.

It's okay, I coach myself. *You'll get that adrenaline back when you need it.*

I bump into the chair Brian was sitting in, and it helps orient me in the dark. Everything feels so much farther away than it seemed.

"Moose, I'm getting better now. Brian is lying; I'm not doing those things anymore."

I ignore him even though the way he uses my nickname

registers in my mind. I couldn't care less if he calls me Moose now. He has never respected me or bothered to take me into account. I don't think he'll ever change.

Soon I'm at the spot under the stairs, and since my hands are tied behind my back, I have to spin and face Dad's direction to use them to feel around for the toolbox.

"It's on the far right. Under the lowest stair," Dad says.

I touch cardboard boxes, plastic bins, then metal in the shape of a box. I work it out from under the stairs until my fingers land on what feels like a clasp. A ripple of pain in my pinky when I accidentally hit it against the metal.

I gasp.

"Careful, don't want the knife to get you," Dad says.

Shut up, monster, I think, but don't answer him. Even so, I slow myself down, reaching blindly behind, using my bound hands as one unit to search for the knife as both my pinky and wrists scream in pain.

A wooden handle with a heavy metal head ... a hammer. No good.

"Actually, bring the box over here and I'll help you look so you don't cut yourself," Dad says.

Jesus Christ, he's acting like nothing happened. Like he didn't just shatter my entire world with his confession of being a pedophile and a murderer. Again, I don't acknowledge him.

I'm on to the next thing—needle-nose pliers—and Chloe has been up there alone with Brian for too long. I have to find the knife *now*.

Bright pain explodes across the pad of my index finger.

"Fuck," I whisper. But it's the first bit of hope I've felt all night.

I found the knife.

CHAPTER 60
NATALIE

AFTER I DELIBERATED for way too long out in the woods, I put on my big girl panties and snuck inside the cabin. It was empty, so I knew there must be a basement and Frankie had to be down there. Jensen too. I had to draw out whoever took Frankie, and get them to come upstairs, where I'd be waiting with my gun pointed right at their head. I saw the outline of a door on the hardwood in the kitchen and I'm guessing that's the way into the basement. I grabbed a dirty plate from the countertop and made my way across the living room to hide behind the wood stove.

Then I threw the plate at the kitchen as hard as I could.

Nothing happened at first, but then I heard Frankie's voice telling me he has a gun.

I'm overcome with relief that she seems okay for now. And impressed that she thought to give me something useful instead of just telling me to run.

But then I wait another couple of seconds, standing behind the stove and wonder why he isn't coming up here.

Light cracks from the floor and I snap to attention, holding my gun with both hands, aiming it so I have a shot right when he appears.

But what I see throws me off.

It's a man in a Bill Clinton mask.

Heat rushes my body and my mind speeds up.

It's him. The one who killed Chloe. The one who held Rachel captive. The motherfucker I've been looking for and here he is, served up to me in an abandoned cabin where I can kill him and get away with it.

I slow my breathing down in order to get my heart rate to settle.

He bends down to close the door and moves into the kitchen. If he would stand still, I'd have a clear shot.

The overhead light flips on and I duck lower behind the wood stove out of instinct so he can't see me. But now I can't see him either.

Fuck. I'd have to expose myself in order to shoot him.

"I know you're not Chloe," he says.

I don't answer. I don't want to give away where I'm hiding, but it's not like he can't figure it out. This is such a tiny cabin with limited options for cover.

His boots hit the wood floor as he takes three steps toward me. I count them so I can picture where he's at. The door to the basement is on the far side of the kitchen floor. Then the kitchen morphs into the main room. The twin bed is closest to me, against the wall directly across from the front entrance to the cabin. He's probably between the kitchen and the twin bed. Maybe five steps away.

"The redhead saved you, huh?" he asks.

The redhead. Rachel. That's who he's talking about. I try to control my breathing but I can feel the irritation at the mention of her. He doesn't get to talk about her.

Breathe.

I can't lose my cool right now.

I adjust to bring my gun up to a ready position. I'll have to pop out to shoot him, risking getting shot myself, and so I need to gather courage and wait for the best opportunity.

"I was glad when I came back and saw that you were gone," he says. "I loved your mom. I never wanted to hurt her, but I couldn't let her get away either. And once you were born, I knew I'd lost her. That she'd never, ever stop trying to escape. I hope your name is Natalie. It was her dying wish." He chuckles to himself and continues, "Imagine my shock when I saw you at the restaurant in McCall. I knew the second you said you were Chloe that you'd be trouble. That's when I put my plan into motion. I knew I could get Frankie up here if I gave her bread-crumbs about you."

Shit. It was him, the guy at Pancake Palace, the whole time. Practically the first person I met when I came down from Montana. I grit my teeth and tip my face to the ceiling, closing my eyes. On the count of three.

One ... two ...

"Your father doesn't deserve prison. I want to take every-thing away from him before I kill him," he says.

My father?

This thought stalls me momentarily.

"That's right. I know who your dad is, and I'm the only one who can tell you that so maybe you should come out from behind the stove and we can talk."

I inhale sharply.

Thoughts crash into each other, each one so conflicting that I can't do anything but hold still.

Don't shoot him until he tells you who your dad is.

No, he's just stalling.

But why? He has a gun. He likely thinks I don't.

Remember this is all a trap. His design.

But I have to know who my dad is.

CHAPTER 61
FRANKIE

I'm grateful for the darkness for maybe the first time in my life because it means my Dad doesn't know I've found the knife.

I hear the murmur of talking upstairs. It's low—must be Brian—and I can only make out a few words at a time.

"Not Chloe" ... *"the redhead"* ...

Not Chloe? My breath hitches in my throat. How? How is she not Chloe?

Maybe Brian is lying.

I can't process it right now. Chloe or not, she needs my help, and if she's not Chloe—the despair punches me in the gut at this thought, but I don't give in—then I'll find out why she lied to me in such a cruel way.

First priority is getting up there.

My stomach twists with anxiety, urging me to go faster.

I turn the knife upside-down so carefully, to be sure I don't cut myself again and that I don't drop it. But positioning it between my wrists in order to cut my ties is so much harder than I thought it would be.

The knife drops in the dirt.

"You found it," Dad says. He must have heard. I hate the excitement in his voice, as if we're in this together.

I feel around on the ground for it, and despite being so cautious, I still cut myself again.

"Fuck!" I'm so frustrated that I want to cry, but I don't. Crying is a luxury I don't have anymore.

"Bring it over here. I'll cut you loose," Dad says.

"No," I say because, fuck him.

"Frankie, let me do this one thing for you," he whispers. I groan in irritation because I can't cut myself free. I need help.

I grip the handle and move back over to Dad.

"You swear you'll cut mine first?" He could cut his own instead and leave me down here.

"Of course. It's the least I can do."

This tone of voice he's using. It's him. It's the dad I know.

He's not who I thought he was, I remind myself.

Even so, I have no choice. I get close to him and his warm hands brush mine as he feels for the knife. I want to pull away at the touch, but I force myself to wait until he has it.

I wait with my back turned to him, trying to hold my hands closer to his reach.

Nothing happens.

"Just a sec, it's kind of hard to maneuver ..." he says.

Then the sound of zip ties snapping once. Twice.

My hands are still bound.

"Sorry, Moose. I need to make this right."

He pushes me away, and since I don't see it coming, I fall on my side, still tied up.

I can't hold the tears back this time. He used me. Of course he did, what did I expect? I try to kick, as if I can somehow stop him, but I don't hit anything.

I hear a knife sawing at fabric—the rope holding him in place. Then his feet scramble on the dirt and I imagine him trying to stand up.

"I'll come back for you as soon as I stop that bastard."
His boots softly pad up the wooden stairs. Dad is escaping.

CHAPTER 62

NATALIE

"You're right. My name is Natalie," I say, still hiding behind the wood stove. "Tell me who my dad is."

But instead of answering, the man gasps in surprise.

Is he shocked about my name?

He grunts and I realize that's not it. Something else is happening.

I want to look. Oh god, do I ever want to see what's going on, but I stay back.

"Put it on the floor slowly," says another man.

What the fuck?

I hear the drop of metal on wood. Clinton Mask must have dropped the gun.

Then the sound of it sliding across the floor like someone kicked the gun out of reach. Is it closer to me? I have to peek. Maybe they'll be busy with each other and not notice.

I move slowly to survey what's going on and then I duck back. Two men. Clinton Mask is standing right where I thought he was. And there's an older guy, salt-and-pepper hair and a goatee. It's Frankie's dad. I recognize him from the articles I've read online and from all my research. He holds a knife to Clinton Mask's throat.

Thank god.

I'm so grateful to have someone on my side here that I'm about to come out and ask where Frankie is when her dad speaks again.

"Who the hell is *Natalie*, and where is Chloe?"

His tone of voice makes a stone drop in my gut. It's icy, hard, and at the same time, aggressive.

I try to make sense of this. Frankie's dad was downstairs with her and Clinton Mask. I assumed he was kidnapped by Clinton Mask too, but my gut says not so fast. I shouldn't trust him, so I hide and wait.

"Natalie is your long-lost daughter, asshole," Clinton Mask says, and my whole world spins.

Natalie is your daughter. Your daughter. Daughter.

The words keep looping in my mind and my knees go soft, making it difficult to hold this squatting position. I want to sit down, but I can't. I need to be ready to move.

Frankie's dad is my dad too.

But Chloe was young—seventeen. And he was her uncle. Not by blood, because Chloe and Frankie's moms were sisters, but still. Chloe would have seen him as family, and when my mind has caught up, my body reacts. I gag, but cover my mouth quickly because I don't want to make more noise. Thank god nothing comes up.

Tears sting my eyes. This is so fucked up and I'm beyond angry. I don't know what I'm feeling, but my heart rate picks up and I squeeze the gun tighter.

"My daughter? What the fuck do you mean? Where's Chloe?" Frankie's dad says—I refuse to think of him as my dad. I'm not ready for that, but his words come fast and breathy. He doesn't seem to know what happened to Chloe.

"Like you don't know, asshole. Natalie is the whole reason you had me go after those girls."

"And you didn't do what I asked, so now she's back," Frankie's dad says. "I also assumed you got rid of the fucking baby."

"The fucking baby"?

I clench my teeth and grip the gun tighter.

"I held Chloe in the prison for months until she had the child. Right under your nose. You didn't even bat an eye when you came to visit the redhead. You simply believed me. That I had dead bodies in that room." Clinton Mask's voice is smug and then he cries out, and I picture the knife pressing closer to his neck.

"... When you came to visit the redhead."

His words swirl in my mind. Frankie's dad was the one who assaulted Rachel. He's the one who needed her to be in pain in order to get off. And he wanted Chloe and me dead.

"So is Chloe alive?" Frankie's dad asks urgently.

Clinton Mask laughs but doesn't answer.

"Tell me she's dead."

A volcano stirs inside of me and I need to take advantage of this moment when they're arguing. I mentally run through scenarios. If Frankie's dad slits Clinton Mask's throat, he'll have the gun and I'll be no better off than I was before he came up the stairs.

Right now, neither of them have a gun, and Frankie's dad is hiding behind the motherfucker who killed Chloe.

Take your shot.

One at a time. First, Clinton Mask.

I move out from behind the wood stove enough to aim for his chest, and I pull the trigger.

CHAPTER 63

FRANKIE

I HAVE to get the knife and try again.

Low moaning breaks through across the room.

Jensen.

"Hey, are you awake?" I ask. I'm surprised because it hasn't been very long, but then again, Brian said he gave Jensen Chloe's dose, and I'm no doctor but a dose for a five-foot-tall woman is going to be way less than what it would take to truly incapacitate a six-three man.

He mutters something unintelligible broadcasting that he's loopy from the sedative.

"Jensen, it's Frankie. I need you to help me. Can you sit up?"

He groans.

I feel around for the knife in the spot where Dad was sitting, but it's not there. He must have taken it with him.

"Fucking asshole!" I say.

"I know," Jensen mumbles. "Sorry."

He thinks I'm talking about him. No sense in trying to have a conversation. I need to get back over to the toolbox and find those pliers I felt earlier.

I move fast toward the spot under the stairs, thinking about my dad up there with Brian and Chloe.

She's not Chloe.

I shake the thought away because I still can't process it.

Since I remember where the toolbox is and what the pliers feel like, I find them immediately and scoot myself over to Jensen.

He's still lying down.

"Get up. I need your help."

He moans, but there's rustling and movement and even though it's still too dark to see, I think he's sitting now. I turn around like I did with my dad.

"I have pliers in my hands directly in front of you. I need you to hold them closed when I tell you to so I can work my hands free."

"Can't," he says.

"What?"

"I can't. My hands are behind my back too."

"Fuck!" That's right. I knew that.

Slow down. One step at a time.

"Okay, can you spin around?"

"Really?"

"Jensen, we're going to die, fucking spin around!"

He gasps softly, and says, "Oh my god. Chloe," like he just remembered.

"Yeah Chloe, and so much more to worry about too. Help me get free."

I move forward a bit to give him space to turn and when I feel his fingers touching mine, I know we're back to back. He takes the pliers from me, fumbling them once.

"I can't squeeze. I don't have the strength yet," he says.

"I don't care how you do it, just hold them closed."

He moves around and I feel the pressure tighten around my zip ties.

"Okay, go," he says.

I pull and saw my hands until finally, the ties snap free. I take the pliers and tug at the ties on my ankles until they come free too.

The sound of a gunshot startles me and I run up the stairs.

CHAPTER 64
FRANKIE

"Fucking hell, you look *exactly* like her."

Because my dad left the door open, I hear his words before I reach the top of the stairs.

"I have your freckles," Chloe says, and I stop cold before they would be able to see me.

What the fuck?

Then I remember my dad's words: "Chloe was pregnant. And I knew it was mine."

Oh my god. Not only is this not Chloe, but she's Chloe's daughter.

How? She would be like ... so much younger than us.

And where is Chloe?

My breathing picks up and my knees turn to jelly like I might collapse, so I sit down for a second to gather myself.

This is my fault. I wanted to believe this was Chloe so badly that I went along with all of her rationalizations for passing as my cousin. The ones she told me and the ones I observed.

Botox.

Baggy clothes.

Thick glasses and gray-streaked hair.

All of it designed to help age her, and any of it could have come unraveled if I had just pulled a little more on those strings. Botox is great, but it doesn't take eighteen years off your face.

I fucking saw what I wanted to see.

Then my thoughts pivot and everything I've learned tonight floods me and in a blip, I remember things.

The extra week Chloe was at Paradise Point without me the summer before she disappeared. She said her mom insisted she go early. Dad was up there that summer. Did he orchestrate that? There's no way Aunt Bertie would have pressed it unless Dad had influenced her. What if he lied and said I'd be up there with her?

But Chloe was already pregnant that summer. So that means it was happening before then, too.

I think farther back to how Chloe never wanted to spend the night at my house that year. We always stayed at hers.

I gag like I might throw up, but swallow down the urge.

"*Let it go, Chloe is gone*," Dad always said. Now I know why. He wanted her to be gone. Probably assumed she was dead.

Is she dead?

I stand and take a deep breath. I don't know what comes next, but I will get justice for Chloe one way or another. For Mom too.

When I step into the kitchen, Dad's back is to me, and his hands are in the air. Not-Chloe holds him at gunpoint across the room.

There's another gun on the floor by the front door, between both of them.

There's a knife a few feet in front of Dad.

Dad turns to see me.

"Frankie, thank god. Get me that gun." He nods his head toward it.

I don't answer him, but step toward the gun, exactly as he

says. Then I pick up the knife too. I don't want to show my cards to either of them.

"Frankie, I have to tell you something," Not-Chloe says. Her voice is shaking and her face is wet with tears.

"Don't listen to her. She lies," Dad says.

I look at her and suddenly, she seems so damn young. Just a child, really. How stupid was I to believe this could be Chloe?

And Dad's absolutely right. She lied to me.

For weeks this woman made me think I had Chloe back, and right now it's clear I never did. And deep inside I know that I never will.

"What's your name?" I ask her.

"Natalie. I'm Chloe's daughter," she sobs. "I'm so sorry I lied to you but I had to know who killed her. This was the only way."

CHAPTER 65
NATALIE

I CAN'T READ Frankie at all. Her eyes are puffy and swollen like she's been crying. Her finger is bloody, and there's more blood all over her tee shirt, and streaked from her left temple to her cheek. But her face is stoic, totally without emotion, and when she picks up the gun, I move mine to aim at her because I honestly have no clue what she's going to do.

"Your dad raped Chloe. And that one killed her," I say, throwing a chin toward Clinton Mask's body, lying motionless on the floor.

"She's no better," Frankie's dad shouts. "She killed Brian in cold blood."

"He kidnapped you! And killed Chloe!" I say, keeping my focus on Frankie.

There's no way Frankie's dad believes she'd have any sympathy for Clinton Mask, right? But there's still no reaction from Frankie. She holds the gun limp at her side, her eyes locking with mine. Tears fill her eyes and run down her cheeks, but her finger moves to turn off the safety.

My body lights up, and I talk faster.

"I killed him because he left me in the cold to die as a baby and then he murdered my mom. Chloe died trying to save me, Frankie. Your dad tortured the woman who saved my life. Her name was Rachel and she was in the prison with Chloe. Chloe freed her right before Clinton Mask killed her, and Rachel saved me. She raised me. She was the only mother I knew. The only family I've ever had."

I break down crying, and can't speak for a minute, but I don't move the gun one inch. It's still trained on her.

"Bullshit," Frankie's dad yells, but he doesn't sound so sure of himself.

Frankie raises her gun and points it at me. "If you're telling the truth, you'll set your gun on the floor so we can talk about it." Her tone is harsh, and I cry harder. She doesn't trust me anymore.

"I can't do that," I say, sobbing. "He'll kill me."

Frankie's dad smirks and lowers his hands and I move the gun back to him. But Frankie is still aiming at me.

"Put your gun down and I'm going to call the police. They'll sort it all out," she says.

No, my gut responds. I can't be here with Frankie's dad the whole time we wait for the cops to show up. She would be the one with a weapon and there's no way she's going to shoot her own dad. He'd probably get it away from her and come after me.

"Call the police first," I say. "I'll put it down when they arrive."

"Jesus Christ, Frankie, either give me the gun or shoot her," Frankie's dad says.

She doesn't flinch.

I keep moving my gun between them, unsure who is the bigger threat, and when I move it to Frankie this time, her dad leaps toward me.

CHAPTER 66
FRANKIE

Fuck!

I was trying to get Natalie's gun out of the picture so Dad didn't get it, but now he's lunging at her.

Everything slows down and I see Natalie's face. Her mouth opens in a scream, her eyes widening as her glasses fly off to the side and hit the floor. She moves the gun toward him, but it's too late. Dad takes her down and the gun goes skittering behind in the same direction as her glasses.

I aim my gun, but my nerve wavers and thoughts bombard my mind.

He's your dad. You can't kill your dad.

Chloe is dead.

But he's your dad. Wait for the cops.

He's the reason Chloe is dead.

Tears blur my vision and I start shaking again.

Natalie is screaming my name. She's bawling and blood smears her face as Dad punches her.

I can't make myself move.

Chloe comes to mind again.

What would she want? If Natalie is right and Chloe died trying to save her, I think I have my answer.

"Get off her!" I scream.

He doesn't listen and instead wraps his hands around Natalie's neck.

I step toward him, close enough he can see me and far enough that he can't get the gun away.

"Dad, fucking stop!"

He doesn't stop. He doesn't even seem to hear me. He's squeezing her neck and she isn't even gasping for air anymore.

I don't want to kill my dad. I want him to go to jail. But Natalie is dying.

Shoot him.

Now.

What would Chloe want?

I cry out and squeeze the trigger.

CHAPTER 67

FRANKIE

I SHOT MY DAD. I just shot my dad. Oh god, oh god.

I'm practically convulsing as I drop the gun and reach an arm out for something to break my fall. There's nothing and so I plop on the floor and wail.

Dad lies an arm's length away from me and a foot from Brian's body.

Natalie coughs hard as she shoves Dad's body off of her and gasps for air. She lies there, very still, and I howl with anger and despair when I see the damage my dad did to her face.

Why did it take me so long to respond?

Her left eye is swollen shut, her nose bleeding, and her lip is cut open. Red marks are starting to appear around her neck.

"I'm so sorry," I sob, crawling over to her. "I should have done it sooner. Are you okay?"

She's still coughing, but she nods and tries to sit up. That makes her wince and lie back down. "My ribs," she pushes out through a swollen mouth. I crawl over to her and sit on my knees.

Tears and blood smear her makeup and I can see her freckles.

My freckles.

The ones we both got from my monster of a father.

The man I killed.

I cry harder, and Natalie pulls herself up slowly to sit, then reaches a hand out to touch my knee. "Shh," she says. "It's okay. I'm okay."

She's comforting me when she's the one who is broken almost beyond recognition.

I move toward her and gently take her in an embrace. All I can do is cry even though I don't know how I have any tears left.

Natalie cries too, but I can tell it hurts her to do so.

Thoughts keep coming, demanding me to process them.

Chloe is dead.

She's been dead since almost the day she disappeared.

This is Chloe's daughter.

Then a new thought:

Natalie is my sister.

I gasp when it lands in my mind.

I never imagined I'd have a sister out there, and now, here she is.

This is what I want to think about right now. Not my dad. Not his horrible crimes. Not my many losses. I want to focus on this one happy thing for a second.

Out of unbelievable trauma, this tiny gift of hope and love.

"We're sisters," I say, nuzzling my face into her shoulder.

She cries louder, and we sit there, holding each other. It feels like neither of us wants to be the first to let go, and so we don't.

ONE YEAR LATER

CHAPTER 68
FRANKIE

Natalie parks the car in front of a stone building out in the middle of nowhere McCall.

"This is it?" I ask.

She nods and takes the key out of the ignition.

We sit in silence for a moment.

The prison where Chloe spent her last couple of days is right there, just yards away.

It's taken a year for me to feel ready to come up here, and I decided to make it a pilgrimage to honor Chloe instead of putting on the annual event for her.

"I couldn't be here for very long the last time I came," Natalie says. "Remember how I freaked out at the Idaho State Pen?"

"Yeah, that was weird."

"It was even worse here. I threw up." She pauses and screws her face up a little, like she's realizing something. "Actually, maybe my vomit is still there. Do you think it will be after a year?"

"Eww," I say and shove her playfully.

She grabs her water bottle, which is practically full, and lifts it like she's showing it to me. "Clean-up crew."

I laugh and shake my head and it feels good to have some levity right now. I'd rather not just bawl, although I'm sure I will anyway.

Natalie's phone vibrates with a text and she peeks at it before we get out of the car.

"It's from Jensen," she says.

I give her a read-it-to-me nod.

Natalie and Jensen have become good friends. He and I are still working on our friendship, but I don't think it's likely we'll ever be close. He annoys me like a little brother would, I learned once I got some distance. But Jensen has been good for Natalie. Sort of a stand-in Dad. Neither of them take each other's shit and I think that's healing for both of them.

She clears her throat and reads his text:

> Aiming to be there around six for dinner.
> Sound good?

"He's cooking for us tonight," she explains.

"Amazing. I've never had any issue with Jensen's cooking. Tell him six. We'll be back and hungry by then."

"We have to prefunk with Huckleberry soft serve before we hit Boise though."

I laugh again. "Sure, Nat. Whatever you want."

Natalie nods and shoots off a reply.

We get out of the car and she points to where she thinks Chloe fell, based on Rachel's description, and where she was abandoned in the snow as a baby, along with the little shed where Rachel found a snowmobile and drove them to safety.

Then we go inside the prison.

My therapist says I need to let emotions move through my body in order to process the trauma, so when the urge to cry appears, I allow myself to feel it. I tell myself I'm safe. We're safe. I tell myself I am willing to feel anything in order to heal and to have my own back.

The truth is that I want to feel the fear, pain, shame, and anything else Chloe and Rachel and the other nameless girls would have experienced. I want to remember that they lived and they matter.

"This was her room," Natalie says, pointing to an open door on the left.

She goes in and uses her water bottle to wash something off the floor and down the drain in the middle. Presumably her vomit, although I don't see anything and I doubt it's still there after more than a year.

"I don't know why I'm doing this," she says. "It's not like it matters."

I look around the room, and noticing the one window, I make my way toward it. My eyes take in the trees and the pine-needle covered ground.

This is the view Chloe would have had. These are the very trees she would have stared at, wondering what was going to happen to her. And to her baby.

I turn and watch Natalie, who seems to be handling this prison experience better than her previous ones. She's not sick yet. It feels like her words from before hover in the air and I go over to her and take her by the shoulders gently.

"This is where you were born. It fucking matters," I say. "Even if the circumstances were horrific."

"Born in a prison, raised by a runaway," she murmurs. "Sounds about right."

"It doesn't matter how you got here. Only that you did. You beat all the odds, Nat, and you're exactly like your mom. The absolute strongest person I know, and when I grow up, I want to be just like you."

BONUS SCENE

Want to know what really happened the day Frankie's mom was killed? Scan the QR code to read a bonus scene called, "It Was No Accident."

(Content warning: references to pedophilia, but nothing explicit or on-page.)

ACKNOWLEDGMENTS

THIS BOOK STARTED as an itty-bitty seed of an idea that I was really excited about. Because of that, I thought I'd write it easily. Six weeks, tops. Total cake.

I was so wrong it's almost unbelievable.

Yet, I couldn't let go of that seed even if I was completely clueless about how to best cultivate it and grow it into a healthy plant. More than any of my other books so far, this one took time, patience, being open to extra feedback, and a whole lot of rewrites. Not to mention loads of encouragement from friends and family. I am truly so grateful for all of the people who invested hours and energy into reading this story and giving me their god-honest, liquid-gold thoughts. Without further ado, I want to thank these gems in my life <taps the microphone>:

First, the book is dedicated to two of my many amazing cousins. Joy Martin and Jessica Stutzke. Close cousins are special because you don't have to share a room or a parent's attention with them, but they really are like siblings. Sisters, in this case. The perfect blend between sister and friend.

Joy and Jess, even though you are on different sides of my

family from each other, you both taught me how to be a friend in your own way.

When I look back on my childhood, I see you both in large swaths of memory, and all my adventures with each of you. Late-night talks, sleepovers, hours and hours (and hours!) spent choreographing dances to perform for the family, summer days blurring into each other, holidays spent hiding out in some corner of a house full of family to share secret confidences while gorging on Grandma's homemade treats. (Different grandmas; both incredible cooks, right?!) All the vacations and dreams shared. The many losses endured, including beloved family members. Thank you for teaching me how to sustain a friendship and that disagreements are not only figureoutable, but a healthy part of a relationship. I love you both.

As for the production of this book, I have to first thank Noelle Ihli, a true and best friend and an absolute genius when it comes to story. Thank you not only for your feedback, but also for telling me I could finish this book all those times I was pretty damn sure I couldn't. You never stop inspiring me on the page and in life.

Thank you to my other thriller author kindreds: Faith Gardner and Caleb Stephens: I'm so happy that our paths crossed, and I cherish our friendship and same-brainness when it comes to writing and publishing. Long live the cult!

Thank you to everyone who beta-read this book and gave honest opinions, starting with my fellow author and dearest friend, Anna Gamel. You are gifted at seeing the best in someone and cheering it out of them. I'm lucky to have you in my life. To Maddy Leary, part-editor, part-reader, your insights are always unique and often propel me further into creativity. I'm so grateful for you! To Jacob Robarts for sharing your thoughts and excitement about the story, and for being a breath of fresh air in my life. To Kelsey Zedwick for an eleventh-hour-save read. You gave me the feedback I needed to cement the story and especially to bring that one Chloe chapter to life. I'm so grateful for our friendship and our history together. Thank you to Kiersten Walmsley and Marissa Hayes, new friends who read and gave amazing feedback just before the book went to final edits. I appreciate your time and love of books.

Thank you to Gregg Olsen for reading an early copy of the book and for encouraging me. I'm grateful our paths crossed even if quite randomly! To my editors, Maddy Leary and Patti Geesey for eagle eyes galore. Maddy, in the developmental stages, for your time and honesty, and Patti as a final look. I'm always amazed at your ability to catch the tiniest things. So grateful to work with you both.

To my family, who are really the best cheerleaders I could ask for. Especially my teens, Cam and Jonny for your love and patience with me as I try to "mom" and also build a career. Best kids ever. To my mom, Denette Dresback, AKA lifelong supporter and the one person who will cry when I tell her my good book news. My sister-in-law, Julie Dresback, who feels much more like a sister than someone who married my brother. Thanks for being my book-hype girl! To my brother, Nate Dresback and sister Rebekah Dresback, for reading all my books. To my dad and retired homicide detective Jim Dresback, for your continued advice on the policing aspect of my books (I still go rogue sometimes though, so any inaccuracies are mine alone).

Thank you to the Booktok/Bookstagram and Facebook Thriller communities for your excitement for my stories and willingness to read and share. There are so many great books available and I'm very honored whenever mine breaks ranks with your toppling-over-TBR and becomes a current read.

Thanks to *you*, too, for reading this book and making it all the way to the end here where even though nobody is handing out awards, I still manage to make a book-Grammy speech. I hope my story pulled you into a wild world where you could forget about reality for a few hours.

There are so many other people I could thank and I'm sure I forgot some of you, but if you had any hand at all in this book, anything from listening to me whine about how I'm never going to crack the story to asking me how it's coming along, thank you! I've pretty much lived on encouragement alone over the past year. I hope I can repay the kindness someday.

XO,
  Steph

ABOUT THE AUTHOR

Steph Nelson's books have been featured in the *New York Times* and *Library Journal*. A lifelong PNW girl, she currently lives in Idaho, and when she's not working on her next story, she's either traveling, hunting for vintage clothing, or reading.

www.ingramcontent.com/pod-product-compliance
Lightning Source LLC
Chambersburg PA
CBHW020246010826

48973CB00006B/1673